BARGAIN OF THE HEART

Richard reached over and grasped Crystal's hand. She withdrew quickly and turned away. What on earth could he do to ease her tension? What could he do to help her through this dilemma? He wouldn't entertain for a second the thought that she no longer loved him—that she really wanted to end the years of joy they'd shared. How could one incident tear apart what had once been a good marriage?

Crystal pushed her plate away from her with half the food left untouched. "Let's get this talk over with," she said finally.

Richard placed his fork on his plate and wiped his mouth with his napkin. Crystal was distant and aloof.

"I have a proposition to make to you," he said.

"What is it?"

"Let's make a bargain for the next three months. Let's try to be a couple—go through a courtship so to speak. Remember our courtship, Crystal?"

She took a deep breath to slow her pulse. "It wasn't working, Richard. Now I want out." She thrust her fingers through her hair. "I won't live like this any longer."

Silence stretched; then he asked, "What do you have to lose?"

"Three months," she finally said. "You give your word that I can have an uncontested divorce in three months."

His body came alert. She could just see the lawyer in him calculating victory. "If you still want out of the marriage."

Other books by Candice Poarch

THE LAST DANCE*
SHATTERED ILLUSIONS
TENDER ESCAPE
INTIMATE SECRETS*
THE ESSENCE OF LOVE
WITH THIS KISS*
WHITE LIGHTNING*
"A NEW YEAR, A NEW BEGINNING" in
'TIS THE SEASON and
MOONLIGHT AND MISTLETOE
"MORE THAN FRIENDS" in A MOTHER'S TOUCH

*part of the Nottoway Series

Published by BET/Arabesque Books

BARGAIN OF THE HEART

Candice Poarch

BET Publications, LLC
http://www.bet.com
http://www.arabesquebooks.com

ARABESQUE BOOKS are published by

BET Publications, LLC
c/o BET BOOKS
One BET Plaza
1900 W Place NE
Washington, DC 20018-1211

All Kensington Titles, Imprints, and Distributed Lines are available at special quantity discounts for bulk purchases for sales promotions, premiums, fund-raising, and educational or institutional use. Special book excerpts or customized printings can also be created to fit specific needs. For details, write or phone the office of the Kensington special sales manager: Kensington Publishing Corp., 850 Third Avenue, New York, NY 10022, attn: Special Sales Department, Phone: 1-800-221-2647.

First Printing: June 2002
10 9 8 7 6 5 4 3 2 1

Printed in the United States of America

ACKNOWLEDGMENTS

My sincere thanks to booksellers and readers who support my books.

The wonderful Pig Picken Cake recipe belongs to my sister's coworker, Sherry Newton of Petersburg, Virginia. She has been generous enough to let me share her aunt's wonderful recipe, and for that I offer my fervent thanks.

As always, profound thanks for support go to my critique partner, Sandy Rangel; my husband, John; my sister, Evangeline, who often accompanies me to book signings; and my family.

One

Late spring had settled in Windy Hills, Virginia, and Crystal Dupree had come home to enjoy it. Up ahead she saw her mountain—at least in her mind the gently rounded peak, bursting with greenery and wildflowers, belonged to her. She smiled, wishing she were at her little cabin sitting on her deck watching the water from the Smith River roll past. She could even picture the vista as sharp and as clear as if she were there.

Crystal drove slowly up Main Street where old glass-fronted shops lined up like mismatched soldiers. On the corner near the drugstore she waved to the Parkers. Janice Parker had taught fifth graders in a classroom next door to hers last year. She'd applied for two years' leave to spend with her new baby. Right now she carried her six-month-old in her arms while her husband, Ray, pushed the empty stroller. Had Crystal not miscarried, her own child would be one month old now.

It wasn't meant to be, Crystal said to herself. If one were to believe that there were lessons to be learned, then she'd have to trust that bad things happened for a reason. But that assessment didn't lessen the ever-throbbing ache that nagged like a broken limb. It was with the miscarriage that her life had begun to fall apart.

In her heart, however, she knew that the downward slide had begun long before then.

She drove on until she reached her husband Richard's office and wondered if she should have waited until tomorrow to see him. Her flight from Japan had left her tired and edgy with jet lag. But Crystal was determined to get this over and done with.

She walked up the cobblestone path to the door where a sign displaying RICHARD DUPREE, ESQ. was tacked onto the wooden panel, and she twisted the brass doorknob.

Richard Dupree glanced at his Rolex, a watch that kept accurate time in three time zones, then rolled down his shirtsleeves and grabbed the navy Armani jacket from the back of his chair. It was one sharp. Footsteps muffled by navy carpeting approached his office door. He glanced up briefly and smiled. Any minute now his secretary, Theresa Daily, was going to rush through the door to warn him to leave *right now* or he'd be late getting to the airport. The woman ran his office as regimentedly as a drill sergeant. He'd canceled two flights already, thrusting her instantly onto the warpath.

"Sheriff Campbell released the Baker boys for lack of evidence," he called out when she didn't immediately appear. He could hear her through the six-inch opening in the door. The Baker boys, one a senior in high school and the other a year younger, were products of too much money and too little parenting. This time they'd been accused of shooting Annie Bedford, Richard's wife's aunt, in the hip three weeks ago. No one had actually *seen* them, except Annie's neighbor, Mavis Prudence, who couldn't see a seven-foot black bear if it were standing in the sunlight ten feet in front of her. The prosecutor wasn't prepared to have Richard haul in two linebackers, stand them a hundred yards away from Mrs. Prudence, and ask her if they were the ones she'd seen leaving Annie's house. So he'd let the boys go while the sheriff's team sifted through evidence. One sticky point remained, however. When Mrs. Prudence had started flapping her arms like a giant bird and screeching at the top of her lungs, the Baker boys had been first on the scene. They'd sworn that they'd stopped to assist the woman because she was waving and shrieking so loudly that they knew something was wrong—just as any other town citizen would have done.

Richard represented them because the boys were more prone to mischief, not actual crime—things like speeding and getting drunk on the moonshine they bought from Old Man Tiber, then staying out the rest of the night, worrying their overprotective, frail mother half to death. Trouble seldom came to Windy Hills—serious crime anyway. Lack of excitement was the lament of the youngsters. For teenagers, Windy Hills was the most boring town imaginable.

Richard wondered how he'd ever explain taking this case to his wife—*if* she ever returned to him. His conscience wouldn't let him slink out of it. He wouldn't let the boys end up as statistics merely because of sloppy investigating.

Still, family was family. He'd have some explaining to do. Annie would understand. He wasn't so certain his wife would.

Richard tucked his airline ticket into his briefcase pocket along with notes from the trial with Cove International, his biggest corporate client. A year ago Cove had moved their cosmetic branch to Windy Hills, and hired him on as local counsel. He and the general manager, Dana Vaylor, were flying out to Ohio this evening. The case of product adulteration was over, but he still had to meet with the corporate attorneys in Ohio.

Two warning knocks rapped against the wooden panel before the door widened.

"I'm leaving right now," he said, stashing his laptop into the case. In the unusual silence, he glanced toward the door. The smile froze on his face. Unnoticed, the briefcase top dropped with a muffled thud.

"Crystal," he whispered. The bottom dropped out of his stomach and he felt as if someone had punched him in his lungs. He couldn't breathe. He wanted to slide into the plush navy chair beside him. Instead, he squared his shoulders and stood, frozen, as time seemed to crawl by.

His wife moved gracefully toward him wearing a sleeveless lavender blouse that clung tenaciously to the curve of her generous breasts and cream-colored slacks that hugged rounded hips he wanted to stroke. She was a feast for a starving man—smelled heaven-sent in her familiar essence that drifted toward him like a sweet dream. Pausing at a captain's chair that faced his desk, she placed a slim golden brown hand on the padded navy-and-cream striped back. Her wedding band and diamond engagement ring gleamed as the light struck them. The fact that she still wore them gave him hope. She was a sight for sore eyes for a man who'd been without his wife for five long, painful months.

Her calm-as-you-please greeting of "Hello, Richard" stung at its lack of emotion. This wasn't the image he dreamed. In his dreams she'd hurled herself into his arms and he dug his fingers into the long ringlets dangling at her shoulders, pulled her body to press tightly against his, and kissed her soft, full lips. His body tightened at the very image. It'd been five months, for chrissakes, and the best she could do was "Hello, Richard"? But even he stood motionless, gaping at her like an inept dimwit, not the powerful lawyer he knew he was.

But those were his dreams, his needs. What were her desires? He watched her, seeking a glimpse of what she felt, hopeful that she was back with him for good. He glanced at the ring again—the ring he'd proudly put on her finger five years ago. The ring gave him hope.

Her silence filled him with dread, and anger surged from the base of his temple. He controlled the anger. He'd promised himself that if she returned, he'd let logic guide him, not erratic emotions. Even though she owed him—and owed him big for what he'd put up with—he dug deep inside for that logic.

She approached his desk, twisting the rings on her left hand. Richard's stomach tensed as the engagement ring slid off easily and as she struggled to dislodge the wedding band. She obviously hadn't taken it off in years. Richard hardly noticed that lighter skin marked her finger as she deposited the rings on the desk blotter. His stomach twisted into a scalding knot. A speeding train pinned him in its headlight and Richard's chest tightened as if something were lodged inside, right along with his temper.

"I'm filing for a divorce."

Logic, hell! "Just like that? Damn it, Crystal." Richard circled the desk. "You've been gone for months and the first thing you say to me is you want a divorce? How about 'It's good to see you, Richard. Why don't we sit and discuss our marriage like reasonable adults'?"

"Because I don't want to talk about it. I've tried talking— for years."

Richard briefly pinched the bridge of his nose and regrouped. "I've been more than patient," he reminded her calmly. Then he sighed, sweeping a glance over her slim form. Dark circles rimmed her eyes. She'd lost weight and she'd had none to lose. This gave her a slightly fragile, delicate look. He softened his voice, realizing that she still hadn't come to terms with losing the baby in November. "Honey, you need more time to deal with what's occurred over the last few months. Here . . . with me this time."

She looked away. "I have already. Is my car parked in the garage?" she asked in crisp tones.

Her biting timbre didn't indicate fragility or reconciliation. Far from it. The hard edge of his jaw tightened enough to crack. She needed his guidance right now. Not separation. "Yes," he said and plunged his hands deep into his pockets to keep from wringing her soft neck. "Crystal, I won't agree to a divorce. You're bent on destroying a perfectly good marriage."

"Not in my book. I'm staying in the cabin until we settle things. You don't use it anyway."

"You'll stay at the house with me, where you belong."

"I've made up my mind, Richard." Crystal hustled to the door and opened it.

Reeling at the possibility of her exiting his life, Richard charged after her and grabbed her arms, spinning her around in the process. "We're not going to end it like this."

"Let go of me." Stony brown eyes that had once been warm and welcoming stared him down—a woman so unlike his Crystal. She looked like Crystal, talked like Crystal, but suddenly he was faced with a stranger. It occurred to him, he didn't know this woman. What had gone so wrong that he couldn't get his wife back? He loosened his hand on her arm and stroked her gently. He held on to their love—felt their love. Nothing could take away what they'd shared. Hope blossomed.

Nothing.

Richard inhaled slowly and eased his hands from her soft arms, staying close in case she bolted again. They were going to deal with this *right now*. Silence stretched as he gathered his thoughts.

The outer door opened. Muffled footsteps carried over the carpet.

"Richard?" Theresa called out, then stopped abruptly. "Oh. Hi, Crystal." The long rose dress she wore blended well with her medium brown complexion. Her natural hair gathered into a ponytail displayed the no-nonsense angles of her face.

Crystal glanced at Theresa and smiled a genuine, albeit shaky smile—one she hadn't extended to Richard. "Hi, Theresa."

"It's good to see you."

"You too."

Theresa glanced uncertainly between them and tapped the watch he and Crystal had given her as a Christmas gift two years ago. "Ah, Richard. If you don't leave now, you'll miss your flight."

Crystal was grateful the attention was drawn from her. She'd known he'd be difficult, but she wouldn't be swayed this time. She focused on the office to bring her raging emotions under control. She wasn't nearly as calm as she hoped she appeared. Her eyes lit on the picture of Richard and her on his wall—the one they'd taken at the Orioles' stadium in Baltimore—and the Hank Aaron ball he'd caught in the stands. He'd propped it on a pedestal and placed it on the edge of the desk. Richard loved baseball. She wondered if he still took the time to watch a game, much less attend one.

It was so much easier to deal with baseball than the emotions fraught with uncertainty from the dissolution of her marriage. It was scary starting over, especially since her life had centered on this man for the last ten years. Their college courtship had been the happiest time of her life, but she couldn't live on memories from the past for the rest of her life.

She watched him, unnoticed. His bronze forehead was creased in a frown. She stifled the temptation to lift a hand to stroke him and smooth the frown away.

Crystal shook her head. Was she crazy? His slight woodsy scent wafting in the air covered her like his comfortable bathrobe—the one she'd worn to tatters because she was loath to throw it out. There was no doubt that she loved him. She simply couldn't—wouldn't live with him. She wouldn't continue to be a widow to his practice. Crystal wanted a life—she wanted a family to share *with* a husband, not in spite of. With Richard she was destined to be alone. She needed more. Children needed more.

She closed her eyes briefly. This should have been easier.

Crystal didn't blame him, though. This was Richard. The law was his wife—she was merely his mistress despite their marriage vows. The realization had taken a while, but she'd finally grown to believe that love alone just wasn't enough. Sometimes one needed to step out of that comfort zone to seek real happiness. Crystal grimaced and shook her head. She'd left a silk blouse behind in Japan, but not that stupid, tattered burgundy bathrobe.

Crystal wanted to hug him good-bye, but suppressed the impulse. Give him an inch, he'd take a mile. One day she hoped he'd come to the same realization she had. One day they could be friends—good friends.

In the background she heard him say, "Call the airport and reschedule for tomorrow morning."

Crystal wanted to leave, but her escape was blocked. She started to edge away. She wouldn't be missed. But Richard stopped her.

"Do you really want me to change that flight?" Theresa asked. "You really should be on that plane."

"Cancel it," Richard snapped.

But Theresa plunged ahead doggedly, just like any good employee whose salary was based on the success of the firm. "It's the last flight out. Your meeting's tomorrow morning. If you cancel, you'll miss your connection at Dulles. There's a pilots' strike. The pretrial conference scheduled here will be over before you get back. The judge will be hopping mad. You don't want to infuriate him again."

Crystal had heard it all before. Richard didn't have a life—didn't want a life—outside of work.

"Don't bother," Crystal said. "I'm leaving. Good-bye, Richard."

"This isn't finished," Richard said, swiping a hand across his short-cropped hair.

"It's finished." She started to move away but he blocked her with a hand that shot out across the doorjamb.

"We've had enough separation between us already. Come with me. To Ohio. Theresa will make the reservations." He stroked the back of his other hand along her face and whispered, "Come with me, Crystal."

Crystal moved from his touch, took his arm, and pushed it away. "No, Richard." Did he think that after years of neglect a small caress would change her mind? Was he that unaware of her needs? She stifled an indelicate snort. Of course he was.

He locked his arm around her shoulder, propelling her from the door. "Let's finish this in the office, shall we?" Unwilling to tussle with him in front of Theresa, Crystal let him haul her back into his sanctuary as he shut the door in the woman's startled face.

"I'm just asking for a little time to talk things out. It's what you've been harping on me about for months and now I'm willing to listen."

Crystal's temper snapped. "Don't use your courtroom summary voice on me." She plunked her hands on her hips. "What do you plan to do? Pencil me in between your meetings with the lawyers and late-night dinners and briefs?"

"We're starting from today. We can't do anything about the past."

Crystal lowered her arms to her sides. "Nothing's changed."

"Things will change," he assured her once again.

About the most useless words she'd ever heard.

"Richard . . ." Theresa called out from the other side of the door.

All those nights of holding dinner until he showed up three hours late. All the engagements she attended alone at the last minute or missed altogether because he never appeared came rushing back to her. But, even worse, the miscarriage. He'd arrived at the hospital four hours late.

Crystal sighed, holding her emotions in check. He and his mother had been plotting political strategies while she was losing their child. And he debated with her now as if the future would be any different. Crystal still wanted children. She'd glanced at the future and she couldn't commit her child to the kinds of disappointment that would be inevitable if she and Richard stayed together. She wouldn't raise her child alone.

It was her fault for letting their marriage diminish to this—and accepting the little he offered for far too long. Now that Crystal knew what the future would entail, she wasn't having it.

Crystal relaxed her stance. With a coy smile, she asked in the sweetest tone she could muster, "Now, how much time did you say you'll spare in Ohio?"

"Plenty." His voice lowered several octaves. "Business shouldn't take up all my time."

She wanted to hit him. "What time is your flight?"

"Richard?" Theresa pounded on the door.

"Two hours. You can make it."

He enveloped her in his arms. A smile crossed his face— the same smile he wore when he won a major case. In the end, that's all she meant to him. Just another trophy to be won, and then he could move on to his next case.

"Rich . . . ard."

He lowered his head and his mouth inched toward hers. Crystal turned her head so that he kissed her cheek. She reached up and grasped his tie, stroking the wall of muscled chest beneath. "Tell you what." She ran her tongue over her lips. "I have a rental car. I'll come to the airport after I unload my luggage."

His eyes glazed. His body tightened. Something below, and Crystal knew exactly what, nudged her in the stomach. "No need," he said. "Leave it here." His voice was husky and deep.

Crystal shook her head. "I have to return the car anyway. You go ahead. I'll be there soon." Crystal pushed off from him and backed to the door, noting the evidence of his desire.

He swiped his tongue over his upper teeth and sighed. "See you in an hour?" He rounded the desk and plucked up his briefcase.

"An hour." Crystal opened the door. Theresa's hand was in the air, ready to knock again.

"Honestly! It's about time," Theresa muttered.

"Crystal's going with me. Make a reservation for her, please."

"Give a person plenty of time, will you?"

Crystal smiled at the peeved woman. "Thanks, Theresa."

"I wouldn't do this for anyone else. Welcome back," she said as she hugged Crystal, then proceeded to her desk. Richard had turned back to his packing.

"Is the battery charged on my cell phone?" he asked Theresa.

"Fully charged and ready to go." She picked up the phone.

Just that quickly he'd completely focused on business again. Crystal knew where she fit in the scheme of things. She could picture herself now, touring all day while he worked. By dinner he'd call a couple of times to tell her he was on his way until about ten when he'd tell her to eat without him. Then sometime after midnight he'd arrive, tired and out of sorts—on a good evening. And he thought she was going to Ohio. Crystal snorted. *Not in this lifetime.*

Mentally saying good-bye, she turned and opened the heavy oak door. Then she sailed out into the bright June warmth, leaving behind this chapter in her life. If anyone had asked her to describe her emotions, she couldn't have done so. She felt no joy, but she wasn't sorrowful, either. Relief, perhaps, that she'd taken the first step in moving on.

She was so intent on her thoughts she collided with Mrs. Potter and almost knocked the older woman on her backside.

"My goodness," Sadie Potter said as Crystal kept a hold on her arms until she gained her balance. Her precious book had fallen to the ground. Luscious fabric strawberries dangled at an angle on the lopsided hat she wore.

Crystal bent and picked the book up, dusted it off, and scanned the title as she handed it to Sadie. "This is your granddaughter's book, isn't it?"

"Oh, yes," the older woman who must have been at least seventy-five said as she straightened her hat.

"*Love's Crystal Flame,*" Crystal read out. "What a beautiful title."

"I always thought so. She dedicated this book to me, you know. And she made up the last poem in the book for me and my husband, see?" Sadie turned to the last dog-eared page. "That way folks will remember it. She said she wanted it to be the last thing people read before they closed the book. It reminded her of the stories I told her about Joe and me." Sadie didn't try to keep the pride from her voice as she carefully closed the precious book and checked it over. Her name was actually in a book. She'd had a hand in making it. A special book her granddaughter wrote.

"That's so sweet. I'll have to get a copy from the bookstore," Crystal assured her.

"They've got plenty—all signed."

"Are you okay?" Crystal asked her.

Sadie nodded, and sadness clenched her heart. "I'm more than fine."

"It's good to see you again."

"I hope you're home to stay."

Crystal looked toward her mountain. "I am."

Sadie watched as Crystal walked to her car. Her granddaughter had written a book. She was so very proud of her granddaughter that she carried that book everywhere she went.

But she couldn't read the poem that her granddaughter wrote—just for her.

Time was running out. Sadie glanced at the beautiful picture on the cover. A bunch of pretty and delicate mountain flowers—pink, purple, and white. Call it pride for wanting to read this beautiful book herself. She wouldn't let anyone read it to her. Folks didn't know she couldn't read—not even her children. She had been good at hiding the fact.

For months, Annie had been teaching her with those Dick, Jane, and Sally books. Sadie had done very well on them, but now she was ready to move on. Annie had gotten herself shot in the hip a few weeks ago, and between the pain of her hip replacement and therapy, Sadie didn't have the heart to bother her.

Just yesterday Sadie had taken her a few dinners to stack in the freezer and the pain was still pretty bad.

Sadie had hoped for some books a little more interesting than the books Annie had used. Her grandchildren had more interesting books with pretty pictures. Sadie remembered looking at the pictures when she tidied up the books after the grandkids fell asleep. But reading was reading. As long as she learned, she'd read anything.

But she had more pressing concerns. Her eleven-year-old grandson was having problems with reading in school. He'd called her a week before school closed. Other kids were making fun of him because he couldn't keep up and it hurt his feelings. He wanted to quit school.

Listening to him talk almost broke Sadie's heart into a million pieces. When she hung up, she sat on the chair and cried like a baby, feeling the pain her grandbaby felt every day from those hateful kids.

If she could read, she would have packed her bags right then and headed to the bus station and gone straight to him. But she couldn't help him. She'd told her daughter to send him to her just the same. She didn't know how she'd do it, but she was going to figure out a way to help her grandbaby.

Sadie watched Crystal get into her car. Crystal. Crystal was a teacher. She had nothing to do all summer. No reason why she couldn't teach their little group and help Sadie's grandson.

"Is anything wrong, Sadie? Can I give you a lift somewhere?"

Sadie came out of her daze and moved forward. "No, no," she said, shaking her head. "I was just taking my daily walk to the store. Thanks anyway."

Sadie watched as Crystal drove away, then looked in her purse to make sure her new glasses were okay. Her new reading glasses. She nodded and closed her purse. They were just fine.

That's exactly what she'd do, Sadie thought as she resumed her walk to the drugstore. She'd ask Annie to ask Crystal if she would give them reading lessons for the summer. She didn't have time to lose.

Two

Crystal stopped by Aunt Annie's white cottage with its cheery blue trim. In her yard, blooming roses exploded in color. But her usually feisty aunt slept fitfully in her four-poster bed, looking frail and delicate in her cream silk gown, a blue and white sheet pulled to her waist.

Crystal wouldn't consider waking her.

Delicate rose essence drifted in the air. On her dresser neat designer bottles of rose water, sachets, and perfumes that her aunt concocted were poised neatly on a ceramic tray.

The only problem was that Aunt Annie liked Richard. In her eyes, Richard could do no wrong. Crystal wondered what Annie felt about Richard now that he represented the Baker boys.

Crystal left a message with Annie's male nurse that she'd return tomorrow and then she made the dreaded trip to the home she and Richard had shared.

Once there, Crystal walked up the cobblestone pathway and climbed the three steps to the long porch. She inhaled deeply and opened the maple door. The stained-glass oval in the center sparkled. As she entered the foyer, she stepped back in time. The colors in the dried flowers she'd arranged in the Chinese vase on the Queen Anne antique table had dimmed. Beside the vase stood a framed photo of their wedding. She looked happy. She *had* been happy on that day.

For the two months before she'd left for Japan, this haven had been a nightmare. She glanced upstairs and wondered if Richard had gotten rid of all the baby things she'd bought. Her sister, Tamela, and her husband had painted the baby's room a pretty green and decorated it with bright yellow, blue, pink, and green flower borders. The colors had been chosen to encourage a creative mind.

Crystal placed her hand on the stained oak banister and slowly climbed the stairs, unmindful of her surroundings. She moved as if she were in a trance as she progressed down the hallway until she stopped in front of a door. She inhaled slowly, unable to budge the sour knot in her stomach. Her hand twisted the doorknob and opened the door.

The room had been repainted off-white. Baby furniture had been replaced with the previous cherry double bed and matching mirrored dresser and side tables. The room had been returned to its guest room status. Crystal slowly exhaled, just realizing that she'd held her breath. In a sense she was glad everything was gone—that she didn't have to look at all the preparations she'd made for their child. She left the room and closed the door behind her. Richard could be thoughtful in many ways. She'd escaped, and he was left behind to put the nursery back in order so that she wouldn't have to relive the horror. But so much had transpired—too much for her to change her mind about the future. So, she sought out the master bedroom to pack her things.

On the way, she glanced at her watch. Richard's plane should be leaving in half an hour. She paused by the door and glanced at the princess phone on the bedside table. Before she could stop herself, she marched across the room and called Theresa, informing her that she wouldn't be going on the trip after all. Then she tried to reach Richard, but his cell phone line was busy. She shouldn't just leave him waiting. Damn it, why should she have a conscience? It was his own fault for trying to manipulate her—he never could take no for an answer. Still, she thought . . . *Just stop it, Crystal, and pack your bags! Don't let Richard do this to you.*

Where the hell are you, Crystal? Richard stood in front of the seat holding his laptop and notes, regarding the faces entering the terminal. The constant drone of airport conversation whirled around him. Latecomers hustled to the departure desk.

But no Crystal.

He pulled his cell phone from his pocket and punched in his home number to check to see if she was at least on her way.

While the phone rang, the night ahead spun in his mind—after the plane landed in Ohio and they'd settled in their hotel room. Crystal in a long, slinky gown—better, Crystal in nothing but glorious silky brown skin, writhing underneath him. The taste of her sweet nipples in his mouth—running his tongue over her honeyed skin, savoring the touch of her hands as they slid over his body. He closed his eyes briefly. He knew just how he'd love her, too. Loving wouldn't be quick—at least for the second go-round. He smiled happily. He wouldn't get much sleep tonight.

He'd only have to stop for an hour or two to make notes on the brief for tomorrow's meeting.

The answering machine clicked on and he listened to the recording of her voice. He hadn't changed it after she left. Sometimes at night he'd hit the announcement button just to hear her voice. Richard pressed END and smiled. She must be on her way.

He glanced down the corridor at the sea of faces rushing to various terminals, mentally urging Crystal to hurry up and get her butt here before takeoff. He shoved the phone into his pocket and sat in the seat next to a man reading the *Post*. Worry was what he got for not insisting that she come with him from the office. He shouldn't have let her out of his sight.

A familiar face headed in his direction. By the time the man stopped in front of him, Richard was on his feet again. Leon Stark. His rival. His friend since elementary school.

"Richard," he said, clapping him on the shoulder. "How are you?" Richard glanced down at Leon's spiffy off-white suit, the jacket thrown negligently over one shoulder. Leon stood a few inches shorter than Richard's six-one but the man made up for his lack of height in attitude.

Richard moved to the side to clear his view in case Crystal came charging toward him. "I'm good. How about yourself?"

"Good, good. Crystal left me an e-mail saying she wanted to talk to me. Do you know when she'll be back?"

Richard's whole body tightened. "When did she e-mail you?" he asked evasively.

"Got it before I left the office."

Richard bit the inside of his jaw. "I see."

"Where're you headed?"

"Ohio. You?"

"New York."

A boarding announcement came over the intercom. "That's my flight," Leon said. "Be seeing you around."

"Sure." As Leon strode to the gate, Richard dialed his office. He scowled as he punched the digits on his phone. Theresa answered immediately.

"Theresa, Richard here. Have you heard from Crystal?"

"I thought she called you. She said she would." Richard heard her sigh across the wire. "She asked me to cancel her ticket."

The boarding call was announced for his flight.

"O—kay." He disconnected, grabbed his bag, and handed his ticket to the agent. Then he plowed down the aisle, found his first-class seat, and sank into it. The seat beside him that Theresa had booked for Crystal remained empty. His visions of copping a feel beneath a blanket evaporated like a puff of smoke.

The stewardess asked him if he wanted a drink. He ordered a scotch and water. In seconds she handed it to him. He sipped his drink and waited.

There wasn't much that Richard expected from other people. He learned long ago to depend on himself and only himself. The exception to that rule had been Crystal. She'd been the one person who had always been there for him.

To thwart the nagging unease that he might really have lost Crystal for good, Richard lifted the glass to his lips and swallowed. The burn down to his insides soothed him like a long workout. He remembered a particularly important baseball game when he was eleven. He'd been selected to play in a tournament and was so eager for his parents to watch him play he'd talked about it nonstop for days—at every meal, at bedtime. He'd garnered promises, even written reminders on their calendars.

On the day of the game, Leon's father dropped them off. Richard watched and waited for his parents. During each inning, each time he went to bat, as he stood at the pitcher's mound readying himself to throw the ball. He hit two home runs that game. He pitched eight strikeouts. Everyone's parents cheered except his. Later on that night, he discovered his parents had been at an important dinner.

He never spoke to them about that game. When the neighbors congratulated them, his parents admonished him for his silence. Telling them about it ruined the excitement of having them there—watching their smiles, hearing their applause, listening to their cheers. Later on, his mother had taken him out to celebrate.

When he sat there without Crystal, he felt like that eleven-year-old kid again—at the pitcher's mound. Alone. With Crystal in his life, he'd never felt alone. She was the one person he'd thought he could always depend on.

Richard drained his glass and handed it to the stewardess. He waited for the coach travelers to finish boarding and stow their luggage, and wished for the plane to be airborne so that he could pull out his laptop and lose himself in his work—to keep from dwelling on the fact that his world was crashing around him.

He reached into his pocket and pulled out the rings she'd left on his desk. He'd brought them with him hoping to give them back to her. Now he rubbed his thumb over the rings and thought of Crystal.

Crystal packed her bags and started her trek to her cabin, first stopping by the grocery store on the other side of town. Since it was the middle of the day, the parking area was only half-full. She greeted several people on her way into the store, but didn't slow her pace enough to make conversation. She grabbed a basket and pushed it down the aisles, tossing in vegetables, fruit, and enough staples to last her a few days. In the aisle with the flour, she saw Gertrude Grant glancing suspiciously at the other end as she held a can of soup in her hand. Then she squinted at the ingredients on the side. The woman looked terribly distressed.

"Hello, Mrs. Grant."

The older woman yelped and dropped the soup, bringing a hand to her chest. "You scared the living daylights out of me."

Crystal approached the woman, bent, and retrieved the can. Then she handed it over and hugged her. Clutching the can in her large knuckled hand, Mrs. Grant squeezed Crystal's shoulders.

"I hope you're back for good," she said, standing back and holding Crystal at arm's length. "We sure missed you."

Sudden warmth flowed through Crystal. "I missed you, too. I'm here to stay."

"Good."

Crystal pointed to the can. "I never knew you to use canned soup."

"I usually don't, but I thought I'd give it a try since it doesn't have a lot of fat and the doctor put me on a low-fat diet. My eyes are going bad and I have trouble reading the small print."

Crystal reached for the can. "Let me read it for you."

"I appreciate that."

Crystal read the various ingredients for the woman, who nodded.

"Guess I have to make my own soup after all. Doc Stone took me off of stuff with a lot of sodium."

"Your soup is better, anyway."

"Well, thank you, dear. You'll have to come for a visit. I'll make you some."

Crystal thanked her and assured her that she would. Then she bought deli sandwiches, cheese, crackers, orange juice, and milk and was soon on her way.

Halfway up her mountain, she stopped at a local winery that produced excellent champagne and purchased three bottles.

Then she climbed the winding hills to her cabin. The cabin had been uppermost on her mind for the last two months. Drinking a mimosa on the deck. Watching the sunset. The day was waning, and suddenly it was imperative that she spend that first sunset on the deck to toast her new beginning.

Virginia offered unique and wonderful views any season of the year. When she'd left the Blue Ridge Mountains in January, snow covered the ground and bare tree branches bent, weighted down by glimmering icicles. Now in mid-June, pretty pink and white mountain flowers dotted the roadside.

Well-meaning friends would say that her marriage had been perfect. Richard was a lawyer. They were financially secure, with a lovely home and mountain cabin. Material trappings.

She wondered sometimes if life would be better if she could accept less. She also wondered that if she lowered the standards on what she felt she deserved from life, would she end up as one of those bitter old women who weren't pleased with anything because their deepest desires were unfulfilled?

Only pleasant thoughts, Crystal reminded herself as she

parked in front of the modern, three-bedroom log cabin graced with huge windows. The flowers she'd planted last spring were in full bloom. So were the weeds that were slowly choking them out. The trees were completely green, though they didn't grow quite as high here as they did at lower elevations.

She quickly unloaded her luggage and groceries. Then she threw open the windows and front door to let in fresh air.

The huge great room was separated from the kitchen by a massive stone fireplace. She stacked her meager supplies in the refrigerator and included a bottle of champagne. Then she threw off the sheets covering the furniture, vacuumed, and dusted. Richard should be on his way to Ohio by now. She felt no joy.

She put away her dust rag and polish and suddenly heard a car door slam outside. A visitor already? For a fleeting moment, she thought that Richard might have canceled his flight and come after her. She ran to the front door.

A stranger stood on her porch, peeping in her screen door.

Dusk was approaching rapidly. Crystal was starving and she wanted to fix her mimosa in time to be on the deck for her sunset.

"Who did you say you were?" she asked through a locked screen door that offered little protection. The medium-brown-complexioned young man sweating in his suit looked innocent enough, but so would Charles Manson if he shaved. The cabin was nestled away in the middle of nowhere, with no one in shouting distance. But this man had the look of a salesman.

"Elzey Johnson."

"I see. I'm not in the market to buy anything today." She started to shut the wooden door.

"I'm not a salesman."

"Oh?"

"Your husband sent me."

Crystal snorted. Richard hadn't wasted time hiring a lawyer. So much for wanting to work things out. She'd spoken to him only this afternoon. Though why would he hire someone who looked more like a law clerk?

Elzey pushed the wire rims up on his nose. "I work with Richard."

"I see." Crystal pinched her lips. "Well, I'll have my lawyer contact you soon."

"I don't think you understand. I've come to see if you need anything for the trip tomorrow."

Crystal frowned. What on earth was he talking about? "What trip?"

"To join Richard. In Ohio. I'm to pick you up at seven to take you to the airport."

Crystal scowled at him. "You've wasted your time. I'm not going to Ohio. Have a good evening, Mr. Johnson." She slammed the door.

And then it hit her. A divorce. The end of her marriage with Richard. They'd been married for five years but they'd dated since she was nineteen—her sophomore year in college. She leaned her head against the cold door, her spirits suddenly plunging. Her world had changed forever and that filled her with an unexpected hollowness.

The trembling started in her hands and spread through her body. Suddenly she was cold. She wrapped her arms around herself as if to hold in the warmth. And she couldn't stop the tears from streaming to the surface and spilling over. Soon she was bawling harder than she'd done in months and found her legs were too weak to stand. She sat on the floor with her back to the door, pulled her knees to her chest. She leaned her elbows on her knees and sobbed with her face in her hands. Oh, God. Her world had been uprooted and she had no idea what her future would entail. Had she done the right thing? Should she have stayed with Richard and accepted what he offered—and lose a part of herself in the process?

She thought she could just waltz into his office, make her magnanimous announcement, and leave and start a new life. But it wasn't that easy—even when she knew from the depths of her soul that she'd taken the only option she could and still hold on to her sanity. Right now it would be so easy to go back to him. But it would be for all the wrong reasons.

Even though she still felt as if there were a gaping hole inside her, her tears slowly subsided and she got up to pluck tissues from the box on the fireplace mantel. She dried her eyes and blew her nose.

The metal knocker banging against the door jarred her out of her gloom. Crystal wiped her face. Then she sniffed and opened the door again.

Elzey awkwardly thrust a business card toward her. He looked shy and out of place, as if he'd rather be anyplace but here.

"I'd like to leave you my home number in case you change your mind," he said as he looked closely at her. "For any reason. If you need anything, anything at all."

Crystal wondered at the insanity of opening her door to a stranger but she opened the screen door anyway and took the card in her shaky hand. She scanned his name and *The Law Offices of Richard Dupree, Esquire,* the address and phone numbers in raised lettering. He'd penciled in his home number.

Crystal glanced at the young man again. He could have just handed her the card and left, but he looked as if he didn't want to leave. Obviously, he'd heard her crying jag. But more importantly, Crystal didn't want to be alone right now.

Elzey had that hungry and tired look about him. Richard had often looked hassled when he started his practice which seemed like eons ago.

Before she could caution herself, she asked, "I was just about to eat dinner. Would you like to come in and share a sandwich?"

"Thank you, yes."

She led the way to the deck and trooped to the kitchen to quickly fix the food, calling herself a dozen kinds of fool for inviting in a perfect stranger even though he did look innocent and like somebody's beloved younger brother.

She slapped the turkey and Swiss cheese sandwiches on a plate with chips, fixed two champagne flutes of mimosa, and carried it all on a tarnished silver tray to the deck, hardly believing that Richard had taken on an associate. He had always handled his practice like a one-man army.

A noisy mosquito landed by her ear, prompting her to run back inside for the repellent that she applied to her exposed skin. She carried the bottle outside so that Elzey could use it, though he had little skin exposed.

Elzey had loosened his tie, placed his jacket on the back of a chair, and rolled up his white shirtsleeves. He stood by the railing. "Your view is even more spectacular than mine."

"Do you live nearby?"

"Three miles from here. I'm renting a cabin from Mr. Walker."

He lathered mosquito repellent on his forearms, neck, and face, and recapped the bottle. She lit a lantern that was supposed to keep the pesky insects away but never seemed quite up to the task.

Elzey joined her at the table and bit greedily into the sandwich.

Crystal's appetite was nonexistent, but she forced herself to nibble anyway. "How long have you been working with Richard?"

"Since May, after I left Roanoke." Elzey picked up his napkin and dabbed at the corners of his mouth.

"And why would you settle in our little town instead of someplace larger?"

"I get to practice everything here. In a larger office, I'd have to specialize, and not necessarily in an area that interested me. And your husband has an awesome reputation."

His eyes lit up as he spoke. Crystal envied his enthusiasm and vigor—that unrestrained hope for the future. She'd always enjoyed the classroom and her children, yet the last semester had been the most difficult in her teaching career. After the miscarriage, it seemed her drive for teaching had vanished. She rubbed her forehead. What would she do? All she'd ever dreamed of since elementary school was teaching. Suddenly fear tingled along the edges of her spine.

"Richard's a great lawyer."

Crystal glanced up at the young man. "That he is. So what do you do for entertainment?"

"Entertainment?" He pronounced the word as if it were foreign.

"Yes." She smiled. He definitely needed her intervention. "It's allowed, you know. Even for lawyers. Have you met many people here?" Crystal thought a moment. If she didn't do something, he'd end up just like Richard. "A summer festival is coming up—at the park. Practically the whole town attends."

"If I have time, I'll go."

"Take the time," Crystal said seriously.

He smiled and nodded.

They finished off their meal and sipped mimosas while they watched the orange glow of the sun slowly sink behind the mountains. The only sounds were sounds of nature. Water rushing past below, tree frogs, a zillion insects. The swing caught Crystal's eye. The two-seater swing she'd installed last summer in hopes of spending lazy evenings with her husband.

Suddenly, she was glad she wasn't alone. Having Elzey here was like having a favored younger brother around, to take away the sting of loneliness—not that Crystal couldn't entertain herself. She'd spent the last few years doing just that. But she didn't want to be alone right now.

Tonight she'd enjoy her view with a new friend. Tomorrow was soon enough to begin to sort out in which direction her life would turn.

At noon the next day, on his way from the law offices of Pratt, Pratt and Stone, Richard finally reached Elzey. "What do you mean, she's not coming? I sent you there to make sure she got on that plane."

"She was adamant. She didn't want to get back on a

plane after her long flight. I went to her house, had dinner with her, and tried and tried to convince her.''

Richard tightened his hand around the phone, wiped the sweat dripping down his face, and imagined Elzey sitting on the deck enjoying the cool mountain breeze. "You stayed for dinner?'' His sweet wife used to leave him a plate warming on the stove, or brewed his morning coffee and scrambled eggs at six, sending him out on a full stomach. His wife who'd at one time come at his beck and call.

"She offered and I was starved. She makes the best mimosas. Not everyone makes them well. The secret is the champagne.''

Crystal had always talked about the two of them sitting on the deck sipping mimosas, watching the sun go down. The fact that Elzey was there in Richard's place left a sour taste in his mouth.

"I sent you there to convince her to get on that plane and you're sitting on *my* deck sipping a mimosa. Do you think that if you spent less time on the drinking and more on convincing her that she'd be on the plane right now?''

A woman passing on the sidewalk skirted a wide path around him. He ignored her.

"I didn't want to antagonize her. Besides, she looked tired.''

"Antagonize her, damn it!'' Richard stifled the impulse to hurl the phone across the street. Instead he punched END. A woman jostled him as she passed. He rubbed the back of his hand across his face to gather his bearings. He'd stopped at the door of a card shop. Shoppers were milling about in the rows and rows of cards and knickknacks. He stood there a moment gazing and then he opened the door. Cool air hit his face. Walking down the first aisle, he studied the various cards—birthday, sick, condolence, graduation, friendship. Suddenly an idea sprang to mind. Crystal had loved getting cards and letters in college. Since there wasn't a snowball's chance in hell of getting her here now, maybe a card would thaw her just before he returned to town.

Three

Richard paced impatiently in Annie's family room. Annie's daughter Stacey had answered the door and now went to get her. He'd stopped on his way to his office Thursday morning after getting permission from the prosecutor to speak to her. Since Richard represented the potential defendant, he wasn't allowed to speak to their key witness without their permission. Had Windy Hills been a large city, he wouldn't have gained permission. He appreciated the informality of small towns. It was still early and he worried that he was bothering Annie before she'd prepared herself for the day. He wanted to talk with her face-to-face—not over the phone. This would be his only opportunity to speak with her today. He'd put it off long enough as it was.

As he waited he listened to Annie fuss in the other room. Her cane thumped on the wooden floor.

He had returned from Cleveland last night. An hour later, he'd received a visit from Leon, his wife's lawyer. He and Leon had been rivals since kindergarten. They still competed in basketball and weekly racquetball games. They'd also remained friends in an odd sort of way. The last thing Richard wanted to hear from the man was that his wife had hired him to handle her divorce.

"Just let me be," Annie snapped. "I can walk by myself. Don't need any help."

"Just don't overdo it," Crystal admonished.

Richard tensed at hearing his wife's voice.

"You've got company, Mom," Stacey announced.

"Who is it?"

He detected a short pause before Stacey said, "Richard."

"What's he doing here?" Crystal asked. "I'll go talk to him."

"He came to see me," Annie said.

"I know that," Crystal started.

"Find something to occupy yourself with. I'll be fine." Annie didn't enter the room alone, however. Crystal threw him a narrow glance and hovered around the older woman, who wasn't that old at all. She was only in her late fifties.

Annie, dressed in a red-print caftan, glared at her daughter and Crystal. "I'm going to send the both of you home. I need some space."

Sweat drenched Annie's forehead. Clearly walking was still quite painful.

"Annie, how are you?" Richard moved forward and clasped her elbow in his hand. His wife, wearing white shorts with a blue tank top, looked cool and very pretty. It had been a long time since they'd been together.

"I'll sit in one of the kitchen chairs. It's easier," Annie said. Richard led her to the table and helped her lower herself into the chair. He was very aware that his wife stood nearby. He also caught the essence of her familiar perfume.

"Hello, Crystal," Richard said after Annie was settled.

She spoke to him and asked if he or Annie wanted something cool to drink. They both declined.

"Why don't you see about my roses?" Annie said. "I promised Ella I'd give her some for the ladies' luncheon. I don't want just anybody messing in my rose garden. Richard and I will be fine, won't we, dear?"

"We certainly will," he said, smiling at this woman who had always been his friend.

Clearly Crystal didn't want to leave, but with her aunt's insistence she had no option but to do so.

She started in on Richard one last time. "This isn't a good time for Richard to be nagging you."

Annie moaned. "I got a hip replacement, not a lobotomy. I can make my own decisions. Just because the two of you are acting foolish doesn't mean I am." She hooked her cane on the table edge. "Early morning while the dew is still on the roses is the best time to pick them."

"Don't tire her out," Crystal warned Richard. She grabbed a basket from the top of the kitchen cabinet and slammed out the door.

Richard pulled his chair close to Annie. "How have you really been?"

"Getting better every day. But I suspect you want to talk about something else."

"You're right." He remembered Annie had always been one for getting straight to the point. "I'm sure you've heard I'm handling the Blake boys' case."

She nodded, her face devoid of expression. "I heard."

"If I thought they had hurt you, I wouldn't have taken them on. But they swore they didn't shoot you. And I believe them."

The older woman nodded.

"Annie, do you trust me?"

Annie regarded him a moment, then sighed—and nodded again.

Richard released a sigh himself. His own wife didn't trust him to keep her happy—to share her sorrow with him—to know that he'd always be there for her. Annie trusted him. Her trust meant more than he or she realized. He wondered if the rest of Crystal's family had Annie's regard. He was afraid to put that to the test. They blamed him for Crystal's leaving—just as they thought he'd betrayed them by taking on this case.

"Thanks, Annie. You don't know how much that means to me."

She patted his hand. "You know I've always respected and admired you. I've always thought your heart was with Crystal."

"I want you to help me find the attacker."

She shook her head, and her short hair, dyed brown, flowed gracefully around her face. "I don't know how I can help you. I didn't see anyone that night. It was dark and his face was covered with something. I only got a glimpse. Then suddenly I was hurting so much."

"What about cars? Did you see any unusual vehicles in the vicinity before you were hurt?"

She shook her head again.

"Did you have the theater money with you?" The robbery had occurred after she returned home from closing the theater one Wednesday night.

"I had money in my purse, but not the proceeds from that night. That's a bad night for a robbery anyway. We make a lot less on Wednesdays. Besides, he didn't even try for the money in my wallet. He seemed to be looking for something specific. I don't know what though. Before he finished, Mavis across the way started screeching and he ran away."

"What was in the car?"

She shrugged. "Nothing. I'd just cleaned it out earlier that day."

"Did you take anything out while cleaning it?"

"No. I keep a clean car. I just vacuumed and wiped the inside down."

Richard pondered that. "So it was one person."

She frowned, thinking of that night. "I only saw one," she finally said.

"I promise you, Annie. I'm going to do everything I can to find out who did this to you."

Annie peered through the window. Crystal was angrily snipping perfect rose blossoms and tossing them into the basket. "Lord have mercy. I hope your wife doesn't ruin my roses.'' She gave him a concerned look. ''My body's mending. I'm more concerned about Crystal and you.''

''So am I, Annie. So am I.''

She cocked her head toward the window. ''Now's the perfect time to talk to her.''

He frowned after his difficult wife. ''I intend to do just that.'' After the way she treated him, anger hovered close to the surface.

''It won't be easy.''

''Don't I know it.''

By the time Richard reached the rose garden, Crystal had almost finished with the roses Ella would need.

He plunged his hands into his pockets and watched her. She continued to snip away and only hoped she was still selecting perfect blossoms. His regard totally unnerved her.

He looked extremely hot—and good—in his navy suit slacks with starched shirt and print tie. The breadth of his shoulders seemed caged. His raven eyes were stormy as if something weighed heavily on his mind. Crystal guessed she was the temporary cause, but their situation would be forgotten soon and he'd move on.

''I admit I don't begin to understand what's come over you,'' Richard finally said. ''I talked to Leon last night. You were going to file for a divorce and not even discuss it with me. That's not like you.''

''I told you my intentions before you left.''

''You stood me up at the airport. You could have told me you weren't going.''

''You wouldn't take no for an answer. I didn't feel like arguing.'' She tucked another blossom into the basket. ''You only listen to what you want to hear.''

Something in Richard seemed to snap. ''Well, think about this. If you *don't* discuss this relationship with me, if you *don't* try to work it out with me, I'm going to tie this case in court for years. Your money will run out long before any divorce papers are signed.''

A fist clutched at Crystal's heart. She found herself taking an involuntary step back. "You can't do that."

He leaned toward her, arrogant and forbearing. "Talk to Leon, your lawyer, about what I can do."

"Why won't you give me the divorce?" Crystal asked. She wasn't going to let him intimidate her. She leaned toward him, the basket separating them. "I don't want anything from you—no alimony, you can even keep the house. I'll settle for the cabin."

"Just the destruction of our family. Don't you think that's enough?"

"No, Richard. We don't have a family. Our marriage was destroyed a long time ago."

"Three months, Crystal," he continued as if she hadn't spoken. "Work with me for three months. If you still want a divorce, I'll consent. Uncontested. Hell, by then we both might want one." The angry retort hardened his features.

Crystal paused. "Are you listening to me?"

"I'm listening."

"Don't put us through three months of torture."

"Severing our marriage is more torture than a short reconciliation—just time to work on our problems. I'm only trying to save a good marriage." He sighed, pulling a dead leaf from a rosebush. "I know the miscarriage was difficult for you. It was for me, too. I know you don't think it was."

Crystal glanced away, not wanting a reminder. Although she was better, the pain still lingered. "That's behind us now. I'm moving on."

Richard shook his head. "I don't think so. Just work with me on this and we'll make it, Crystal." His voice softened. "Don't let one tragedy destroy all we've meant to each other."

His eyes were so heartrending, Crystal was forced to glance away from the naked desire. "You're acting as if it was the baby that separated us. It wasn't. We were falling apart long before my pregnancy. We're not happy together."

He reached out and caressed her cheek. "I was happy."

She shook his hand from her face. "You don't know if

you were happy or not. We hardly saw each other. I just want a clean break where we can separate as friends, not as enemies."

"People who love each other the way we do don't separate as friends. It's too painful. We belong together."

Crystal closed her eyes briefly. "I thought so once. I don't believe that any longer."

He inhaled as if she'd stabbed him. "I'm sorry you feel that way. The decision is yours."

A sudden chill hung on the edge of Richard's words. He turned away and started walking away in long and angry strides. Before he turned the corner at the house, he said, "If you're willing to work with me, meet me for dinner at the Moon Crest at six."

Moments later, Crystal heard the motor to Richard's car start. She ran into the house and dialed Leon, only to hear his secretary say that he'd left for court. She left a message for him to call her.

"You're all done with the roses?" Annie said as Crystal disconnected.

"I'll put them in water." Crystal's gaze jerked to her aunt. She reached under the cabinet for a vase with trembling fingers. "Would you like for me to stay longer?" she asked.

"No. Stacey is taking me to the park. I'll be fine. You go on and do what you have to do."

"If you need me, you have my number."

Annie nodded. "Richard's a good man. I hope the two of you can work it out."

Crystal didn't want advice right now. Her marriage wasn't the strong one that her aunt's had been.

"I saw Tina French at the hospital visiting a neighbor the other day." Tina was the principal of Crystal's school. "She asked if you were coming back in the fall. They could certainly use you."

"I don't know if I can continue teaching. I'm going to take the summer to think things over."

"Not teach! You've always wanted to teach. You'd been play-teaching to your dolls even before you started school."

Crystal rubbed her forehead. "I know. I just . . . I can't explain it. The spirit isn't there any longer."

"I'm sorry about that, Crystal. You take the summer to come to grips with whatever ails you."

Annie watched her niece climb the stairs to get her things from the spare bedroom. She wished there was something she could do to make two people who loved each other see the light.

This thing with teaching went back to the miscarriage, Annie was sure. Losing a child had the tendency to rip a family apart. Richard loved her niece. Love was a precious gift. Annie and her husband had shared a rare kind of love. She'd hoped for the same for Crystal and Richard.

Annie sighed and started down the hall to the first-floor bedroom to change clothes. She was taking her first trip to the park today. She was afraid. Afraid her hip would give out and she'd make a fool of herself and fall flat on her face. Still, she wouldn't allow herself to stay in the house any longer. She couldn't remain an invalid—even if it was only in her mind.

Sadie was taking her daily walk when she saw Annie sitting across the street in the park. The sun was bright and hot. Sadie adjusted her hat to shade the sun. She didn't know why she continued with this walking ritual. It wasn't doing her any good. In good time, the end would come, and walking wasn't going to prolong the inevitable.

What did worry her was that she wasn't making progress in her reading. Her grandson arrived the day before and precious time that could be used to help him was wasted. Before she knew it, the summer would be gone. He would be home in the same predicament. The idea of asking Crystal to teach her had been plaguing her for a week now. But she didn't have the nerve. Annie might think asking her niece was an insult. Crystal was Annie's niece. Annie could ask her.

Sadie hated to worry Annie. But she didn't see another

option. She waited for the walk sign, the only one in Windy Hills, to indicate it was safe to cross the street. Just a few cars were in the vicinity this time of the day, she noticed as she crossed the street.

"Hi, Sadie. It's good to see you," Annie said from the wooden bench under the pecan tree.

"How are you feeling, Annie?"

"Better. Thanks for asking."

Sadie lowered herself onto the bench and placed her hat beside her. Her head felt cooler. A small breeze shook the leaves.

"That's a mighty sassy hat you're wearing."

Sadie glanced at the hat. Today she'd pinned a group of silk wildflowers to match her rose-colored slacks.

"I've never seen anyone with as many pretty hats as you."

"I love my hats."

Annie was holding a rose in her hand. "Why don't you take this?"

"Thanks, Annie."

She watched Sadie closely and Sadie glanced at the kids playing on the swing set and monkey bars.

"You been feeling okay?"

"Couldn't be better." Sadie didn't worry about her business getting out. She trusted Annie to keep her business to herself. "There is one thing that's been troubling me. I don't want to put you to any trouble, but I've been wondering if it would be okay to ask Crystal to teach our little reading group—just until you're feeling better."

Crystal had too much on her mind already, Annie thought. She didn't need another obligation. She needed to deal with Richard and their marriage.

Annie remembered their conversation. Crystal was taking the summer to think. Annie couldn't put these people on her niece.

She glanced at Sadie. The woman must be at least eighty. Three months ago, Sadie had come tearing into her house, raring to learn to read, to read her granddaughter's book.

Sadie wasn't looking herself. She seemed to have aged years over the last year. Annie had wondered many times if Sadie was having medical problems. Annie also knew Sadie was a private person. She didn't like to talk about her business. She'd been that way since Annie moved to this town after she married William.

Annie sighed. The whole world wasn't going to be put on hold while Crystal worked on her problems. Then, too, teaching these people three hours a week wasn't going to put that much of a hamper on Crystal's thinking. Ultimately the decision would be Crystal's. Annie wasn't going to pressure her. She'd let Crystal make the decision. Perhaps teaching adults would get her into the mood for teaching children again. Perhaps teaching them would bring back the joy her niece had experienced. Not everyone could reach children the way Crystal could. If Crystal didn't come back to her profession, the loss would not only be felt by her but by the children whose lives she'd touched through the years. Perhaps teaching these people who craved so dearly to read would bring her out of the depression she'd fallen into.

"I can't make any promises. But I'll ask her, Sadie."

Four

Watching a bartender mix drinks was like observing a magician perform magic, Richard thought as he studied the bartender's efficiency behind the bar. He nursed a scotch and water as he waited impatiently for Crystal and wondered why he'd arrived fifteen minutes early. He shouldn't have. It left too much time to wonder how his life had come to this.

He swiveled the drink in his glass. Ice clinked against the side. The bartender wiped up after a customer who left. Richard didn't bother watching the TV tucked into the corner as the after-work crowd gathered in. Business was picking up by the minute.

As the liquor fired up his insides, he wondered if she'd even show—if she'd call his bluff. Had she sensed that he'd issued an empty threat—that he couldn't possibly hurt her? Couldn't she see that he was trying to keep her from making the biggest mistake of her life—of their lives? Richard sighed. Perhaps not. Crystal wasn't in the frame of mind to make drastic decisions. Richard knew he was doing what was best for both of them. He wasn't looking out for himself alone. It was his job to protect Crystal. She was his wife.

A person could only be protected up to a point. Would she just ignore him and go ahead with the divorce—just like the scene at the airport? Richard tightened his grip on his glass. He hated being stood up. It was just like her and the mood she'd been in lately to do it again. He glanced at his watch. Five fifty-five. She'd make him sweat it out down to the last minute—if she showed up at all.

Six came and went. Richard went from his one-drink limit to Pepsi, which did nothing to soothe his mounting temper.

By ten after six, he'd finished his Pepsi. Crystal finally wandered into the restaurant. He left the bar and joined her at the door. "Took you long enough, didn't it?" he snapped, at the edge of his patience.

She glared at him, watched the waiter approach. "I didn't want to come at all."

"Talked to Leon, did you?"

She lifted her chin, meeting his gaze straight on, then tightened her lips and positioned her purse more securely on her shoulder.

Oh, hell. Richard knew right then she was going to fight him tooth and nail.

He followed the waitress who escorted them to their table—one that gave them a scenic view of the rolling hills. One silver lining in this God-forbidden awful situation. As soon as they were seated Richard opened his menu, distancing himself, trying to decide how to get things back to normal. He didn't see one item on the list. He only used the menu as a means to simmer down.

"I'm not really hungry. I just came here to get this over and done with," Crystal said, closing her menu and placing it by her plate.

He glanced at her over the top of his own. "You're looking scrawny. You need to eat."

"What I don't need is you ordering me around," she said with an angry movement of her hand.

Two old ladies at the table beside them watched with open mouths. Vacationers.

Richard glared at her. "You're bent on making us the spectacle of the whole town."

Crystal lowered her voice. "How we're presented to the town is what's wrong with this marriage in the first place. Well, I don't care how it looks. I'm living my life the way I want to for a change."

"Since when did I stop you from doing the things you want to do? Have I interfered with your career? Have I been a demanding husband?"

A waiter arrived and asked if they were ready to order. In a silence as thick as pea soup, Crystal ordered chef's salad.

"I'll have steak, medium well." Richard had said the first thing that came to mind. The waiter detected the tension and must have decided not to exchange town gossip as he usually did. He quickly excused himself.

Richard didn't want to talk about their problems during dinner and fought for a neutral topic to break the oppressive silence. Crystal made no effort to be cordial.

"Did you enjoy Japan?" he finally asked.

"It was fine."

"Annie's looking much better."

"She's getting along well considering the circumstances."

"How often will you be staying at her place?"

"Not often. Wednesdays and weekends when Stacey's at the theater."

"I see," Richard said, admiring the pretty blue silk sundress she wore with the pearls dangling at the top of her breasts. "And the rest of the time?" He focused on her face.

"I'll be at the cabin."

"I see."

"How are your parents?" she managed to ask.

"They're fine. It wouldn't hurt you to see them." Richard wanted to shake her and say *Wake up! You're talking to the man who loves you!* yet they were acting like polite acquaintances. Just thinking about it tore at his insides.

"Right now, it would be awkward. For both of us."

Strangers, Richard thought again. The situation between them had never been this strained before. Never.

After a few more awkward attempts at communication, dinner arrived and although the five-star restaurant's food was eloquently prepared, it could have been paste for all the appetite Richard had. Crystal merely picked at hers.

His wife was tense and angry—and beautiful. Dark circles outlined her eyes. Stress lines appeared on her face. She'd changed so much since the miscarriage. He was well aware that she had not forgiven him for not being there. He wished that he had gone straight home that night. That he hadn't stopped off. He would have done anything to prevent the loss of their child. After the miscarriage, she barely noticed he was around. He'd taken time from work, but she hadn't noticed that either. He'd wanted to share their loss with her, but he couldn't. She'd closed him out of her heart. And he couldn't talk about his pain to anyone else. To others he needed to present a strong facade. He didn't talk about it. The loss was something he should get over. He was supposed to move on, but he couldn't move on without his wife. They were hanging in limbo, together—yet mentally they were a world apart.

Richard reached over and grasped Crystal's hand. She withdrew quickly and turned away. What on earth could he do to ease her tension? What could he do to help her? He wouldn't entertain for a second the thought that she no longer loved him—that she really wanted to end the years of joy they'd shared. How could one incident tear apart what had once been a marriage dreams were made of?

Richard sipped his tea in the tense silence surrounding them. He knew a bargain would be the best for both of them. Maybe if they could work together, her perspective and drive for life would return. Perhaps she'd willingly come back to him, become the woman she'd been before the pregnancy.

Crystal pushed her plate away from her with half the food left untouched. ''Let's get this talk over with,'' she said finally.

Richard placed his fork on his plate and wiped his mouth with his napkin. Crystal was distant and aloof.

"I have a proposition to make to you," he said.

"What is it?"

"Let's make a bargain for the next three months. Let's try to be a couple—go through a courtship so to speak. Remember our courtship, Crystal?"

Crystal watched him warily. "Why should I have to go back that far?" She swiped a weary hand across her face. "What difference would it make? We haven't been together in years. Even when you were here, mentally you were a million miles away."

"Forgive me for having a career to build—for supporting my family." Couldn't she see that her stubborn behavior hurt both of them?

"I have a career, too. We also had a marriage, which always, always took second place."

"Crystal, marriage isn't a romance that ends on page three-fifty. It isn't lace curtains, romantic flowery comforters topped with a zillion pillows, dancing in the moonlight seven nights a week, endless romantic candlelight dinners on the patio, or sweeping up the stairs with you in my arms like the perfect romantic hero. Hell, I'm tired after a day in the office. You were too." Richard sensed immediately that he'd said the wrong thing, but he couldn't seem to stop himself.

Crystal reared back as if she'd been struck. How could he belittle her offerings to keep the marriage alive? She leaned toward him. "I'm not stupid. I don't expect to do those things nightly, but little gestures once in a while don't hurt. At least it would indicate you care. Otherwise, what do we have?" She pointed a forefinger toward his chest. "I'll tell you what. We have nothing." Crystal knew she'd been tired too, but she still put hot, nourishing meals on the table, which he didn't eat half the time because he didn't make it home for dinner. A punch in the stomach wouldn't throb nearly as much as his words had struck her heart.

"We have different interests."

"We have to share something together," she said, her voice suddenly quieter. "You spent more time with your friends than you spent with me. I sat home alone most Friday or Saturday nights."

"Being married doesn't mean we have to be each other's shadows. But you seem to find time to spend with just about everyone else."

Crystal threw up her hands. How could he be so obtuse? "I don't expect that. But you're not hearing me, and why isn't that surprising? In the twelve months before I left, I can count on both hands the times we spent together. They were political functions with your parents and dinner at your parents' home, which is about the most stress-provoking thing we could do because your mother hates me."

Frustration flowed through him in waves. "Honestly, Crystal. You're not married to my mother."

Crystal took a slow breath to slow her pulse. "It wasn't working, Richard. Now I want out." She thrust her fingers through her hair. "I won't live like this any longer."

Silence stretched; then Richard asked, "What do you have to lose?"

"Another three months of our lives."

Richard pinched the bridge of his nose and sighed. "Three months isn't too much to ask for. If it doesn't work out, you'll get your divorce."

Three months or three years. Leon had warned her of how difficult a divorce would be without Richard's compliance. She hadn't believed him. Richard hadn't been vindictive before. She stared at a stranger—her husband, the lawyer—and knew by the set of his jaw that he wasn't bluffing. She also wondered how she could have fallen in love with a man so hard, so calculating and cold. Sadness of another kind came forth. It didn't have to come to this.

"Three months," she finally said. "You give your word that I can have an uncontested divorce in three months."

His body came alert. She could just see the lawyer in him calculating victory. "If you still want out of the marriage."

Oh, she'd definitely want out. No more arguments. She'd

have her freedom to live in the town that she loved with no interference from Richard.

"Deal."

"I'll help you move your things back to the house."

"I'm not living with you."

"How do you suggest we work on our relationship?"

"With as much distance as possible."

He frowned. "Cooperation is part of the deal, Crystal. We have to be together to work out our differences or at least try to."

"You can't possibly expect us to take up from where we left off. I'm a different person." She raked him with a malevolent glare. "You're certainly a different person. Hell, I've made friends after I left whom I know better than I know you. And I learned a long time ago that you can't make a marriage based on good sex. I'm not moving back home."

Richard tightened his lips. "We have to at least see each other. Date. Eat out together."

With this bargain, she'd just jumped from the kettle into the fire. But she knew that the newness would soon wear off. She only had to hold out for three months.

"I'm staying at the cabin," she said again. She'd spent most of her summers there. A modest-sized three-bedroom log cabin several miles up the mountain. The road was almost impassable in winter. The back porch looked out onto the Smith River, and across the river, spectacular mountain peaks floated in a sheen of snow in the late spring and entertained any lucky onlooker. This year she'd missed the show. But not next year. Next year it would be hers, and she wasn't leaving that home again.

"Fine with me. You've always loved it there."

She nodded and pushed back from the table. "Well, I have a long drive ahead of me."

"Crystal, for us to work on our relationship, we have to spend time together. We haven't resolved that."

Crystal closed her eyes and rubbed her forehead. She

was buying time, not working on their relationship. "Two evenings each week, and not always weekends."

"Twice a week? That's it?"

"It's two more times a week than I saw you when we were married. Take it or leave it."

"You seem to be calling all the shots—for now. I'll take it," he snapped, leaving Crystal with the impression that she wasn't getting very much of a reprieve at all.

"If you cancel because of business, that'll be it. There are no make-up days. Mondays and Thursdays," she said.

How long would it be before he took on a project that would monopolize his time? There would always be time-consuming projects.

Annie loved early evening and the approaching twilight. Both she and Crystal enjoyed sunsets, Annie thought as she pondered how to approach Crystal about teaching reading skills to the group of five. No sense in delaying, she thought as she sat at the kitchen table staring out the window with the portable phone in her hand. She dialed her niece's number. The phone rang and rang. Crystal refused to get an answering machine. Annie disconnected and hazarded a glance at the clock. It was a quarter to eight. She'd try again later.

A cup of tea would be nice, she thought and it would help her sleep more peacefully. She forced herself out of the chair, put water in the kettle, and turned on the stove.

Her daughter had left a few minutes ago to do some grocery shopping. She'd be back before long. Annie stretched out her leg. She could do so now without it screaming for mercy. Just the other day her doctor had said she was mending well. Two more weeks, he'd said, and the pain would be much more manageable. The water began to boil in the kettle. On her way back to the stove the doorbell rang. Annie sighed and went slowly to the door. There stood Travis Walker, tall and handsome as the devil himself. His profile spoke of power and ageless strength.

Annie's heart jolted. Her pulse pounded. A brisk breeze blew through the screen door, fanning her. His hair looked slightly damp as if he'd washed it without drying it completely.

"Evening, Annie," he said in that fine bass voice that reached right down to her toes. "You look to be doing fine."

Her hand shook slightly as she unlocked the door. He handed her a bunch of lilies. "I hate to visit so late, but I was late with the farm work. How are you doing?"

"A lot better." She hooked the screen latch and led the way into the kitchen hoping he couldn't tell how foolish she was acting. She smelled the flowers. They had a nice fragrance to them.

"The flowers are pretty," she said, reaching in the cabinet for a vase.

"I hoped you'd like them." He held a hat in his hand. Travis was a courtly kind of man. Very mannerly. Very strong. Very solid. Something pleasant stirred within her and refused to settle down.

"I was fixing tea. Can I fix you a cup?" By now the kettle was whistling. Annie hoped she'd put enough water in it for two.

"Let me get that for you," he offered, placing his hat on the coatrack by the kitchen door.

"I can fix tea," she said as she carefully placed the vase of lilies on the table. She took two cups and saucers out of the cabinet, and put a tea bag in each cup. Then she poured the water.

Travis leaned close to take the cups from her. He smelled nice. Masculine with a touch of spice, she thought as she watched him carry her burden to the table. The china looked like tiny playthings in his large hands.

The two of them settled at the table. He put a spoon of sugar in his. She used a package of Sweet 'N Low.

"I was worried about you there for a while," he finally said as he stirred his tea.

Annie didn't know what to say except, "I was a little worried myself."

"I talked to the sheriff. He still suspects the Blake boys."

"Richard doesn't think it was them." Annie was past menopause but she swore she felt a hot flash coming on.

"I'll feel a whole lot better when they find whoever it was." His square jaw tensed visibly. Reflected light glimmered over his handsome face like beams of icy radiance.

"You and me both," Annie said and groped for a conversational piece other than her hips. "How're your crops coming?"

"Looks like a good year so far." He sipped on the tea again. He had a kindly mouth. His handsome face smiled warmly down at her. "Who's teaching the reading group now that you're laid up?" he asked.

Annie cleared her throat. "I'm going to ask Crystal to do it. Haven't done it yet though."

"Hmmm. She'd be good at it. I'm surprised they don't have a program in place already. More people need help than you'd realize."

Lightly Annie fingered one of the fragrant lily blossoms. "I didn't realize until recently that so many people couldn't read."

"Back in the day, not everyone had the opportunities." He sighed. "Seems like a long time ago when farming was the main business in these parts. Now even farming is part of new technology."

Annie nodded. Travis had come by every week since she'd been hurt, offering help and bringing dinners and flowers to brighten her day. What a thoughtful man.

"How is your nephew, Sam, working out?" Annie asked. Sam had taken over the paperwork for Travis after his wife died a couple of years ago. Annie hadn't seen much of him until her accident. The single ladies all across town had been chasing him. Eligible men were scarce and Travis would be a wonderful catch.

The warmth of his smile echoed in his voice. "He's been a big help to me since Rosalee passed away."

"That's good. Kids can really come through for you when you need them."

"That's the truth." His hand shook slightly as he picked up the cup again, changed his mind, and set it down. Annie's brows rose in question.

Travis sat straighter, gathering courage. Annie wondered what was wrong.

"I've been wondering . . ." he finally mumbled.

"Yes?"

He cleared his throat. ". . . if you'd like to spend the day at my place Saturday," he said in a rush.

Annie thought about that. Spending a couple of hours on a park bench was one thing, but a whole day with Travis?

"I'm getting some new baby chicks," he said quickly.

Annie stifled a smile. "Oh, yeah?"

The beginnings of a smile tipped the corner of his mouth. He looked sheepish after he thought of what he'd said.

"A chicken coop isn't the most exciting thing, is it? But baby chicks are some pretty little things. I have a separate little house made just for them."

"Hmmm." There was something warm and enchanting in his gesture. He looked so hopeful. She didn't have the heart to turn him down, but her hip wasn't up to walking around a farm yet. Unconsciously she rubbed her side.

"You wouldn't have to do a lot of walking or anything. Just sit on my porch. I'll have Gertrude fix us lunch. That way your daughter won't have to worry about you. Dinner too." Gertrude was his sister.

"Crystal's going to be here Saturday."

"She can come too. Or," he said, watching her intensely, "she could take the day off."

"I guess she could."

"I'll drive the truck. Be easier on your hip getting in and out."

Baby chicks. Annie couldn't work up too much excitement about seeing chicks, but spending the day with him . . . now, that was another matter.

"All right. If it's a good day."

"I'll pick you up around eight. Give you time to get straight."

"Eight?" Baths took three times longer now.

He laughed, embarrassed.

She liked that shyness about him—that caution. She also knew he was a hound. Women loved him. He stayed aloof, which made him even more appealing. He'd chosen to take her out. She shouldn't put too much stock in it. Maybe she was building this up to be much more than it was. A neighborly gesture. But the look he gave her was much more than neighborly. The feelings stirring around her definitely surpassed neighborly feelings.

"I forget everybody's not on farmer's hours," he said. "I get up at four. Nine okay?"

Goodness. She'd have to get up at six to get a bath and put herself together. Annie nodded. "But call first. Make sure I'm ready by then."

He nodded, glanced at the half-filled teacup, and stood. "Thanks for the tea," he said, gathered his hat, and twisted it in his hand. "I'll lock the door behind me. Don't you get up," he said, when she started to rise.

Annie settled back in her seat. "Good of you to stop by. Thanks for the lilies."

Annie heard his footfalls disappear, then the door close softly. Soon after, a truck door slammed.

What on earth was that all about? she wondered. Had the man been working himself up all these weeks to ask for a date? She smiled, patted her hair—and almost screamed. Her hair was a fright. She grabbed the portable phone and left a message at her hairdresser's. She needed a new do. *Baby chicks,* she thought as she disconnected, unable to stop the smile that reached not only her face but down to her core.

Richard stormed out of the restaurant. His mother had asked him to stop by this evening. He'd made the excuse of having a prior engagement. *So much for my private engagement,* he thought as he watched his wife drive away.

He had an entire evening ahead of him. He might as well go by and see what his mother wanted.

He wasn't in the mood to talk to anyone right now, but what was the sense of sitting around home stewing over his dinner with his wife?

He drove down the tree-lined street the two miles out of town to his parent's stately brick colonial. He parked, exited, and loped to the front door.

"Dear, I'd hoped we could go out to dinner," his mother said as soon as he entered.

"Not tonight, Mom. I've had dinner. But I'll run out to pick up something for you."

"No, no. I have plenty in the fridge." Although it was evening, Claire Dupree was elegantly dressed in silk slacks and a matching tunic.

"What did you want?"

"Don't stand in the door. Come. Let's have a seat."

They wandered into the den, Richard's favorite room. It had wall-to-wall bookshelves. Volumes of Langston Hughes, Shakespeare, Zora Neale Hurston. He'd lost himself in there as a boy. He fixed his mother a sherry, nothing for himself.

"I understand your wife's back," she said, accepting the drink.

"She is." Richard sprawled in a captain's chair with a rich burgundy upholstery.

His mother puckered her lips in annoyance. "I hope she has come to her senses."

"She's just going through a difficult time. The miscarriage was hard on her."

"I realize that, dear. It was difficult for you, too. The best thing to do in a situation like that is to get busy. Get back into the flow of things. Complacency leaves too much time to think. She'll come back to herself."

Richard nodded.

"I'd like the two of you to come to dinner Sunday."

Richard rubbed the back of his neck. "I'll ask her, but I can't promise anything."

"I see. Well, she really needs to start supporting you with your judgeship. Everything needs to look on the up-and-up, even if it isn't. You don't want there to be any excuse for them to turn you down."

"Other members of the bar have gone through divorces. They don't use that against you anymore."

"Divorce?"

"We're not there. I'm merely saying that Crystal's and my relationship should have no effect on my selection."

She narrowed her eyes. "Are you sure things are fine with you?"

Just damn perfect, Richard felt like saying. He nodded, hopped up, and poured himself a club soda.

Claire narrowed her gaze. "You would tell me if it wasn't, wouldn't you?"

Richard felt restless and irritable. "Did you invite me here to talk about Crystal?"

"Actually, no. Don't get annoyed. I've been thinking of your commission. Have you talked to the selection committee yet?"

"Just before I left for Cleveland."

"It wouldn't hurt if I talk to them as well."

"I appreciate your offer, but don't."

"Every little effort . . ."

"Don't. I'm a big boy now. I can handle it."

His annoyance grew when she wouldn't let the topic drop.

"I've always supported your father. I'm here for you too."

"Thank you, Mom, but there are some things I have to do alone."

He set his glass on the bar, glanced at his watch. "I've got some briefs to go over tonight."

"You just got here," she wailed.

"I know. Where's Dad?"

"At a commissioner's meeting."

"I'll see you, soon."

"I'll set up lunch with Crystal. Someone has to get her on the right track."

"Stay out of it."

"I don't like to pry, but—"

"Then don't."

More silence. "Does this have anything to do with the rumors that are spreading around town? Is Crystal after a divorce?"

"Right now, we're trying to work things out." Did they have to hash the whole damn problem in the midst of the town? Couldn't anything be done in private in this godforsaken town?

"Once she heals, things will go back to normal."

Claire quirked an eyebrow. "Are you sure about that?"

He was hoping. "I'm sure."

"A wife shouldn't stand in the way of her husband's progress. I always stood with my husband. His election to mayor has been as much my success as his."

"Not everyone is cut out for public life."

"You are destined for greater things. You won't always be able to take time off because your wife . . . Perhaps you should consider whether Crystal is capable of functioning as your wife in the role you aspire to."

"If there's a choice between my wife and these 'greater things,' then I choose my wife."

"You may feel that way now. But how will you feel ten years from now?"

When Richard started to respond, his mother held up a hand. "It seems you've been through this before. It was barely more than a year ago when you had to put your life on hold to bring Crystal to her senses. She's proving to be unreliable. Just something for you to consider while you work out your problems."

"Crystal is the most important part of my life."

"I understand that. But, Richard, I am your mother. I think it's my place to talk to her."

"Stay out of it. I mean it, Mom."

"Well, I never!"

What was it with women today? He couldn't do anything right.

"I'll see you later." He left his mother sputtering on the couch.

On his drive home, Richard shook his head. He couldn't rid his thoughts of Crystal. Moving her back into his life where she belonged wasn't going to be as easy as he thought it would be.

Richard felt guilty. He was letting his mother down. His problems weren't her doing. His issues didn't start and end with her. Yet, he'd been short and irritated with her. She was the one person who'd always been there for him. Elementary and high-school games, special occasions. His father had been tied up with civic duties. His mother even helped build his practice by sending people his way, convincing them he was the best attorney for the job. Soon he had a reputation, not by his mother's machinations, but by his results as a capable lawyer. Still, he owed her and he was letting her down.

But he was a married man. His first responsibility was to his wife. His mother should understand that. Her first priority had always been his father.

Richard needed this time to get his relationship back on track. He thought he could do it all. Now, suddenly it seemed he'd lost control of his life.

Relationships. What trials one went through in the name of love! He seemed to be paddling against the tides right now. There had been good times—many good times—that made what he and Crystal shared worth fighting for.

Richard thought back five years—the night he called Crystal from the office to tell her he'd be home in an hour. When he'd arrived, the house was dark except for a low beam beckoning from the bedroom. And he was starved.

He headed to the bedroom, hoping to coax Crystal into fixing a plate for him. When he got there, he found her stretched out on the bed in nothing but illumination from the velvety glow of candlelight. Her natural brown tresses styled in shoulder-length ringlets were splayed invitingly against the white silk pillowcase. Soft music played in the background. Slowly, she draped a hot-pink feather boa between silky butterscotch-toned breasts. The boa stroked her satiny skin. Both ends dangled between her thighs. Hunger of another kind sizzled through Richard—as hot as glowing coals.

The most glorious two hours passed before Crystal left the bedroom to fix him a plate.

Richard restrained the desire the image invoked. *Give Crystal a divorce? Never!*

He wiped the sweat from his face, put on his signal light, and made a left turn into his driveway.

He was disappointed that she'd done this to herself. Angry that he had to dance to her tune to keep his marriage together. He wanted that woman, the one with the pink feather boa, back in his life.

When Richard pulled into the yard, a man stood beside a beige, nondescript car. His back was toward Richard as he leaned against the door. When the headlights from Richard's car flashed on him, the man turned.

Aaron Stonehouse. He'd moved here ten years ago and opened a small high-tech company. He had grown up in D.C., but his mother was reared here and moved to D.C. after graduating from high school. His grandparents still lived nearby.

Richard didn't often see Aaron. For the most part the man kept to himself. It was public knowledge that he was the technical genius in the company while his partner ran the financial and management areas.

As Richard exited his car, he wondered what brought Aaron out here this time of night. The man looked haggard, as if he hadn't slept in days. His clothes were rumbled as if he'd slept in them for the little sleep he'd managed to grasp. His white shirttail was half in, half out of his pants.

"Aaron," Richard said, "come on in."

The man grabbed his jacket from the seat. While he put it on, he must have realized his shirt was hanging out and hastily stuffed it into his wrinkled slacks.

"I need your help," Aaron said as soon as Richard closed the door.

"Let's have a seat and then you can tell me all about it." Richard liked to use the low-key approach. Often when people thought the world was coming to an end, it ended up being a small matter, easily settled.

"I can't sit," he said and paced the length of the room. "I'm going to lose my business."

"Why?"

"My partner, Jack, has been robbing the company. It takes two to sign off on checks and I think the accountant is in on it with him."

Richard didn't ask if the man was sure, because if Aaron didn't have proof, he wouldn't be pacing in Richard's living room.

"How much has he stolen?" Richard asked.

"More than a couple million. The company was flush with money. I wouldn't have known anything if he hadn't gone on vacation with Sally. She's the accountant. Sally's assistant took over and found some discrepancies in the books and brought it to my attention. I had an audit done." He raked trembling hands over his head. "I don't think the business can survive this, not unless we recover that money."

"When are they due back?"

"At the end of the week."

This sounded like it could turn into a major case. If Richard planned to spend more time with Crystal, a case of this magnitude was the last thing he needed right now. "Tell you what. I'm going to give you the name and number of a good lawyer who can help you."

"But you're the best around. I need you if I'm going to save my business at all."

"This lawyer . . ."

"I need *you*. I've worked my tail off growing this business to where it is today. I read about what you did for that cosmetic company. I need you on my side."

"But . . ."

"It's not just me. If I have to close the company, all my employees would be out of work. The economy's bad. I've got to uncover some of that money to survive. Don't tell me you won't take the case."

"Look, I have a few things I'm working on . . ."

"You hired an assistant. Everyone's been talking about it."

Richard sighed. Life wasn't going to take a hiatus just because he needed a break. Could he take this case and find time for Crystal, too? She was only giving him two days a week. He had another five to work his cases. Elzey was taking some of the work off him.

He glanced at Aaron. The man wasn't yet thirty-two, but he looked as if this setback had aged him several years. He gave the same answer that had gotten him in trouble with his wife in the first place. But he didn't see any other option.

The case with the cosmetic company was finished. He had more time than he had a month ago.

"All right," Richard said finally. And he began to interview Aaron so that he could start work on the case.

Five

Richard struggled with Princess, his neighbor's dog, shoving her to the side so he could see how to drive. Princess loved riding in the car, although she wasn't content sitting in the passenger seat. The golden retriever all but climbed onto Richard's lap.

"Move over, will you?" Richard snapped, gently pushing the dog aside again, and made a left turn into his driveway. He parked in front of the garage, glad they'd made it this far. Taking the creature up the mountain was going to present a problem.

He grabbed hold of the short leash and fought to get the animal out of the car. When he tried to bring her up the front steps, Princess strained toward the SUV.

"Come on, you mutt." He had second thoughts about giving her to Crystal. If he had this much trouble, would she be able to handle her?

Crystal, however, loved the dog. Raymond Byrd had brought Princess to visit her often before Crystal left for Japan. Princess was putty in her hands. After much coaxing Richard finally got Princess into the house and down the stairs to the basement. But she wanted to play.

"We don't have time for that. Time to get this business over with." The dog knew Richard, barely. Hopefully the gift of the dog would give him some brownie points with Crystal.

Once they made it to the basement, Richard gathered up soap. The dog hated water—hadn't had a bath in God knows when. The dog's usually lustrous fur was matted with brambles and dirt. Richard and his SUV had the smelly dog scent. Richard turned on the shower and waited for the water to warm. "In you go," he said, trying to coax the dog into the shower.

Princess pulled back.

"You can't take a shower out here." Admonishment didn't help. After several attempts, Richard kicked off his shoes, picked up the dog, climbed in with her, and shut the curtains. She clawed at the curtains. Richard admitted he wasn't the best at dealing with animals. The fact that they were both wet by the time he soaped her down was a good indication. He scrubbed her body vigorously and brushed her fur. Princess licked his face, then shook her body. Soapy water flew everywhere, dousing Richard—dousing the shower.

"Ah, damn." Richard's shorts and T-shirt dripped with water.

"We've got a long way to go, pal."

By the time he finished, he understood why he didn't have a dog. He shivered as cold water ran off him. His patience hung by a thread. He threatened to return the dog to Raymond. He couldn't. The animal was an olive branch.

He toweled, then blow-dried the beast. Golden fur was soft and shiny. Hmm. She needed something else. Then he remembered Crystal's favorite perfume. He took the dog upstairs, realized he shouldn't put fragrance on her skin, so he sprayed his hand and wiped the scent on the dog's fur and sniffed. Smelled better on his wife.

Glancing at his watch, he realized he needed to get his shower and get a move on. Annie had told Crystal not to come today. She was spending the day with Travis.

Which meant Crystal was free to spend the day with him—and Princess.

Travis parked a couple hundred feet from the back of his house. A fenced-in area housed the chickens. Annie was grateful they were fenced in and not running around wild on the lawn. Chickens might be cute, but their droppings weren't.

"Let's see the chicks now so you won't have to navigate the stairs again," Travis said.

"You didn't bring me here to see chicks, did you?" Annie asked, as she cautiously climbed out of the truck with Travis's assistance. She wasn't that enthusiastic about going into a chicken coop. Most of the chicks wandered inside a fence.

Travis sighed, tightened his grip on her arm. "No. I wanted to spend the day with you." His gaze was direct. More so than last night when he seemed nervous about asking her out. "You'll like the chicks, Annie."

Annie smiled tenderly under his regard. "I'm glad you asked." They continued to stare at each other like young teenaged simpletons.

"I see. Since I'm here I may as well see them," Annie said finally.

Travis coughed lightly. "They're the cutest things, Annie." He grasped her arm in his by tacit consent, and they both turned and walked slowly side by side.

"Ummm," Annie said. She could do without the chicks. She'd heard talk of stinking chicken coops. From what she'd heard, one could barely find a place to step safely.

They plowed ahead. She hated using a cane. As they neared the coop, she saw two young men coming out of the chicken house. They wore rubber boots and carried shovels. Each had a large bucket in his hand. Annie didn't want to think too closely about the contents.

They spotted Travis and her almost immediately.

"Thought I heard your truck, Uncle Travis. It's all cleaned up."

"Annie, you know my nephew, Sam, don't you?"

"We've met," Annie said.

"Sam grew up in Roanoke with my sister. Troy is his best friend. They play in the little band together."

They all spoke at once. The boys groaned at Travis's mention of "the little band."

"I'll have to take you to hear them some night. They're good."

"He's prejudiced," Sam said.

"But true, I'm sure," Annie agreed.

The chicken coop was clean, and when Travis directed her into the little chick house, she was instantly enthralled. "They're beautiful." Tiny little chicks that could easily fit into the palm of her hand lingered around the feeder, pecking up bits of corn and oats.

Travis smiled easily. "Told you you'd like them." He dropped her elbow, bent to pick up a little chick, and handed it to Annie. A seed dropped from its mouth.

Annie stroked the feathers as it wiggled in her hand. The chick was soft and fluffy. She found it impossible not to return Travis's disarming smile.

"How did you get them?"

"They're shipped by a carrier from Ohio."

"You're kidding."

"No. When I was a boy, they were delivered by regular postal service. Today we use special delivery so they'll arrive within twenty-four hours."

"They're just babies. Don't they starve before they reach here?"

"No, they're shipped in bunches of twenty-five soon after they're born. They have enough in their systems at birth to sustain them a few days. The trick is to make sure they're warm enough, which is why they're shipped in a large group."

"That's amazing." She tried not to think about the babies

being separated from their mother right after birth. It seemed harsh somehow. Life was harsh.

Sam and Troy entered the coop, distributed more food, and looked the chicks over.

"Chicks require a lot of special attention for the first couple of weeks," Travis said.

Annie handed the chick back to Travis. He placed it carefully on the ground and gathered a wire basket hanging from a peg. They went to the other coop and gathered eggs. Some were pale green, some brown, some white, some pale blue. Annie had never seen the varying colors of eggs before, though she knew they existed.

"Where does the color come from?" she asked.

"From different kinds of chickens. I have a nice little variety here."

"Do they taste different?"

"Not enough so you can tell. The colorful eggs are called Easter eggs."

Travis carried the eggs in a basket in one hand while he helped Annie to the truck with the other. As he drove to the house, Annie held the basket on her lap. Soon she was seated on the porch in the swing. This had been her most invigorating morning since her accident.

Travis disappeared into the house to tell Gertrude they were ready for breakfast. His sister prepared most of his meals, though she lived alone about a mile down the road. She was also one of the women in the reading group and had brought Annie some of the most mouthwatering cakes she'd ever tasted.

So far, so good, Annie thought as she waited. It had been several weeks since the shooting. Her hip was healing better than she thought it would. She'd had to take the stairs to the porch carefully, but other than that, things were fine. More than fine. She was having a grand old time.

Travis's house was at a higher elevation than her home. He must have been thinking of the view when he built it. She looked off into the mountains. The blue haze had worn off to display the beauty of the trees and slopes.

Annie was feeling blissfully happy, and being near Travis, she felt . . . alive again.

It had been years since she'd enjoyed herself so with a man—not since her dear husband, William, passed away. She wasn't a prude. Just that it wasn't so often that someone so dashing came along.

Crystal cast the fly into deeper water.

"That's a good one," her father said. He'd been fishing on the river below since sunrise—in fisherman's bliss. He loved to fish and would have been pleased with just his own company, standing in his hip boots, in the Smith all day long.

She'd joined him an hour ago. Even before she and Richard built the cabin, they often got away during the summer to go fishing. She'd prefer taking a brisk walk through the forest—or perhaps a leisurely walk, but her competitive nature kept her pinned to this spot. She wanted to catch the biggest fish. After all, she classified this river—mere yards from her deck—as her river.

Fishing wasn't so bad though, as long as her father cleaned them.

She watched the water gurgle over rocks. Her father had finally relaxed.

From her peripheral vision, something caught her attention. She looked up. Richard was being led by a dog down the rocky incline. Richard and a dog? She peered closer.

"Princess?" she shouted and almost dropped her pole. "It can't be. She's grown so huge." Turning, Crystal hurried out of the water and dropped her pole on the bank. She ran to the dog. Richard let the leash go. Dog and woman met halfway. She bent and rubbed the lustrous, tan fur. Hmm, clean.

Princess yelped, set her paws on Crystal, and licked her face.

"You remember me," she said.

"They don't forget," Richard replied, finally reaching them.

Laughing, Crystal hugged the dog, burying her face in the thick softness, inhaling freshly washed fur. Was that her favorite perfume she smelled on the dog? She glanced at Richard. "What're you doing with her?"

Terrible regret coated his voice. "Raymond's going into a nursing home. He can't take the dog with him."

"Oh, no." Crystal's euphoria burst. She swallowed the despair in her throat. "What's wrong with him?" Her father came out of the water to join them. He was frowning. He didn't know Raymond. He wasn't from here.

"Alzheimer's," Richard said. "There's no one to look after him."

"How terrible."

"That's a sad thing," her father said, shaking his head. "More and more people are coming down with it. How are you, Richard?" Her father wiped his hand on his shirt and extended it for a shake.

"I'm fine, sir," Richard said, shaking her father's hand. Then he slid his hands into his pockets. "Raymond's been a good neighbor."

"Where are they taking him?"

"Not far. They've built a new retirement complex a few miles away. Close enough for us to visit him."

Crystal nodded, not commenting on the *us*. "He's going to miss working in his vegetable garden."

"Since his daughter lives close by, he'll have the opportunity to putter in her garden. She really wants to keep him, but she works. She needs the income."

"Are they selling his place?"

Richard nodded.

"It isn't going to be the same without him." Crystal tugged gently on the leash as Princess paused at the cooler holding the fish. She would miss Raymond terribly. He'd walked over often with Princess, offering fresh tomatoes and greens from his garden. She would serve him a glass of tea on hot summer mornings and they'd sit on the porch talking about his family or hers for a few minutes before he'd be on his way. He was a kind, gentle man. She'd miss opening the kitchen door to find him on her doorstep.

Then suddenly Crystal realized, she wouldn't be there either.

"There's an extra pole over there if you plan to stay," her father said to Richard, returning to the river.

"I've got the entire day," Richard murmured, sending a gentle, loving look her way. "I'm going to get my gear from the house."

With a deliberately casual movement, Richard turned and climbed the rocks. The climb emphasized the force of his thighs and the strength of his shoulders. Crystal was acutely conscious of his tall, powerful physique. She had to conquer her involuntary response to his kindness—to him.

This wasn't an image she'd observed often in the last five years. Jeans and a T-shirt. More often he wore suits. There was a certain earthiness about him in jeans, she thought as she unhooked Princess from her leash. The dog wouldn't roam too far. Raymond had trained her well.

"Come on, girl. Let's catch some fish."

With a taste of freedom, Princess splashed into the river.

"Darn dog," Crystal's father muttered as the dog started to chase after a fish, scaring others away.

Crystal had expected Richard to make a nuisance of himself last night. But he'd shared a fish dinner with them and left shortly after her father had. Perhaps he was taking this dating business to heart. Not pushing the envelope, so to speak.

At church Sunday morning she received the expected odd looks. People didn't know what to think. Since she spent last summer in the mountains, her presence there was no indication of the state of her marriage. In the absence of facts, people tended to fabricate. It was none of their business, Crystal thought as she marched down the aisle behind

Annie. This was Annie's first visit to church since the surgery.

Richard had already arrived, she noticed. They sat two rows apart. There were no empty seats on his row. She could always pretend she hadn't seen him. It wasn't unusual for them to drive separate cars, especially when he was thick in a case. He was known to work before and after church services. But for most of the time, church was the one activity they attended together.

She put her worries behind her as Reverend Toler preached a moving sermon on forgiveness. His sermons usually left her feeling good and refreshed. This one only served to bring on the guilt. Had she made the right decision in leaving Richard?

No! Crystal, stop second-guessing. Forgiveness didn't mean one had to continue putting up with repeated negative situations. She held nothing against Richard. She was merely moving on. The service ended and she wanted to make a quick getaway, but was waylaid by friends and family. People wanted to talk with Annie and her. They wanted to know about her trip to Japan. She hadn't visited anyone except Aunt Annie in the two weeks she'd been home. Her family of strong-minded women would want to dispense advice, but Crystal didn't want any advice. She wanted to continue to rest without constant reminding about the miscarriage. And the sad look on faces really threw her for a loop. The best part about Japan was that no one knew about her troubles. They left her alone—didn't treat her like an emotional cripple.

When she and Annie could finally slip away, they drove to Annie's place. It was a lovely day. The temperature hovered around the mid-eighties. Crystal fixed a snack and they sat outside near the rose garden under the oak tree. The wind slapped her in the face with the strong rose scent.

Roses were Crystal's favorite flowers. She tucked a blossom into her hair and she cut one for her aunt, too.

There was a certain vivaciousness with Annie today— her spirits had been greatly lifted.

"How was your day yesterday?" Crystal asked her aunt, sure that Travis was responsible for this new facade.

Her aunt blushed and picked up her glass of lemonade. "Just fine."

"Uh-huh. What's this with Travis?"

Annie gulped. A trickle of lemonade spilled on her chin. "Nothing. Just a friend," she said, dabbing her napkin at her chin.

"Hmmm," Crystal said. Her mouth trembled with the need to smile.

Annie narrowed her eyes, tried to maintain a serious expression that fell short. "Don't you start it," she said.

Crystal held up her hands in an innocent gesture. "I'm not starting anything."

"I had a good time," Annie finally said, leaning back in her chair.

"I'm glad you did." Crystal regarded her aunt with amusement. "You know what they say about farmers."

"I'm sure you're going to tell me."

"I'll let you find out on your own."

"I can't wait."

The women laughed.

"Your hip okay after your excursion?" Crystal asked.

"My hip is just fine." For an instant, wistfulness stole into her expression.

For moments they sipped their drinks and basked in private thoughts. Then Annie smiled, reached up, and patted Crystal's hand. "I'm glad you're here, dear. This is my most favorite place."

"Mine too."

Annie exhaled an exaggerated breath. "This is a good day for me. I've had many bad ones since—well. I just have to get outside."

"I'm glad you're doing better." Crystal took a bottle out of the sack at her side. "I brought you something. I saw this at an antique store in Japan. Thought you'd love it."

"Oh, my!" her aunt exclaimed as Crystal placed the bottle within easy reach. "It's absolutely lovely." Annie regarded the intricate Japanese designs. "You couldn't have given me a more perfect gift."

"You're welcome."

"When you were little, you loved to gather the roses with me and stay underfoot whenever I was in my rose garden. And antiquing. You'd find the prettiest little bottles that cost a pittance. I've kept them all. If I were to research them, I'm sure some are quite valuable."

Crystal smiled. She had fond memories of that time. Just the two of them.

"You were the most eccentric aunt a girl could have." Crystal nodded. "I had fun. You are a special aunt."

Sadness stole the warmth from Annie. "But you don't enjoy my roses any longer."

"It's not that I don't enjoy them. It's that ... I don't know what's going on." She floundered in an agonizing maelstrom.

Annie reached across the table and patted Crystal's hand. "Give yourself time, child. Sometimes the body needs time to heal. We're in this fast-paced era right now. We feel that we have to rush from place to place. Rush to do this and that. Sometimes, Crystal ... sometimes we just need time to relax. If we're quiet long enough, the answer will come. Everything will fall into place." She took a bite of her cookie. "You don't have to spend so much time with me anymore."

Crystal watched Princess lounge in the garden. "I enjoy spending time with you. Besides, what will I do in the meantime? Keeps me from moping around the house."

"You take long walks with Princess. Go antique shopping. You don't have to buy anything, it's the journey that counts."

Both women fell into silence.

"I do have one more favor to ask of you," Annie said. Crystal sensed her disquiet. "What is it?"

"I've been teaching some adults to read. It's hard to believe that so many still can't read and write. But some of them grew up on farms and they were kept out of school.

They only went between the harvesting and planting. Often they fell so far behind the rest of the class that they dropped out altogether. But one of the things they've always wanted to do was to learn to read. I would like for you to take over that chore for me.''

Crystal's face clouded with unease. ''I don't know if I'm the right person. Someone trained in adult education might be better.'' Truth be told, Crystal wasn't fond of teaching again. She needed time *away* from teaching.

''You'll do fine. It will only be until I can get on my feet again. I'm not very good at teaching, but I do the best that I can. You have to do better than I do. They've been weeks without instruction. I don't want them to forget what they've learned.''

Crystal thought back to her last days in the classroom in Japan. She had struggled through each and every day. The walls had closed in on her, she had felt . . . suffocated. How could she return to that atmosphere? How could she turn them down? Wasn't that her purpose in the first place—to help others?

''They asked specifically for you. They value their privacy. So many times, they try to fit into a reading world, but can't. They trust you. They feel you'll be discreet.''

Crystal only half listened as she struggled with her conscience. She could barely breathe.

''I have a schedule.'' Annie took sheets out of the pad on the table beside her and slid them across to Crystal.

''They're all free after five. Perhaps you can take a couple of them each night.''

''Do you think they would mind if I teach all of them together? Are they on the same level or at least close?''

Annie nodded. ''I started teaching them around the same time.''

''I'll teach two nights a week.'' Crystal thought for a moment. Richard had chosen Monday and Thursday nights for their dates.

''Sadie wants three nights. How would Monday, Wednesday, and Friday work? They might be able to meet earlier on Fridays."

"We could meet here on Wednesdays."

"You don't have to."

"I insist. I won't leave you alone."

Annie sighed a disgruntled sigh, but underneath Crystal sensed that she was thrilled that so many people cared. "I guess it'll work," Annie said. Then she described her students' progress so that Crystal would know where to begin.

Suddenly, her aunt sat straighter in her chair and fiddled with the lemonade glass. Crystal heard footsteps in back of her. Princess barked and sprang forward. Crystal caught her by the collar and patted her.

It didn't take a genius to guess who caused that reaction from Annie. Crystal glanced around to see who was approaching. It was Travis Walker. Big surprise. She glanced at her aunt again, then at the tall man approaching them—looking as if he were on a mission.

Travis held his church hat in one hand and a fruit basket in the other. He'd discarded his suit jacket. His massive shoulders filled the shirt he wore. His shoulders weren't doing anything for Crystal, although she could appreciate them, but the man's physique was disturbing her aunt plenty.

Crystal saw this as the perfect opportunity to exit before her aunt talked her into anything else. More time to shop, her foot. Annie was a crafty old bat.

Crystal glanced at her aunt with the intention of making a hasty exit when she noticed the sexual awareness on the woman's face. Annie straightened the silk caftan, smoothing the lines. She had it bad.

"I'll get more lemonade," Crystal said. She greeted Mr. Walker and went inside. He barely noticed her. His eyes were for Annie only. Crystal regarded the couple from the door. This was good for Annie.

Suddenly Travis Walker leaned toward Annie and kissed her on her cheek in a courtly fashion.

* * *

On Monday afternoon, Richard was walking to his desk when he spotted his wife walking in the direction of his office. She held one of those big bags on her arm—the kind women carried books, papers, and just about everything in. Princess was straining on her leash.

Richard rushed out the door and strode a few paces down the sidewalk to greet Crystal. He had no illusions that she was coming to see him. His luck hadn't run that well lately.

"Where are you two off to in such a hurry?" Richard asked as the door slammed behind him.

Crystal gritted her teeth. She patted the bag by her side. "Just going to the library to make copies."

"Why didn't you make them in the office? I have a perfectly good copier. Besides, I don't think they allow animals in the library."

"I'll tether her outside. Besides, copies are reasonable at the library."

He took her elbow in his hand. "Won't cost you a dime here. Can't get a better price anywhere."

"Thanks for the offer, but . . ."

"You aren't avoiding me, are you? Theresa's been asking about you."

Crystal gently tried to remove her elbow from his grasp. Richard held on. "Richard, I'm almost there. Next time I'll stop by your office."

"We don't have to be enemies."

"I never said we were."

"It would help if we get accustomed to seeing each other on a casual basis." He rubbed the dog's fur. Princess licked his hand and did a dog groan in bliss.

Crystal sighed.

Richard pretended he didn't hear it. "Are you enjoying the cabin?" he asked as he ushered her toward the door.

"When I get the time."

He opened the door.

She'd always made things too easy for Richard, Crystal

thought as she and Princess passed him. But was it worth putting up a fight over some copies? *Pick your battles, Crystal.* She didn't want to seem churlish and ridiculous. He held the door for her and she entered the office and spoke to Theresa.

Richard asked Theresa to make the copies for Crystal.

"Actually, Theresa, I can make them. You continue with what you're doing."

Theresa frowned. She didn't like dogs, liked them even less in the office. She was a cat person. "You've got a mighty big brute there."

"She's just a teenager now. But sweet."

"Hmm. I hope she won't grow any larger."

Crystal smiled and went to the copying room. Richard followed her, slid his fingers sensuously over her arm. She removed her arm from his grasp and went to the copier.

He lounged casually against the door frame and played with Princess. He seemed to be peering at her intently.

Crystal took in his tempting, attractive male physique. Every fiber in her body warned her against him. It was all an act. Still, the line of his body was too enticing by far.

"How is Annie? You all were surrounded by such a crowd yesterday I didn't get an opportunity to speak."

"She's doing well."

He shifted positions, stopped ruffling Princess's fur. The dog wined. "I want to thank you for giving me this chance with you."

Crystal scoffed. "As if I had a choice. You browbeat me into it."

Richard shrugged his wide shoulders. "You always have a choice."

Crystal finished her copies. Richard would put up a good fight to get her. But once he did, things would go back to the status quo. She knew it. He knew it. She wouldn't be fooled this time. No matter how attractive he was—no matter his efforts now.

She shoved her copies into her bag. "Thanks for the copier."

"You're welcome." He narrowed the space between them. "Put on your dancing shoes tonight. I'm taking you dancing."

She glanced up. "Dancing?"

He nodded.

Being held in his arms. Unwanted sensation ran up Crystal's spine. She wasn't completely immune to him. She didn't relish the idea of being in his arms half the night. She almost felt the sexual magnetism that made it so hard for her to resist him. Intimacy had never been a problem between them.

"You have to work tomorrow."

"I'll manage," he whispered. Slowly and seductively, his gaze slid downward.

Crystal's heart rhythm accelerated. She tugged on Princess's leash and approached the door. With his eyes he stoked a slow-glowing flame in her. Richard moved back, barely giving her enough space to exit without touching him. Not enough to escape without whiffing the heady cologne that she loved. It had a very light scent. One she wouldn't have smelled at all if she didn't know him so well. This dating business wasn't such a cool idea.

Richard walked her out the door, his arm brushing hers too frequently to be happenstance. "I'm looking forward to tonight." His voice was low and smoky.

She was immune. Or so she told herself. Her body knew differently.

She cleared her throat. "I may be running a little late. Come after six, okay?" After showing up unannounced the other day, he didn't have room to argue. She couldn't complain, however. He'd brought her a precious gift.

Princess.

She made her way to her car and drove to the grocery store for dip and chips. She was waylaid several times by friends.

Soon she put the top to her car down and she and Princess were navigating the curving roads with the wind ruffling around them. By the time they reached her cabin, Crystal had relaxed considerably.

Early this morning she'd prepared a banana pudding for the group. Some of them didn't have an opportunity to eat before they arrived. She'd give them a fifteen-minute break in the middle of class and serve the banana pudding and dip.

Richard watched Crystal drive away. She was as skittish as a fly on hot coals. He smiled. She might say she wanted a divorce, but she wasn't immune to him. Not by a long shot.

In his office, Richard worked on Aaron's case. Aaron had sent over copies of cancelled checks and invoices. Jack and Sally were living up a fine life with the money they'd bilked from the company. Since Aaron had paid no attention to the financial portion of the company, they probably thought he'd never find out about the embezzlement.

Six

Crystal forced herself to eat a sandwich after looking over her lesson for tonight. She glanced at the clear blue sky. Right above the trees, an eagle soared free and majestic. The weather was simply beautiful. There weren't any rules that dictated she and her class couldn't enjoy studying outside. She went inside, dragged a card table and extra chairs onto the deck. The days were long. Hours of daylight were left.

Princess bounded off the deck and chased after a squirrel. When it ran up a tree, she barked several warnings before she returned to the deck to flop down.

Crystal had never taught adults before. She was more apprehensive than she let on to Annie.

Her grandparents had regaled her with many stories of how difficult life had been even for children in the early to mid 1900s. Many worked gathering crops from September, the beginning of the school year, to November. When they attended school in November they were far behind the other students. March through May was planting season and they constantly chopped wild grass to keep the crops from being smothered out.

After a while, many students would quit school, never to return, never really learning to read and write.

Her grandmother had been a teacher. She'd told Crystal many times how, after she received her degree and taught at her first one-room school, she would drive to school in the mornings and, seeing others in the field, she'd thank God for granting her the opportunity of an education. She'd used her training to help so many others. Aunt Annie had taught a few years before she married Uncle William and opened the theater.

Teaching must have run in the family, because after listening to Grandma's many stories, Crystal had wanted to teach, too. To help out in some way. Perhaps this was her opportunity.

Crystal went into the house for the pitcher of lemonade. She'd just set it on the table when she heard a car in the driveway.

Sadie arrived first, bringing Crystal dinner. Pork chops smothered in onions and gravy, kale, and mashed potatoes—cooked from scratch, not dried flakes. Crystal's stomach growled just from the aroma.

"There's enough for you and Richard," the older woman said. "I figured you wouldn't have the time to cook before the class began." She wore a plain summer hat, pale blue to match her blue dress trimmed in white lace.

"You shouldn't have, but thank you," Crystal said, accepting her offer. Princess rose from her resting spot, wandered over, sniffing at the contents. Crystal held it out of the dog's grasp and stored the dinner in the fridge. "You'll get the bones after I'm done," she told Princess. She'd have dinner after the class left.

Blond-haired Betty Wright brought a bag of kale from her garden. Betty had grown up on a poor farm in West Virginia and moved to Windy Hills after she married. She'd worked the last thirty years as a housekeeper at the hotel near the college and retired a year ago. She sat at the table and pulled her knitting needles and yarn from her bag.

Ricardo Lumas brought her fresh strawberries from his garden. He was a gardener at Windy Hills College.

Gertrude brought a jar of honey from a neighbor's beehive, and Jimmy Blowe brought a bottle of wine from his bar.

"I'm making you a hat, Crystal. I think you'll like it," said Sadie.

Betty glanced up from her clicking needles. "I'm making you a sweater."

Not to be outdone, Gertrude said, "I'm making her a patchwork quilt."

Crystal held up a hand. "Please don't bring any more gifts. I really enjoy teaching. I'm looking forward to this. I don't expect gifts."

"We're thankful that you're helping us out," Sadie said as she sat at the table with Able Nivens. "And no calling us by our last names. Call me Sadie. Otherwise you'll spend half the night calling out Mrs. and Mr. You're the teacher, after all." The others nodded in approval.

Crystal was touched by their generosity. They all took seats. Her kids had never settled down so easily and eagerly. Sadie pulled a miniature tape recorder from her huge bag, set it on the table by her tablet. Crystal began class by having them read from a book to assess their skills.

Sadie settled her new glasses on her nose and looked at the pages Crystal handed them. "No Sally, Tom, and Jane books?"

"We'll be reading other materials," Crystal said.

Sadie nodded. "Good."

"Okay, Able, your turn."

The older man of at least seventy clutched the papers in his arthritic fingers and began to read, haltingly.

"That's *down*," Sadie said, pointing a finger on Abel's paper.

"I know what it is."

"Well, why didn't you say so?"

"If you mind your own business, I'll get around to it. You aren't the teacher."

What did you do with a fighting group of grown people? "Okay. Good job, Able. Continue, please."

Able twisted his papers to the side so Sadie couldn't see, and continued to read. Crystal made a few corrections along the way. He was progressing nicely. They all were. Crystal was genuinely thrilled and humbled by their efforts. They could so easily have given up, but here they were struggling, even at their ages.

What did that say for her? Crystal thought. She'd been floored by her tragedy but she should have been able to move on. She shook her head, tearing her thoughts from herself. These students had already proven one was never too old to learn and move forward.

Forward. That was the operative word.

After the last student read, Crystal taught them a new lesson. By then they were ready for a break so she served the dip and banana pudding.

Before they left, Crystal handed out homework. Her aunt had done a wonderful job with teaching them, she realized. Tonight no one left immediately. Sadie, Betty, and Gertrude began to talk about a study group while the men looked on.

"You can study at my place," Jimmy said. "I've got a private room we all can use."

Aunt Annie said they were embarrassed because they couldn't read. In this private room, their business would probably stay with them. Crystal didn't know if keeping silent was a good thing. If the word spread, others who needed help with reading might come forward and the county could institute a program.

"You going to join us, Able?" Ricardo asked. "We're meeting for dinner tomorrow night."

"My granddaughter works the evening shift. If we have problems, she'll help us," Betty said.

"I'll be there, bright and early." Able turned to Crystal. "That was the best banana pudding I've ever tasted. Thank you."

The others thanked her and everyone left.

It was well after eight and the sun hadn't set. A huge

orange ball was slowly disappearing behind the mountains. Crystal still had time for her sunset. She cleaned up the dishes and showered. Then she settled down with a glass of lemonade and a well-fed Princess beside her. Crystal scratched the dog behind the ear. The sunset was nicer for having company—even a dog.

Richard was late. Why wasn't she surprised?

Crystal might not have been thrilled with her date with Richard, but that didn't stop her from looking her best. She dressed in a sleeveless silk turquoise sheath, and draped around her neck the pearls Richard had given her as a birthday gift two years ago. The effect was stunning. And he hadn't shown up, as usual. She felt like a fool.

Anger started to build. She could be doing other things like preparing for Wednesday's class, or resting in comfortable shorts and a T-shirt. She got up and headed inside. Forget Richard. She was changing into jeans.

Crystal stilled. Did she want to knock Richard off his feet? She was trying to get out of this marriage, not string it along. His actions were just another reminder that he couldn't be counted on. This wasn't exactly a V-8 moment. Hadn't she already known that?

Just as she headed to her bedroom, she heard his SUV pull into her drive. Angrily she strode to the door and opened it. He was freshly showered and looked good enough to eat in his slacks and sports jacket. Crystal stifled her anger. She could play the role of a rational individual. There was nothing to gain by erupting in anger. Richard would soon slack off and her time would be hers. She could act with the best of them for the time it took him to revert to his previous role.

"You look stunning," he said with a heart-stopping smile.

Even with acting, Crystal couldn't contain the pleasure that sprinkled over her like a warm summer drizzle in hundred-degree weather. "Thank you," she said. "You look handsome." His words weren't going to her head, she assured herself.

"I hoped you'd approve."

He kissed her on the cheek. The subtle scent of his cologne stirred emotions she didn't want to ponder. *You're acting, Crystal. Remember that.*

They ended up eating Sadie's dinner. Afterward, Richard patted his flat stomach. "I need to work off that dinner. Let's go dancing."

"Now? The drive isn't worth it."

His gaze was riveted on her face, then moved over her body slowly. "To me it is."

Uh-oh. I don't want to go there, Crystal thought as a tingle ran down her spine. But this was his night. She wouldn't argue. He was bringing her right back here, however.

On their drive he talked about what had gone on in the town while she was away. They listened to an oldies CD—slow, deep soul. The kind that stirred the blood, and created a deep tingling that raised the hair on her arms and had butterflies dancing in her stomach. Her body felt on fire, as if he were stroking her with the music.

It had just been too long since they were last together. And she was only human.

Richard's voice had lowered too. It was soft, creating an atmosphere of intimacy. Crystal lowered her window. The breeze washed over her hot skin.

It helped little.

Finally they arrived at the lounge. Not a minute too soon, Crystal thought as she raised her window.

"They have a lot of new equipment," Crystal noticed as the band began again.

"Oh, yeah. They're doing very well."

"Their manager must be good."

Richard shrugged. "By the looks of things he must be."

The band struck up a ballad. Before she knew it, she was dancing in Richard's arms. It had been almost a year since he held her this close. She ran her hands along his back—liked the feel of him too much. She also liked the feel of herself pressed against his strength.

Where was *her* strength? Why wasn't she fighting this? It was as if all her senses were attuned to him. She didn't want to fight. She decided she'd just enjoy this a little while. It wouldn't hurt for one night. The song ended not a moment too soon. They returned to their seats and the waitress came to their table.

"What would you like, Crystal?" Richard asked.

"Daiquiri, please."

Crystal saw several people she knew. Many stopped by her table to welcome her home. In a few minutes the band took a break.

Sam Walker, the band's leader, came to their table.

"You're very good," Crystal said, sipping on her drink. She'd better take it easy. She'd had two already.

"Thank you."

"If we don't watch it, you'll be playing in the big leagues soon."

"Speaking of the big leagues, next month we're making a music video and see where things go from there. It's taken a while because everything about this business is expensive. But we hung in there and we're finally almost where we want to be," he said.

"Congratulations. I'm happy for you." Crystal loved when people realized their dreams. Travis was a good man. Sam came from a good strong family. They knew that success didn't come without hard work.

Another band member joined them, handing a soda to Sam. He introduced them, but Richard seemed to know him already.

"Troy's my right-hand man," Sam said. "Don't know where I'd be without him. And he's hell on drums."

"Pleased to meet you," Crystal said, well into a good buzz. Everything was okay with her.

Troy gave a crooked smile. He seemed shy. He wouldn't look her straight in the eye. Well, if he was to become successful, he'd better get over his shyness in a hurry. But he wasn't shy on the stage, she'd noticed. He played those drums like the skilled musician he was. After talking to Richard and her another few minutes, the young men stood.

"We have to get back to work," Sam said.

"Good luck on your video," Richard murmured.

He gathered Crystal's hand in his and kissed her knuckle.

The band started up again and played a fast song. She and Richard were on the floor getting down. Then the band played a slow number and dedicated it to Richard and her. When their arms closed around each other, they were winded. Crystal's heart pounded against his chest. She felt the rhythm of his heartbeat against hers. Strong and masculine and heady. A lullaby comforting her like a blanket around a baby.

His body felt familiar and wonderful, reminding her how long it had been since she'd felt his touch.

They danced a few more numbers and then they left—to Richard's house. While Crystal was still under the smoky haze Richard had created, she found herself unbuttoning his shirt.

He kissed her neck. He pulled the dress over her head and kissed her body, building up a heat so intense she was ready to explode with wanting him. Her body danced to his touch. He knew her body well.

Her fingers thrilled at touching every inch of him. And then they were kissing—deep, drugging kisses.

Crystal's world somersaulted as Richard carried her up the stairs and placed her on their bed. Something nagged at the ege of the sensual cloud. And then he was touching her again, kissing her nipples, stroking her thighs, and she forgot whatever it was that briefly interrupted her.

There wasn't a spot left untouched. She was caught in a magical web.

And suddenly he was inside her and Crystal closed her legs around him, welcoming his fullness. The emotions sprang so tight and urgent. They were moving, moving as one. She couldn't get enough. The pressure built. Pleasure expanded—until she exploded. And then she heard his deep male moan of exultation.

* * *

Richard sighed, the aftermath of intense pleasure flowing through his body. Crystal was sleeping softly in his arms. Sleep was slowly claiming him, too. He caressed her face, kissed her cheek, and cradled her in his arm. He pulled the sheet to cover them. It was comfortably cool in the room.

Crystal's head rested on his shoulder. From the moonlight outside he studied the rise and fall of her breath. The silhouette of her face. The house seemed full again—alive. It wasn't meant just for him. It wasn't a home without his wife beside him.

His wife was finally back. Richard tightened his arm around her. Back to where she belonged.

Crystal awakened the next morning and felt a heavy arm around her waist. She heard rhythmic breathing nearby. She drew still. Slowly, she turned her head. Richard slept peacefully beside her. She shifted positions. She was naked. She sensed his nakedness beside her.

Last night rushed back in glaring detail and she groaned at her stupidity.

Oh, God, how could she have let this happen? She ran a hand over her face, then started to ease from the bed. His arm anchored her waist. She pushed it aside, slid from beneath the covers, and headed to the bathroom. Cool air rushed across her skin, further reminding her how foolishly she'd acted.

"What's wrong, Crystal? Wait up, honey. I'll join you." He did a slow sensuous stretch and kicked the covers aside. He lay there confident in his male glory.

She didn't let herself be moved by his act. "I'm taking a shower. Alone."

"More fun with two." He sat up and moved off the bed.

"Not this time, buster." She shut and locked the bathroom door behind her.

"Come on, honey. This isn't the way to start your first day home."

She knew he'd do that. Crystal snatched open the door. The way he stood there told her he thought he had it made.

She glanced at him with burning reproachful eyes. "It's not my first day home. If you thought that little act last night was going to make a difference, think again. I'm going back to my mountain. I knew I couldn't trust you."

His expression clouded in anger. "I wasn't making love alone and I didn't force you. You know you wanted me as much as I wanted you. Why don't you just stop this acting? Stay here where you belong—where you want to be." He leaned toward her. "Your body doesn't lie."

"Acting! You're the actor here. You should get an Emmy." She slammed the door. He hit the door and stormed off.

She showered in record time, hanging on to her anger. After she dried off and lotioned, she glanced to the counter at the lotions she usually used. It was as if she were away for a short vacation and were coming back. And that was how Richard was treating the situation—as if she were away temporarily.

Crystal wrapped the towel around her, marched to the closet, and selected the first thing that looked presentable.

Richard stomped into the shower after her.

Again, her closet was filled with clothing as if her move were only temporary. Perhaps that was why Richard wouldn't accept that their relationship was over. Her things were still here, as if she would return. It was time she gathered her belongings. Then maybe he'd get the picture.

Perhaps she had put this off because severing their relationship completely was more than she could deal with in one step. Perhaps Richard didn't believe her because, unconsciously, she was still holding on.

Richard never realized how lonely a drive could be with two people in a car. He and Crystal were on their way up the mountain. She pouted against the door. Right now he struggled with a fiery anger that was unfamiliar to him.

"I didn't rape you last night. You were coming on to me as much as I was coming on to you. You were with me every step of the way. I didn't even have to coax you. Just admit that you wanted me every bit as much as I wanted you," he finally said half an hour into the drive.

"I didn't say you raped me. I take full responsibility for acting stupid."

"It's your first sane act in months." His voice was quiet, yet held an undertone of cold fury.

She tightened her lips and glared out the window. "You don't have to worry about a repeat performance," she sputtered, bristling with indignation.

"Just tell me, what's wrong with intimacy between husband and wife?"

"In this case, everything."

He gripped the wheel so tightly he had to relax his fingers consciously. "You belong with me."

"I'm just your possession, one that you don't want to give up. At least admit that much."

"Crystal, that isn't true. I've always loved you. From the very beginning."

Crystal shook her head. "You're lying either to me or to yourself. You know that you're playing me until you get what you want. It's always the chase with you. Nothing's changed. Once I move in with you—if I were that stupid—the relationship will go sour. I don't want to keep going through this. Let me go and be done with it."

Anger swept through Richard like a mountain thunderstorm. "If it wasn't what you wanted, you wouldn't have complied. Since we can't have a decent conversation without throwing blame, just remember you agreed to three months. I'm holding you to our agreement."

Crystal swept a hand through her hair. "Just prolonging the inevitable."

"Hey, what's three months out of a lifetime?" he said stubbornly.

They were silent during the final fifteen minutes to the cabin. A thousand remarks flew through Richard's mind, but none that wouldn't result in an argument. Crystal was in a fighting mood. He'd planned last night to be the beginning of a lifetime—a rejuvenating of their love together, what they'd meant to each other over the last five years. Not the beginnings of a one-night stand. Which was exactly what she wanted to make of what had been very special for him.

Crystal's students met at the restaurant that evening as they had agreed. This was not one of Sadie's good days. She knew the group wasn't going to agree to lessons with her grandson present. They liked their privacy as much as she valued hers. She hated to put more work on Crystal but she wasn't capable of teaching her grandson. She needed help.

She wasn't so out of it that she didn't notice Gertrude's distress.

Sadie looked out the door to see what had caught the woman's censure. It was only that New York fellow. He was in town all the time. It was bandied about that he was doing good with the boys. He was going to take them to stardom. Wouldn't that be something? Sadie's daughter was a famous poet. She hadn't been able to quit her job just yet but one day she would. Her poetry was every bit as good as those famous authors on that Oprah's show.

Sadie wished she could get her granddaughter on the Oprah show. Then she'd have it made. She wouldn't have to struggle with another job to eke out a living. She could come to the country and write her beautiful poems. The country offered plenty of atmosphere. So much peace. Sadie wondered how she could write at all in the noisy city.

Sadie nudged Gertrude in the side. "Anything wrong, Gerty?"

Gertrude shook her head. "I don't trust city folks," she said.

Sadie thought about her granddaughter. "Not all city people are bad," she said. Gertrude talked as if they were aliens.

Her eyes narrowed as she watched the manager. "I don't know about that manager. Looks too slick to me."

"At least he's making some videos for them," Sadie said. "My grandson loves those videos that come on TV. But I don't know about those half-naked fast gals doing all sorts of nasty things. Lord, the women were all over the men. Rubbing against the men in front of *everybody*. Enough to stir a boy's blood to boiling. I made him turn off the TV right then and there. I got rid of cable, too. I told them I wasn't going to have that mess in my house." She looked around and made sure no one else was listening in. "I know he sneaks and watches them anyway when he's at home. Now, that's between him and his parents. He isn't going to do wrong in my home." She glanced at the manager again. "You don't think that manager is going to allow that garbage in the boys' video, do you? If so you need to put your foot down. Have the reverend talk to him. That'll set him straight."

"Wouldn't do any good. It's not the women I'm worried about. It's him," Gertrude said as they watched him talk animatedly on the cell phone.

Sadie moved her chair to get a better view. *Almighty*. She never seen anybody talk so much on the phone in all her days. What all did they have to say that they couldn't even eat a meal in peace?

Sadie patted Gertrude's hand. "Don't you worry. Having fast gals on the video isn't the worst thing that can happen, you know."

The next morning Richard traveled to Roanoke, an hour's drive from Windy Hills, to argue a case. He was truly in a quandary about what to do about his wife. Nothing worked with her. He'd done everything he could think of to make things better. Maybe Crystal just didn't want to get well. The things women could put a man through, he thought as he made it into the city.

He was listening to Tim Toyner, talk host of the HISS

radio show. A guest speaker talked about her latest book on relationships. Theresa was always lamenting because she missed the Oprah shows about relationships and self-discovery. Richard finally told her that if the shows were that important to her, perhaps she should tape them. He couldn't get out of the office before four and neither could she. Damn, who had time to sit around and listen to talk shows?

Women, that's who. And that was where they were getting these foolish ideas on how a man was supposed to act. Damn it, you couldn't act normal anymore. You needed a book for everything.

The author was now talking about men and women being like night and day when it came to what they expected in relationships.

You can say that again, buddy, Richard thought. He considered it a racket, but, hey, he didn't have a problem with how people chose to make a living.

"If you want to find out how to please a woman, read my book."

"Yeah, right." Most folks who bought the books didn't read them cover to cover. They stopped long before they reached midway. A few months later a new book would catch their interest. They'd buy that one too and read a few chapters before they shelved it.

He should know, Richard thought. How many books had Theresa bought? Every time he turned around she had another of those books. He'd ask her if she'd finished it. Her answer was always no—always. They'd be better off with a romance novel. At least they read those to the end— the good ones two and three times.

This book would go the same route as the others, Richard thought as he parked near the courthouse.

He was finished with his case by eleven. He went down the street to purchase lunch. He'd skipped breakfast. He was starved. On his way, he passed a bookstore. In the window was the relationship book the author had spoken about that morning. Once in the store, he glanced around to make sure no one he knew was in the vicinity. He wouldn't be caught dead buying one of those women books.

Curiosity had Richard reading the back cover and thumbing through the book. It didn't seem very logical to him and he put it back on the shelf. His stomach growled. He headed for the door.

God knows, women should be able to understand each other, he thought as he neared the door. It really couldn't hurt to pick up a few pointers. His footsteps slowed. Damn it, nothing else had worked.

Richard made a hundred-eighty-degree turn back to the self-help section and took the blasted book off the shelf.

He stood in a long lunchtime line and paid for the book, then made his way back to Windy Hills where Aaron Stonehouse was waiting for the appointed meeting.

Richard led the man back to his office where they settled with cups of coffee neither one touched. He glanced at the two boxes of records piled by his desk.

"I've gone through the invoices," Richard said. "In the stack there was a group of invoices paid to bogus companies."

"Bogus companies?"

"They aren't real, just set up on paper. The money went into several dummy bank accounts."

Aaron released a long breath.

"I'm turning this over to Elzey," Richard said. "It's taking more time than I realized it would."

"I don't know . . ."

"He's qualified to handle this case," Richard assured him. "He's older than he looks and he worked at a District Attorney's office for three years before coming here. He's dealt with situations similar to this before."

"You'll be working closely with him?"

"Yes."

Aaron nodded and Richard pressed the intercom, asking Elzey to come in.

Richard introduced the men. With regret, he watched the men leave his office. He had to make changes someplace. This could have been a really interesting case but it wasn't worth his marriage.

Seven

Friday's class had been changed to Saturday morning. A couple of students had other things to do.

Able arrived ahead of the others. "Ms. Dupree," he said with a nervous gesture. He swallowed hard, boldly met her gaze with bulging eyes. He wasn't the most handsome man, but if you could get past the five o'clock shadow and grave expression to the heart of gold beneath, you'd find plenty to admire. When a foot of snow fell, he'd be the first to dig driveways and not ask for a dime for his efforts.

"Call me Crystal."

He chuckled at that. "If I'd a called my teacher by her first name I would have gotten my knuckles rapped."

Crystal smiled, trying to imagine the rawboned man beside her at age six, and couldn't picture him.

"Things are different now," she said.

Able cleared his throat. "I was wondering ..."

Crystal placed a stack of papers on the table and weighted it down with a paperweight, giving him her undivided attention. "What is it?"

His jaw worked for seconds. "Could I have my classes on a different night?"

Crystal knew he was retired. Aunt Annie had said any night would do for him. "What days don't work for you?" she said gently.

He looked down at his large scarred hands, which looked to be permanently stained a dark color. He'd worked as a farm-equipment mechanic before he retired last year. "It's not that," he said.

"What is it, then? If the night is a problem, perhaps we can change class nights for everyone. We can discuss it tonight."

"I don't want *them* to change nights. Just *me*," he said on a frustrated air. There was also a touch of defiance. Able was usually pretty easygoing but right now he had that mulish look on his face. What was going on?

"I see," Crystal finally said. He was on the same level as everyone else. This course was no different from any other class she'd taught. Some students caught on faster than the others. He fit right in the middle. "May I ask why?"

He jerked his head to the side. "I don't like being near Sadie," he said in a rush, then pressed his lips together tightly. He sounded so much like Crystal's younger students she stifled a laugh. Crystal coughed, started to ask why not, then decided she already knew.

"That's not a problem. I'll make sure you're seated next to someone else."

He glanced skeptically at her. "I'm not sure you can handle Sadie."

"Don't worry. I've been dealing with difficult students for years."

He nodded and placed his notebook on the table.

When Crystal returned to the house for the lemonade and paper cups. Sadie drove into the yard.

She came directly into the house, not taking the time to put down her books and purse.

"Crystal, I need to talk to you."

This seems to be the day for tête-à-têtes, Crystal thought. She set down the tray she'd just picked up to carry outside.

"What is it?" she asked, giving the woman her undivided attention.

"You know my grandson's spending the summer with me."

Crystal nodded.

Sadie sighed, pulled out a chair and dropped into it. "He's got a reading problem and I don't know enough to help him. I hate to add more to your schedule but I don't know where else to turn. You know how mean kids are nowadays. They tease him."

"Bring him to class," Crystal said.

Sadie was shaking her head before Crystal finished talking. "I don't think the others would like that. Besides, he needs special help so next year he'll be up with his class."

"Okay, Sadie." Crystal's heart went out to the troubled child. She wouldn't consider turning down Sadie.

They took a few minutes to agree on a time for Sadie to bring him by. When Sadie got up from the chair she'd commandeered, she looked years younger. And as the older woman joined the others on the deck, her usual bounce was back in her step.

Crystal put the tray in the fridge.

She'd serve fresh cut-up vegetables with the dip today for a snack and the Pig Picken cake she'd baked this morning.

She still wondered why she'd fixed Richard's favorite cake. They hadn't talked since their lovemaking the other night and their argument the following morning. Just thinking about their next encounter made her nervous. Oh, well, she wouldn't have to deal with it tonight.

Richard had difficulty finding a place to park when he arrived at six-thirty. Several cars were parked in Crystal's driveway. It looked like a party was going on. He recognized Abel's 1985 Cadillac, Travis's new Lincoln. What was going on? he thought as he climbed out of his car. The noise came from the back of the house. He rounded the house and pulled up short.

Several people were snacking on dip and eating Crystal's delicious cake—the cake she baked from scratch that she hadn't baked for him in more than a year.

Sadie saw him first. "Come on and join us," she said as she cut a bite with her fork and tasted it.

"I hope I'm not intruding," he said, really not caring one way or the other. This was his home, damn it. He had every right to be here.

"Of course not," Sadie said, rising from her chair. "Pull up a chair. I'll fix you some lemonade. It's good."

He'd just bet it was. "I don't know. Seems like I'm crashing the party."

Crystal came out of the house just then with Princess on her heels. By then he was deep into conversation with Sadie and Gertrude. Gertrude must have been driving Travis's car since he didn't see the man anywhere.

"Your wife is doing a great job with us," Gertrude said.

"Before long, I'll be able to read my granddaughter's book," Sadie agreed with a touch of pride.

Able set his cup on the table. "I'll be reading the paper all the way through pretty soon," he added.

"Nothing but trouble in the papers," Gertrude warned. "The Bible might be a better idea. That's what I'm looking forward to. Then I can go to Sunday school. Won't be embarrassed because I can't read the lessons."

Jimmy leaned back in his seat. "I expect I'll follow the stock markets."

"I'll be getting my GED," Ricardo said.

For a moment Richard didn't know what they were talking about. A book, the paper, the Bible. Then it hit him. They couldn't read. Crystal was teaching them to read.

"Keep at it and you'll be reading like pros in no time," Richard said.

Sadie nodded, proudly.

It was five minutes before Crystal thought of an excuse to get him into the house. He carried his plate with him. Princess bounced in on their heels and wagged her tail for a treat. Richard reached under the cabinet for a dog biscuit. She took it and flopped in the corner on her pillow.

"You're early," Crystal said.

"I know. I was in the vicinity on business and decided to stop by on my way home." He leaned against the cabinet, took a forkful of cake. "You must have been planning for me. You baked my favorite cake."

Crystal looked heavenward. "After the break, you have to leave so that I can finish my class."

"I brought work. I can sit on the front porch. I won't disturb you. Princess and I can sit there together. We won't be a problem." He perfected the puppy-dog look.

Crystal stood indecisively for a moment, then blew out a long breath. Princess glanced up at the exclamation. Crystal didn't have time for an argument right now. "I'm not fooled by this," she snapped and started to leave.

Richard grasped her arm. Ever watchful, Princess moved forward.

"Sit, Princess."

The dog stood at the ready.

He set the plate down, brushed the hair from Crystal's face with his finger. "I think what you're doing for these people is wonderful."

Crystal glanced out at the group as they happily ate around the table. "I think *they're* wonderful."

Richard let her go and she went outside to join her students. He wished he knew what she was thinking. At one time he could read her as easily as a book. Then again, at the rate things had been going lately, it might be a good idea that he couldn't read her as well, he thought as he joined the others during break. It might be too discouraging.

Princess eased out of the door to join Crystal. She reached down and scratched the dog by her ear. Richard glared enviously at the dog. He could use a warm touch from his wife. He turned from the scene and started walking to the front porch. He knew it was bad when he was competing with the dog for affection.

* * *

Crystal had that hemmed-in feeling again. She didn't know what it was that made her so edgy. She only knew that along with the pressure from Richard and the constant reminder of her marriage and the baby, the oppressive feeling was growing with no limits. She just wanted to go into the cabin and be alone with Princess. She smiled. Princess, who was full of boundless energy, was her one true joy right now.

Richard. She couldn't blame him for the way she acted the other night. If she were honest with herself she knew their lovemaking had been her fault. Even today she couldn't answer why she'd drunk so much. She shouldn't have let her defenses down. She wasn't a drinker.

She'd wanted Richard. But she couldn't have him. Her actions Monday were a disservice to him. She'd given him false hope where none existed. She knew she wasn't going back to him. How on earth was she going to convince him now?

Crystal placed a bowl of cold water on the deck for Princess. Her class had left.

Richard had seen them off, then come around the back of the house. "When you said Saturday, I didn't think you meant first thing in the morning. Why didn't you call first?"

"I thought you knew."

"I didn't mean the entire day." Crystal narrowed her eyes. "Or are you just spending the afternoon?" She stacked the platters together.

Richard kept all expressions from his face and beckoned to the dog. "All day. Evening too."

The dog sidled up to Richard. He reached out to scratch her behind the ear.

"I'm having coffee as soon as I finish here."

"Mind if I join you?"

Crystal wiped the table down, thinking she should have

chosen another make-up day. Her plan had been to take a walk and think about her future after reading the paper. She went into the house, grabbed a cup and saucer, and set it in front of Richard and took her own seat. She glanced out at the view. At least the blue haze still covered the mountains.

Richard carried the platters inside, then returned for the pitchers.

"I'm starved for real food. I didn't get much of the snack," Crystal said.

"Would you like to go into town?"

Crystal shook her head. "I have sandwich fixings inside."

Richard joined her as she fixed two sandwiches—smoked turkey piled high with lettuce, tomato, and pickle. She added chips to their plates.

This was their first encounter since Monday—the day of the big fiasco. She'd canceled Thursday. He'd asked to see her today. Prolonging only served to make her even more weary. She just wanted the day over.

When they ventured outside, Princess smelled food and whined. Crystal broke off some of her meat and fed it to her. The dog wolfed it down and came for more.

"You can't be hungry. I just fed you." Crystal went inside and poured dog food in Princess's tray.

Princess was no fool. She sniffed it and came back for some more of someone's sandwich.

Richard pointed at the dog bowl. "Go eat your food, Princess."

Princess barked and slithered over to her bowl.

It didn't take long for Crystal and Richard to eat the sandwiches. They both seemed tense.

Crystal realized they needed to clear up the misunderstanding. She shoved her plate back. "Richard, I may have given you the wrong impression Monday night."

"It's over with. It was too soon. I know that now."

"Richard."

He sighed, scrubbed at his chin. "Leave it be, Crystal. If you say that what we shared was less than our feelings for each other, I won't believe you."

"That's just it. You only see what you want to see."

"Let's say it was too soon and leave it at that, because we still have months to work on our relationship."

Crystal started to say something. She looked at the determined slant of his jaw and knew it was useless. He was so damn stubborn.

Richard already knew that she wanted to tell him Monday had meant nothing. She believed that even if she couldn't see that she'd let the real Crystal come through, he realized. He wasn't going to let her analyze it to death. He knew that Crystal, who'd only had two or three drinks, was his wife once again. Everything else was just fuzzy details. They had other issues to air right now.

After lunch, Richard and Crystal donned hiking boots and with Princess bounding ahead of them, they hiked through the wilderness.

Richard was deep in thought. In the book he'd read that it helped to talk about problems. Crystal blamed him for not being there when their baby died. As much as he didn't want to broach that subject, they needed to clear the air before they could move on. Richard realized he didn't have any real problems outside of convincing Crystal that she belonged with him. But she needed to work through her problems first. She had to blame someone, and that someone was him.

Here goes World War III, he thought as he said, "Crystal, I think we need to talk about the baby."

She glanced sideways at him. "What about it?"

"You . . ." The book said not to say *you,* to talk in terms of him. "I feel that you think that the miscarriage was my fault—that you blame me."

"I don't blame you for the miscarriage, Richard. I felt alone."

"I tried to be there for you. Once I discovered—"

"You knew I was having problems that night, and yet you still stopped by your mother's on the way home."

"I thought it was morning sickness. You always felt lousy. You always said it was normal morning sickness."

"I remember telling you I was going to bed because I was feeling horrible."

"You went to bed early every day since the pregnancy began. I thought it was part of the pregnancy. You seemed to need more rest. I didn't see anything unusual in that." Terrible regret assailed him.

"You should have come home."

"I know that now, in hindsight. Do you think that my coming home would have prevented the miscarriage?" He stroked her cheek. She moved away. "If I'd thought for a second that you were seriously ill, I would have come home. After everything is said and done, I hope you know me that well."

She pressed her lips firmly together, looking away from him.

He stopped walking, reached out to stop her. "We need to talk this through."

"What's done is done. There's no use in hashing it out over and over."

"We need to clear this up so we can move on."

"Move where?"

"Work with me on this."

Storm clouds grew in Crystal's eyes. "I don't blame you for losing the baby, but at least you could have been with me. I wouldn't have gone through it alone." Crystal turned and hopped over a log, distancing herself from him. "I realized that night that you were never going to be there for me. You wouldn't have been there for the baby, either. As far as I was concerned, the marriage ended when I lost my baby." Crystal crossed her arms over her stomach and gulped in deep breaths. It was all coming back just as painful as it had been that day.

Richard walked up behind her and enclosed her in his arms. "A day hasn't gone by that I don't wish I'd gone straight home that night. When Mom called, I told her you weren't feeling well. She said that she had fixed your favorite

meal and to stop by to pick it up. I told you I was going to
pick up something from the store on my way. I thought that
would be better. We started talking about . . . Well, it really
doesn't matter. I stayed longer than I'd planned to. I know
words don't help. I am really sorry for that.''

His voice was raw. Crystal couldn't stand it. She remained
silent. She was too full to speak.

''I loved our child, too,'' Richard continued. ''That night,
I lost the baby, and in a sense, I lost my wife too. I couldn't
read your mind. If you were really sick, beyond morning
sickness, I wish you had told me. I can't cook a lavish meal,
but we would have made do.''

Crystal's throat was raw, too. ''Our problems went beyond
the miscarriage,'' she finally said. ''Don't you understand
that's been the story of our marriage? We have so little
together. I know it doesn't make sense to you. The baby
was holding us together.

''You spend long hours on cases. What's left over is spent
with your family on your family's political affairs. There
isn't time left over for our marriage. If we were blessed
with children, you wouldn't have time for them. I'd raise
them alone—just the way your mother raised you. I don't
want that. I want a marriage where both parents raise the
children. Where I have some kind of family life. You
wouldn't make a good father, Richard. Your children won't
know you.''

Anger swamped him. ''That's not true. Where do you get
these ideas?''

She turned to face him. ''Think about it. How much time
have you spent with your father outside of political affairs?''

Richard started to respond, then stopped.

''Don't tell me. You think about it.''

*Damn it, this talk is worse than the book said it would
be.* He'd tried to be reasonable, but Crystal punched below
the belt.

''I spend plenty of time with my father.''

''Be honest.''

''I don't understand why you're dragging this all out. We

already know the outcome because I'm not giving in this time.''

Fear coursed through Richard. He couldn't give her up. The book said that the beginning could be painful, but if they continued, they could solve their problems. He grasped at straws—anything to make this terrible distance abate. ''Would you consider counseling?''

''Counseling? I don't need a counselor to tell me what the problem is. I already know.''

Richard couldn't believe he was suggesting this. ''But we're too close to the problem. A third party could see more clearly than we can.''

She swiped a hand through the air. ''Would it keep you home some nights? Would it help you spend more time with me, or a child?'' she asked. ''I don't think so. You don't spend time with me because you don't want to. In the scheme of your great career and civic duties, our family comes last.''

She could have bowled Richard over with a feather. ''That simply isn't true, Crystal. I love you.''

''It's one thing to *say* you love me. It's quite another to show it. Let's go home. We've spent enough time together today.''

She started off and Richard followed slowly behind, deep in his thoughts. He was a lawyer, good at reasoning. Right now he wondered if one logical thought formed in his brain. It seemed his reasoning skills had vanished in the face of their problems. Had their marriage really been that bad? It hadn't seemed so to him. He couldn't leave it at that.

''Crystal—''

''Richard, leave it be.'' She kept walking faster a few paces ahead of him.

Richard caught up with her. ''I can't—''

''All right,'' she snapped. ''It was me. I failed, okay? I lost our baby. I did something wrong that caused me to lose our child.''

Richard was stomped. ''Crystal—''

''Just say it. It was my fault,'' she screamed at him. Her eyes filled with tears.

Richard gripped her by the arms, shook her once. "You stop talking like that. It wasn't your fault. It's nobody's fault."

"Babies just don't . . ." The tears that spilled over broke Richard's heart.

"Yes, they do. You aren't God, Crystal. It isn't your fault—your decision. You did everything right. I was there. I watched you eat the right foods, take daily walks, get regular checkups, take your vitamins. Some things you can't plan. Some things you just can't control no matter how much you want to." Richard felt better when she was blaming him. He could take it. But this blaming herself for something she had no control over was a thousand times worse.

"You've been blaming yourself all this time?" Richard closed his eyes. He hadn't been there to tell her any differently. She hadn't trusted him enough to discuss it with him. Perhaps she was right, he thought as he closed his arms around her and pressed her head against his shoulder. There was so very much they needed to talk about. So very much in their marriage that had been simmering and now seemed to be boiling over.

Richard held Crystal until she quieted. Then they walked silently back to the house. Even Princess sensed the tension in the couple walking with her. Instead of tromping after squirrels, she stayed close to Crystal.

"I'm spending the night with you," Richard said when they reached the door.

Crystal shook her head. "No. I want to be alone."

"You've been alone too long. I just want to be with you. I wasn't with you before, but I'm here now." When Crystal started to say something he held up a hand. "We won't make love. You have my word on it. I just want to be with you. Don't push me away. Not this time."

Her mind was in neutral, without hope. "Nothing's changed."

Richard nodded. "I know." But a lot had changed. More than either of them realized. Crystal's desire for distance from him was much deeper than the fact that she felt he wasn't good husband material. And since she wasn't willing to see a therapist, it was up to him to help her heal and get on with her life—with him. He hoped that in the process he wouldn't drive her further away.

Richard patted the dog on the head. Since when did their cabin get to be hers? he wondered. It had always been hers. Since the spring three years ago that they bought it. He could probably count on one hand the number of nights he stayed each year. A Saturday here, a Sunday there, and then back to the office bright and early Monday morning.

What struck Richard most was that Crystal was so close to the truth. He had planned to court her and then get back on schedule with the things he'd planned for his career. In his family their lives centered on career and civic duties. He knew that Crystal came from a less formal background. They had strong personal ties. They participated in volunteer work, but they also were known for huge family reunions. He'd even taken time from his full schedule to attend a couple of them. They'd been loud, playful, and fun—as foreign to him as Russia.

Parties with his parents were tasteful, and formal. One wasn't less than the other, just different. He'd always thought that that difference was what made them a special couple.

Crystal didn't know what had prompted her to tell Richard the truth about what had been plaguing her since she'd lost the baby. He had a way of picking at her until she'd do anything to get him off her back. And she'd ended up telling him her fears. Now he wanted to stay close to help her heal. Didn't he realize there was nothing he could do? She'd been healing on her own. She'd do much better if she had space.

Crystal put the last dish in the dishwasher in her aunt's house and went outside to sit under the oak tree. It was hot, but the shade from the tree lowered the temperature several degrees. She was also blessed with a lovely afternoon breeze.

Crystal began to prepare for Monday's class. She had worked for ten minutes before she heard a car drive into the yard. Annie had been hurting all day. Crystal had given her a pain pill that also helped her sleep. To keep the doorbell from waking her, Crystal went around front to see who'd arrived. Travis climbed out of his pickup truck.

Crystal met him at the porch. "Aunt Annie is sleeping right now. This hasn't been a good day," she said to the man. He held a hat in his hand.

"Just as well," he said. "I've been meaning to have a talk with you."

"Come around back. I was enjoying lemonade. Share a glass with me." Crystal started to the back door. "Have a seat under the tree. I'll be right there." She disappeared into the house. When she returned with the tall glass, Travis sat in the seat as if something weighed on his mind. He'd placed his hat on his knee and he ignored the glass she placed on the table in front of him.

"It's a nice day today, isn't it?" he asked.

Crystal wiped the sweat from her brow and looked up at the sun glaring down. "Not too bad," she said. It was much better in the shade.

Travis was a proud man who ran a very successful farm in a small valley midway between her and her aunt. His wife had died two years ago, and since then his nephew helped him with the chores. He was one of those gentle men with an unassuming but proud air. He seemed very tense and nervous today.

"I hope the lemonade isn't too sweet for you," Crystal said.

"I like it sweet." He still hadn't touched his glass.

Crystal poured some of the liquid from the pitcher into Princess's bowl and added a couple of ice cubes. Princess lapped hers up in seconds and glanced longingly at Crystal's glass before she flopped down beside Crystal. Crystal scratched her behind the ear.

Travis seemed to be stirring something around in his mind. Crystal didn't have a clue of what it was. She'd always respected him as one of the town's quiet but strong and generous citizens. If anyone met with a disaster, he was always the first to give food, clothing, and anything else that was needed.

Could it be Gertrude?

"Is Gertrude well?" Crystal asked.

"Oh, no. No. She's right as rain."

Crystal nodded.

Finally, he said, "I know you've been teaching reading lessons."

Crystal held a sigh of relief. "Yes, I have. The lessons are going very well."

"Everyone is pleased. Gertrude can't say enough good things about you."

"I'm glad to hear that."

"I was wondering ..."

"Yes?" Crystal asked.

"Well, when my wife was living, she'd take care of all the farm paperwork. Now, my nephew, Sam, does it. No telling how long he'll be around. If that band of his takes off, he'll be gone before you know it."

Crystal nodded. "I heard them at the club. They're very good."

Travis nodded. "I was wondering." He cleared his throat. "The church has asked me to become a deacon."

"That's wonderful."

"Problem is ..." He seemed to think his thoughts privately before spilling them.

"Yes?" Crystal urged.

"I've never told nobody, but I can't read. It's always been my dream to be a deacon, and as much as I want to be one, I can't since I can't read from the Bible."

"I see."

"I can read a little. When Gertrude started with the reading group with Annie, she'd teach me what she'd learned. Also I bought one of those phonics sets. I've been listening to the tapes and following the book. But I need more. I want to get my GED one day."

"I think that's wonderful," Crystal said.

He looked out toward the mountains. "I can't court Annie properly until I get my GED."

"Why not? You're not less of a man for not having one. You're very successful."

"For now. I need to take some college courses—to go further. Farming's not what it used to be. It's more technical now. I can't even read the magazines on new technology. My wife used to read them to me." He looked earnestly at Crystal. He was filled with anguish. "I need to be able to do those things for myself. Annie's different from my wife. Annie's got her degree. She wouldn't be satisfied with someone who can't read."

"Are you sure of that? Have you talked to her about it?"

"No."

"There's much more to a person than that. My aunt has more depth than that."

"The world revolves around reading."

"I agree with that. As an educator, I think learning to read is the right thing for you. But don't sell my aunt short."

"I hope I can trust you to keep my confidence."

"You can."

"After I get my GED, then I can pursue Annie. Right now I can only be her friend."

He seemed to have made up his mind. She could see the pride in his words. There was nothing she could do to change his mind. It wasn't her place to do so.

"I was wondering if you'd teach me how to read. You've never been one of those gossips. I've always liked that about you." He took a sip of his lemonade. "I'll be glad to pay for your services."

No one else was paying Crystal. It wouldn't be fair to charge him. She'd given up on free time. It just wasn't meant to be. Crystal wondered when she'd have time to think about her future course. Since she was leaving Richard, she needed a steady source of income. Teaching would do it, but she no longer wanted to teach. Still, there was no way that she could turn down this proud man and live with herself. Call her a marshmallow. No wonder Richard thought he could walk all over her. "I'll be happy to teach you."

"I'd be mighty obliged if you can fit me in."

"I teach the other group on Monday, Wednesday, and Friday nights. How does Tuesdays and Thursdays fit your schedule? I'm usually home by three-thirty."

"That suits me just fine."

"If you have a few minutes, I'd like to see where we need to start."

"I'm in no hurry." He seemed to relax for the first time since he'd arrived.

Crystal went to the house and gathered a couple of books. She smiled. Travis was serious about her aunt. Very serious. Her aunt deserved some happiness after all this time. She hadn't taken anyone seriously since her husband died years ago. Annie had loved Uncle William very much. The women in her family were known to make successful love matches.

Crystal thought of her own predicament. She had followed the family tradition—up to a point.

She *had* made a love match. But hers hadn't been successful.

The next day, Crystal met with Sadie's grandson and assessed his skills. A wide range of problems could be responsible for difficulties in school that would get worse the older he got if it wasn't corrected. The good thing today was with proper attention he could be reading on grade level and actually enjoy reading. Luckily there were teaching materials she could borrow from school that would make his instruction fun.

In addition to private tutoring she enrolled him in summer school class. A couple of days later, his teacher told her his problem wasn't as bad as they thought, which Crystal was happy to report to Sadie.

Crystal set it up so that he would read to his grandmother for an hour each day, which would help them both.

Eight

Annie's Taurus didn't hug the road as smoothly as Crystal's sporty Jaguar. After hearing a strange knocking sound, she'd put her baby in the shop for repairs and borrowed Annie's car. The car had only been driven once or twice since the shooting.

Now Crystal rushed home for her Monday class. It had been an unusually rushed Monday, she thought as she zipped around another curve and stepped on the brake. She readied herself for the next curve when nothing happened. No brakes and the car continued to accelerate down the hill.

Crystal pumped the brakes again. Still nothing. Panic careened around the edges. In a little while she'd be nearing a really sharp curve that overlooked a cliff.

Crystal shifted from drive to second and lurched against the seat belt as the car forcibly slowed. In seconds she shifted into first and lurched again. The cliff was approaching. She pumped the brakes with her right foot and the emergency brake with the other until the car finally slowed on the gravel a yard from the cliff. She managed to engage the emergency brake completely.

Crystal's heart thumped in her chest. She pried stiff fingers from the steering wheel. Her hand trembled as she reached for the door. Slowly she opened it and stepped out of the car on rubbery legs. She clutched a hand to her chest and walked closer to the incline, glancing over into what seemed like an abyss that ended miles down the mountain. She backpedaled to the car, closed her eyes, and sank to the seat with her feet on solid ground. She couldn't get completely back into the car . . . not yet. Fear, stark and vivid, knotted inside her. She felt like howling with tears, but that wouldn't accomplish anything. She tried to concentrate on the fact that she was still alive . . . that she'd survived.

Crystal retrieved her cell phone from her purse on the floor. Then with shaky fingers, she dialed the garage in town for a tow truck.

Crystal got out of the car again and paced. She checked the time. She'd be late for her class.

In five minutes, she heard a car approaching. It was much too early for the tow truck. In seconds, Sadie's ancient Oldsmobile rounded the curve. When the older woman saw Crystal, she stopped.

"Car trouble?" Sadie asked.

"Brakes gave out."

"Oh my word!" She looked Crystal over slowly. "You okay?"

Crystal nodded, waves of apprehension sweeping through her. "A narrow miss, but I'm okay."

Sadie opened her door and climbed out. "Want me to take you home so you can call the garage? We're closer to your house than mine."

"I've already called. I've got a cell phone."

Sadie looked around and put her hands on her hips. "Don't like the things but they come in mighty handy at times like this. Not safe being on the road alone. I'll wait with you."

"That's kind of you," Crystal said and wondered about the brakes. The car hadn't really been used in weeks. Was it possible something had gone awry? Crystal couldn't stop the unease she felt as she looked out across the rounded mountain peaks while trying not to look down on the town. She wouldn't look down again.

When Richard heard that Crystal had almost driven over Passion's Cliff, he nearly came unglued. Icy fear clutched his heart. By the time he reached the car, the scene more resembled the one he came upon at her house. Four of her students had stopped to lend help and moral support.

"Howdy there, Richard." The hood was up. Able peered under the car. Then he gingerly stood. "Mighty close call."

"You can say that again. See anything?"

Able shook his head. "Not a drop of brake fluid in her."

"How can that be?" Crystal asked.

"That's what I want to know." Richard still hadn't simmered down.

He saw how close she'd come to the edge. He touched her to assure himself that she was all right. And damn it, he had a right to hold his wife. He dragged her into his arms and held her close. She felt good and solid. He kissed her with a rough and quick urgency, then gently. It was merely a quick kiss, but a thorough one nevertheless.

Able cleared his throat. "Well, I've done all I can here. I guess I'll go on to your house, Crystal, to tell the others what happened," he said, trying to avoid looking at them.

Crystal touched a hand to her lips. "I appreciate that. Oh, I forgot my papers in the backseat." Crystal untangled herself from Richard and dashed to the car just before Junior hauled the car onto the tow truck. She grasped a zippered canvas bag out of the seat.

Richard insisted Crystal drive his car to the house while he rode the tow truck to the garage.

He'd had Annie's car checked only a week before Crystal returned home. With the car just sitting there, the brakes should have been fine. He glanced at his wife and then down the mountainside.

He couldn't stop wondering. The holdup of Annie still nagged him. Were the failed brakes meant for Crystal or for

Annie? Did someone want Annie dead? And if someone *was* after Annie, what could the gentle woman have done to make such a formidable enemy? He hated even to think it, but where were the Blake boys? He shook his head. He couldn't see them hurting Crystal. Still, he wasn't taking any chances. Not with his wife.

With the brake failure, things had started to get more serious. They had been serious enough from the beginning.

The promise of a generous tip assured him that Crystal's car would be looked at immediately.

Perhaps it was merely a leak somewhere. Perhaps he was making trouble where none was. Either way, he wanted to know. If Junior had missed something, he was changing mechanics. Mountain roads were no places for sloppy work. But he knew Junior was a careful worker; his own car might be old, but it drove as smooth as velvet.

Someone from the sheriff's office came to investigate while the mechanic worked on the car. It didn't take long for the mechanic to check out the line only to discover that it also had no oil.

"I could have told you that. The question is why?" Richard asked.

"You ever known me to slight you when it comes to brake fluid?"

"I wasn't implicating you. Can't you tell me why there's no fluid?"

Junior hovered under the hood and then beneath the car for a time while Richard paced impatiently waiting for his response.

Junior rolled from beneath the car. "Looks like the line's been loosened. She should have seen the oil on the ground," he said, taking a soiled rag from his back pocket and wiping his hands.

Who would want to hurt Crystal and her aunt?

The deputy scratched his head. "When Crystal called, the first thing I checked was the Blake boys. They've been out of town the last week with their parents. Which doesn't absolve them. This could have been done any time."

"They're certainly your obvious focus."

"They're our suspects," the deputy reminded him.

Or could someone be after him? Did he have enemies who would hurt Crystal to get back at him? No . . . maybe if the brakes had failed in Crystal's Jaguar, but not Annie's car.

How would that tie in with Annie?

"I'll talk to them when they return," the deputy said before he left.

Not before Richard talked to them.

Richard drove Annie's car to Crystal's house. When would he stop thinking of it as Crystal's place and think of the cabin as theirs? By the time he arrived, the class had ended. Crystal was freshly showered and smelling sweet, dressed in his old bathrobe. There was something erotic and warm about seeing her in his bathrobe.

He handed her keys to her.

"What was wrong?"

Richard explained about the brakes, ending with, "I want you to move to the valley with me."

Crystal was shaking her head again before he even finished his statement. "Absolutely not. It could have been a fluke. Accidents happen."

"Nothing was wrong with the lines. It was filled a month ago. The connection with the cylinders was loosened."

"Anyone can make mistakes. That's all it was. One of those freak incidents. I survived."

"And if it wasn't a freak occurrence?" His response held a note of impatience. "What if it happens again?"

"I have to believe it was. Who would want to harm me? I haven't made any enemies."

"What if the person was after me? What if they knew that by hurting you, they'd hurt me?" Richard wished he could get her to see reason. "What if it wasn't those boys? What if it was someone else and the boys were merely blamed for it? What if it's a connection to Annie?"

She looked irritable and agitated. "Don't try to upset me with this cloak-and-dagger business. You're defending the boys who hurt her."

"Crystal . . ."

"I don't want to talk about this right now. I've had a long day." Their eyes met. "Thanks for bringing me my keys. You better get back to town before it's too late. I'm sure you have an early morning scheduled."

Richard pinched the bridge of his nose. "I'm not leaving. I'm spending the night."

"No, you aren't."

"Crystal, be reasonable."

"I'm fine." She plunged on carelessly. "The brakes were a fluke. Go home."

Richard tried for calm. "Would you let your stubbornness keep you unsafe?"

"If I really believed I was in danger, I'd move to town. But I don't believe that I am. Can you honestly give me proof that someone wants to harm me?"

Richard shook his head.

"Good night, Richard. I have Princess for protection."

Richard approached her, bent, and placed a light kiss on her cheek. "Good night, Crystal. Take very good care of yourself. I'll be very upset and angry if anything happens to you."

He dropped her hand and walked out the door, shutting it quietly after himself.

Crystal released a breath and patted Princess on the head. She listened for Richard's car to start.

She had no enemies. She was certain no one was trying to harm her. Richard was blowing a simple accident all out of proportion. Still, she didn't sit out on the deck that evening. Instead she checked the doors and the windows to assure herself they were securely locked. She settled at the kitchen table, thinking about her class—trying not to think about her close call. She gazed out the window. It was pitch-black outside. Feeling she was alone in her hermitlike existence, she usually didn't close her blinds, preferring the bright morning sun pouring in. She found herself hopping out of the chair and closing them tonight. Richard had her feeling paranoid and for no good reason. She wasn't going flying back to the valley in fear. She wasn't going back to him.

She remembered she didn't hear Richard's car start. She peered out the window. Richard looked as if he was comfortably settled for the evening, sitting in his car.

"Oh, for goodness' sake."

In the end she went outside.

He slept in the spare bedroom.

"Richard, you've been very antisocial lately," his mother said to him near lunchtime the next day. She wore olive slacks and a matching short-sleeve jacket draped with a multicolored scarf.

"Work has kept me busy."

"I can certainly understand that. But I suspect it has more to do with our—shall we say small disagreement? You've never acted this way before. I've never known you to carry a grudge. You know I was only trying to help, don't you?"

"Of course I know that. Believe it or not, I have other things on my mind."

"Are you sure, dear?"

"I'm sure." He checked his watch. He had nothing planned for the next hour. "Just to prove it, have lunch with me," he said.

She smiled. "I'd love to."

They walked the two blocks to the restaurant and were soon seated at the table—his mother with a cup of hot tea and he with iced tea.

His mother sipped delicately from her china cup and placed it back on its saucer. "I don't care what you say, I wish Crystal hadn't decided to choose now to act up. This doesn't look good for you."

Richard stifled his annoyance. "I'm sure they won't hold my personal relationship against me. Divorce rates are high among lawyers. Haven't you heard? We make horrible husbands.'' A trace of bitterness that he couldn't stifle slipped before he could stop himself.

''Oh, rubbish. Crystal just refuses to be part of the family structure. Her rightful place is beside you, not stirring up trouble. I've always wondered if maybe you needed a more—worldly wife. A wife who enjoys civic and political matters as much as we do.''

''Let's not talk about my wife. Crystal is and was the right choice. We love each other. That's all it takes,'' he said.

His mother pinched her lips together. ''That may be, but she doesn't support you. You're a politician. I've always supported your father.''

''I know you have. Crystal has been a good wife. She has supported me in other ways.''

''Then where is she now when you really need her? Chances like these come along once in a lifetime.''

Richard raised a brow. ''Where's Dad now?''

''He's at the office, holding a meeting with Judge Reynolds. It wouldn't hurt you to spend more time with him.''

''Right now, my caseload is full. I need time to deal with Crystal. She still isn't over losing the baby.''

Claire sighed.

''My marriage is important to me.''

''Is it as important to her?'' his mother asked quietly.

''Of course it is.'' Richard had to believe that it was. If the marriage hadn't been, then Crystal wouldn't have fought so hard for them before. Perhaps it was his turn to fight for her. She wasn't making it easy.

His mother patted his hand. ''Well, think about the future. Your career couldn't be in a better position. And you can't afford to lose this opportunity.''

Left unsaid was whether he wanted to hold on to Crystal. A judgeship would give him evenings at home—time to spend with his wife and, God help them, children. If only Crystal would hold on a little while longer, everything she ever wanted would be theirs. Their future was hinged on his winning the judgeship.

He also wished he could get Crystal to believe losing the baby wasn't her fault.

Richard glanced at his watch. For once, Crystal should have come into town to dine with him. He made a mental note to call her when he returned to the office. He was very worried about her being alone on the mountain. Although she believed that the mishap was an accident, he wasn't as trusting.

"Try to come to dinner Saturday night."

"Afraid I can't."

"We're having the judge over."

"Sorry, Mom. But I'll see what I can do."

"Bring her. This is important."

"Another time, maybe." He placed his napkin on the table and signaled for the waiter. As he paid his bill, he noticed Crystal heading to a nearby table.

In the library, there just hadn't been enough of the books Crystal needed for her class. She now carried a tote bag of books she'd checked out. Since most of the readers were at the same level, she wanted them to read from the same books. She might be forced into going to her old school for materials. She could try some of the national reading programs, but her class had work to do in the meantime.

She reached Richard and his mother before she noticed them sitting at a corner table.

Richard stood. "Join us, Crystal."

Crystal stifled an inner sigh. She preferred lunch alone, but she couldn't be rude. "Hello, Claire."

Claire gave a disapproving smile. "It's good to see you, dear."

The waiter held a chair for Crystal and she sank into the cushions. "I won't stay. You've completed your meal."

"I'd welcome the time to see you. We see so little of you now."

Claire was nothing if not diplomatic.

"What brings you to town?" Richard asked.

"Books. I was hoping I could get the books at the library I needed for my class, but unfortunately they don't have enough of what I need." The fact that the group met at Jimmy's place was common knowledge in town now.

"Crystal is teaching reading to some adults in the area," Richard explained to his mother.

Claire looked on with interest. "That's wonderful, Crystal. I'm sure there are national programs from which we can get the materials you need. You know, I hadn't thought about an adult program here."

Crystal smiled. "I was thinking of driving into Roanoke to the bookstore."

"Before you do that, let me see what I can get for you." Claire was at her best when she was arranging things.

"It's really not—"

Claire patted Crystal's hand. "Think nothing of it, dear. I'm happy to help in any way I can."

Crystal knew that Claire was a powerhouse with charitable causes. If anyone could fulfill her needs, this woman could.

Claire glanced at her watch. "I have a meeting. It was really nice to see you again, Crystal. I trust that you are well?"

Crystal nodded. "Very."

"Good." She glanced at Richard. "If you can make it, dinner is still open Saturday night—for both of you."

"We'll see," Richard responded, rising to his feet.

Claire left with a flourish of subdued Chanel. Richard sat down and regarded Crystal.

"How is the car?"

"I was a little nervous after yesterday, but all went well today."

He covered her hand with his own larger one. "Take care of yourself, Crystal."

Crystal looked away from the naked need in his eyes. "I will."

"I'm looking forward to tonight."

That's all she needed to put her on edge again.

This foolish bargain, Crystal thought. Why had she even

made it? In the end the result would be the same. Chances were that she wouldn't be able to conceive again, and if she were able to do so . . . Richard would want children, not that he'd spend much time with them, but he would. If she were so blessed, she would need a man like her father—like her uncles. Her next child would probably be the only one she would have. And she wanted to give him or her the very best life had to offer. The best was a father who was around.

Why had she told him about her fears, her anguish? She hadn't spoken to anyone about it before, yet at a weak moment, she'd spilled it to him—the man she was trying to sever ties with. Only leaving Richard wasn't easy. Crystal closed her eyes briefly. Nothing with Richard was ever easy.

Back at his office, Richard told Theresa he was going to Annie's.

"You need to be working on that divorce case," she called after him.

"It'll hold," he told her. Truth be told, he'd lost his taste for divorce cases. He didn't like them anyway, but in a small town, one couldn't exactly specialize. Most of the lawyers handled all kinds of cases. He was no exception.

It was roaring hot outside. Richard started the air conditioner and drove the few miles to Annie's place after getting approval from the commonwealth attorney.

She was stirring around in the house when he arrived.

"I'm glad to see you're better," he said.

"Be a few months before I'm good as new, but I can do most things now. I'm glad of that."

"So am I, Annie. So am I."

She eased herself into a chair. "So what brings you out here on a workday?"

"Your car. I want a list of your employees. I don't believe it's a onetime occurrence," he said. "I also understand you've been seeing Travis lately. Think there are any jealous ladies out there?"

Annie blushed. "He's just a friend. He only stopped by a few times to see how I was. And he started visiting me *after* the shooting."

Richard nodded.

"I'll get that list for you. They're all local kids for the most part. Good kids."

"We must look somewhere. You were on your way from the movie theater that night, weren't you?"

"Most of my employees were there."

Richard stood. "Let me know as soon as you get that list."

"I'd like to know what's going on with you and my niece."

Richard swiped his tongue over his front teeth. "So would I. I'm working on her."

"Well, pay her some attention. That should work."

"I'm trying, Annie. I'm trying."

"Does she know you completed the application to take Judge Reynolds's place?"

"No. I want it to be a surprise—if I get the appointment, that is."

"That'll give you more time with her at least."

"It will."

"Of course, your daddy's campaigns will still take up time. That shouldn't be a problem. Nobody has the nerve to run against him."

"It won't always be that easy."

"Well, I'll let you get on your way."

Richard rounded the table and kissed Annie on the cheek. "You take care."

"I will."

Travis had been thinking for a long time that he needed to repay his nephew for sticking with him these last few years. He had no hope that anything would come of that band. They'd gone through this once before. The boy had lost every dime. Borrowed money from Travis and lost that too. If he purchased the theater from Annie, it would give his nephew something of his own. The boy would be good at running a theater.

Annie didn't always get the latest movies that the kids raved over. If she did, her business would be more profitable. She'd probably be able to open it most days during the summer.

She threw a couple of coats of paint on it every other year, but it was still wearing around the edges. Right now the seats needed replacing. If she purchased the right movies, she'd have more customers and the profits would grow.

Soon, he and Gertrude would be able to read and could keep the farm books. Although he could still use his nephew, he wouldn't need him as urgently as he did now. Farming wasn't in the boy's blood.

Yes, he could just see his nephew running the theater. Maybe he'd even marry Annie's daughter and the two of them could run it together.

He had no doubt that his nephew's sidekick would be there with him every waking hour. The boy was loyal. He could say that much for him.

Annie would have the time to rest. She deserved it after all these years.

He rang the doorbell. He glimpsed Annie through the screen door. She looked good in her long sleeveless dress, and she wore no makeup. She didn't need it on her flawless skin. She looked bright and cheerful as a mountain spring. He just about lost his concentration—and his nerve. He didn't know what came over him when he was around Annie. Around anyone else, he didn't act like a fool. Around her his mind took a holiday. She must have thought he was a simpleton the way he carried on.

She had a somber look on her face as she approached the door. As soon as she saw him, she perked up. Her step was a little more frisky. Maybe she was as affected by him as he was by her.

In no time he found himself on the porch sharing the rocker and a glass of iced tea with her. Sitting close to her, he felt the warmth of her skin. It elevated his temperature several degrees. They talked about nonsense for a time, and about Crystal and the near miss. Finally, he worked up the nerve to broach the topic weighing heavily on his mind.

"Annie, I've been wondering if you'd ever thought about selling the theater."

She twisted in her seat and eyed him closely, a puzzled frown on her face.

"My husband and I built that business from scratch. No. I've never considered selling."

"I know. But it's a lot for you to take care of now. You need time to rest."

"My daughter is working it now."

"It's a lot of work for you ladies."

"You act like ladies can't run businesses." Her tone was quiet and Travis felt safe continuing the topic.

"I didn't say you can't, but, Annie, you've worked hard all your life. If you sell the theater you'll have time to rest— get rid of some of the worry."

After all, in a year or so he hoped to get his GED. He'd have the equivalent of a high-school diploma. He'd ask her to marry him. He'd take care of her.

"I'm still in my fifties. I'm too young to retire. The proceeds from the theater won't take care of my daughter and me for the rest of our lives."

"Your daughter can still work there." He faced Annie and gathered her smaller hands in his. "Annie, I want to buy the theater from you."

"Why?"

"My nephew's going to be disappointed if that video isn't a hit. I don't have much hope for that manager of theirs. I don't see that he's doing much for them. Sam will be at loose ends when it's all over. If I can offer him the theater, that'll give him something to work with. I think he'll enjoy it. He and your daughter can work together."

Annie looked incredulous. "I can't sell the theater to you."

"It needs things—like new seats. The place is falling down."

Annie took her hand from his and slid away from him. He saw immediately that he'd made a mistake. "I didn't mean that you aren't doing your best, but businesses like that can drain your wallet."

Annie was quiet. He wished that she would say something—anything. The longer she remained silent, the more nervous he became. He always said the wrong thing around her. The words got all twisted on his tongue.

Annie fiddled with her watchband. "Have all these visits been about the theater?"

"Of course not, Annie. I . . . care about you."

"Well then, why haven't you come by before now?"

He didn't have an answer for that.

"I think it's time you leave."

"Annie—"

"I'm tired. I need my rest."

He started to say something, but he didn't know what to say to her. He twisted his hat in his hand.

He caressed the side of her face with a calloused hand. "The theater has nothing to do with the way I feel about you. I hope you believe that."

Annie got up from the rocker and made her way back inside, locking the screen and the door this time.

He looked at the solid surface. Yes, his approach had been all wrong. He didn't mean that she hadn't done a great job. Only that the young needed it so much more. He wanted to take some of the strain and pressure of a business off her.

But he'd done it all wrong. He wondered what to do to get back in her good graces.

Nine

The Baker boys were back in town. Richard's secretary finally tracked them down and they arrived at his office soon after Richard returned.

Right now they sat in the captain's chairs—both wearing jeans and muscle shirts—looking as if they'd just finished playing basketball—smelling like it anyway.

"I've got a problem," Richard said.

"What is it?" Rodney, the older one, asked.

"The brake fluid from Annie's car suddenly drained yesterday. My wife was driving the car. She almost ran off the mountain road."

"And you think we did it?" Rodney asked.

Richard swiped his teeth with his tongue. "You tell me."

"We haven't been near Annie's car. Why would we attack your old lady when you're helping us?" Alonzo said.

Rodney swiped a hand over his face. "We didn't attack Annie."

Alonzo looked worried. "Does this mean you're going to dump our case? You've got to believe us, man. We wouldn't hurt anyone."

"I asked myself those questions." Richard steepled his

fingers beneath his chin. "Let's revisit the night Annie was shot. Did you see anyone in the area that night? Or anything unusual?"

They both shook their heads no.

"We were just driving by when we saw Mrs. Prudence running into the yard," Rodney said.

Alonzo nodded. "It was real dark."

Rodney frowned. "I saw the tail end of car lights in front of us, but I didn't pay it any attention. Mrs. Prudence was carrying on so, we were worried about her."

"Right now, I'm worried about my wife."

"Get her to move back to town. It'll be safer for her here," Rodney said.

Alonzo stretched his long legs. "It's not safe out there up in those mountains."

Richard sighed, rubbing the bridge of his nose. "I wish it were that easy. What were you doing on that road? Annie's road leads to the mountains, but it's much more difficult to navigate than Mountain Drive."

The boys glanced at each other.

The silence irritated Richard. "This isn't the time for secrets."

"We were coming from Old Man Tiber's place," Rodney finally mumbled.

Alonzo continued cautiously, "Sometimes the sheriff puts up roadblocks on Mountain Drive, especially when they think teens have been going to Tiber's place."

The sheriff had tried to put Tiber out of business, but the wily old man moved his still often. The sheriff never knew where he was setting up business. The wilderness was thick and overgrown in this area.

"Do you know where Tiber's still is located?"

Both boys shook their heads—too quickly. They knew.

"If I'm to help you, you have to be honest with me," Richard said.

"We just visit him now and then. He's an old man. We're too young to drink. Besides, he wouldn't sell to us," Alonzo assured him.

Now Richard knew they were lying. Tiber would sell to anyone who paid ready cash.

Richard thought about Tiber; then he tossed around an old beau named Rufus that Annie had called him about. The relationship with Rufus had been when Annie was twenty-two. By now, Rufus should have forgotten about Annie. But one never knew in affairs of the heart.

Richard had called an investigator in New York to check him out. He wasn't leaving anything to chance.

On Thursday afternoon Richard arrived early at the cabin—earlier than Crystal had expected him to—and placed a bag on the table. She was curious about its content but wouldn't touch it or ask. He hadn't mentioned plans for the evening, so she was dressed in jean shorts and a spaghetti-strapped top—the same clothing she had worn when Travis arrived for his lessons. Travis had been eager and grateful for her instructions. He'd studied and studied the words and sounds she'd given him. One thing she'd noticed already about her students—they were an enthusiastic lot. They all wanted to learn with an uncanny zeal. Right now she was stacking the eggs Travis had brought from his farm in the fridge. At the rate they were going, she wouldn't have to buy groceries often.

"Those eggs must be very interesting," Richard said from the hearth. He seemed moody as he regarded her, his hands dug into his pockets. One of his cases must be troubling him.

"It's been a long day, that's all."

"You should have rested this summer."

"I'll get bored. I need something to do. I wasn't so certain at first, but now I'm glad Aunt Annie asked me to teach this class."

"You need time to heal."

"My doctor gave me a clean bill of health. So there."

"I'm glad to hear it, Crystal."

She disregarded the longing and need in his voice and

looked at the hand dangling by his side. Absent was his briefcase. She'd come to think of him and his briefcase as a pair. Somehow that assessment had changed lately. Still, as solicitous as he was being, she couldn't trust her and Richard as a pair any longer. She couldn't relent. Because the attention Richard was paying to her was short-lived. Soon, he'd be in his own little world and she'd be in hers. She couldn't forget that. But God, was it hard when he lavished such attention on her! She was consumed with a mixture of need and anger and lethargy. She purposely held on to that lethargy with Richard because she couldn't afford to let go. She couldn't let him see her weaknesses, because then he'd pounce—relentlessly, like the wolf he was. Sleek, graceful, and intoxicating.

Remnants of their lovemaking came back to her. She thought too much about Richard. A relationship needed more than spectacular sex. She glanced away from him and put the last egg in the tray. She could endure this for three months. Three damn, long, endless months. She shut the fridge door. *You can play the role for three months.*

"Have you had dinner?" she asked.

"No. Want to try the winery?"

"Not this evening. I fixed a macaroni and tuna salad. Will that do?"

"Like ambrosia."

Crystal took the macaroni out of the fridge. She got a loaf of sourdough bread she'd bought when she was in town yesterday and drinks. Richard set the plates out.

"Why don't we sit on the deck?" he asked, heading outside with the dishes.

Crystal regarded his back. She didn't want memories of him on her deck, but she grabbed the bowls and followed him. After all this time, he suddenly wanted to eat on the deck with her. A year ago, she couldn't convince him to share a meal up here on the deck or anywhere else with her. The strange surge of affection she felt building within her was frightening.

She'd wait for her mimosa until after he left, but he

circumvented her in that too. He took a bottle of champagne out of the bag, fresh-squeezed orange juice and other ingredients, and began to prepare two flutes.

"You may not want to drink and drive back down the mountain," Crystal said.

"One glass with dinner won't hurt."

"Suit yourself." She carried the bread outside and lit the lantern to keep insects away.

They sat down to dinner. Crystal barely tasted the salad she loved so much. She resented the fact that he was even here. They made strained small talk through the dinner. By the time it was over, even Richard was wearing thin around the edges.

"Richard, this isn't working. We can't go through this for three months. We'll hate each other. Can't you see that?"

"You aren't even willing to try."

"I've tried."

"I'm trying too. The least you could do is meet me halfway."

"Now that you're putting in a little effort, I'm supposed to stop everything and believe that you're willing to become an active participant in this relationship. I know and you know that as soon as I move home, there won't be any more mimosas on the deck. There won't be dinners together."

"I'm here now."

"Now isn't good enough! Let's part while we're still friends. Not as enemies. I don't want that."

"I don't want that either. But I want you to give us this chance." His tone was relatively civil in spite of his anger.

Crystal hoped he didn't snap the stem of the glass.

She tried to keep her heart cold and still. Crystal snatched up the dishes and carried them inside, stood at the sink running water to wash the bowls.

Richard brought the rest of the things from the table. "We can use this as a new beginning for us. A different beginning," he said quietly as he gently stroked her shoulder.

"I don't trust you." Her whispered voice was hoarse with frustration.

Richard felt as if she'd thrust a knife in his gut. He had to be way out in left field if his own wife didn't trust him. If she didn't trust him, whom could she trust? He gritted his teeth to keep from saying the wrong thing.

"That's one of the things we need to work on," was all he managed.

Crystal turned toward him, the dishcloth hanging in her hand. Disbelief was clearly written on her face.

So many issues, Richard thought, to get his marriage back where he wanted it. He dared not ask if it was worth the effort, because to him it was. He'd never love another woman the way he loved Crystal. He doubted he'd find someone to love him the way she did—had. That kind of love didn't just disappear overnight.

The destruction of their marriage didn't occur overnight, either. It occurred slowly over the five years they were married. And he only had three months to fix five years of destruction.

He'd burned the midnight oil many a night to win a case. He couldn't offer any less to save the most precious and dear thing in his life.

"Crystal, we need to be together to work on this."

"No" was her only answer.

"I'll drive here every day."

"I want to be alone." She wiped down the countertop.

"You were never this disagreeable before. Never this stubborn."

"If I had been, maybe we wouldn't be where we are right now."

"I realize I didn't spend enough time on us. I felt I needed to build the law practice. When we . . ." He hesitated. "When we had children, I wanted you to have the choice of staying at home if you wanted to. I didn't want to force you into that decision. I just wanted it to be an option. Is that so bad, Crystal?"

"Children need two parents."

"I would have been there."

She shook her head. "You wouldn't have."

Damn it. Didn't his work mean anything to her? Why did it all have to be her way?

"This lifestyle isn't cheap. The house, the cottage, your car. They all cost money."

"I didn't ask for all this."

"You're enjoying it all the same," he retorted in cold sarcasm.

"I work too, remember? You didn't buy all this alone. I would have preferred a husband to material trappings any day."

"Damn it! You've got one." The hell with tiptoeing around her. He had feelings too.

"I don't *want* one anymore."

"The hell with what you want!" Richard shouted. "What about what I want?"

"You always get what you want. But not this time. For once in your life things aren't going to turn out the way you want them to, just because you want it that way."

"For three months they are," he snapped, his control history. Richard got his jacket and slammed out of the house. Who the hell could reason with a woman when she was in this frame of mind? From the very beginning she'd been disagreeable. Deliberately so. And he was falling right into her trap. And he couldn't help it. He couldn't take her ambivalence any longer.

The next morning at five, Richard played racquetball with Leon at the club. Seeing Crystal—loving Crystal and not having the intimacy they shared—was driving him crazy. He couldn't even kiss her good night. Sexual frustration was building to the breaking point. Richard needed the physical activity. And he put all of his sexual frustration into hitting the ball. They were both sweating profusely by the time the game ended.

"What's with you today?" Leon asked on the way to the locker room.

"Nothing's with me."

"I think your wife had better come home, else you're going to wear yourself out."

"Stuff it," Richard said. He took his towel and wiped his face.

"What's up?" Leon asked, wiping his own face and eying Richard closely. "You'll get over it. Wrap yourself in an all-consuming case and the pain will ease away. One day you'll forget you were even married—at least for a few minutes during the day. Now, night is a different matter. But then I take my briefcase home and don't stop work until I nearly pass out."

Richard scrubbed a hand up his face. "Hell of a life we have."

"Isn't it just? And speaking of our life, you check out the new doctor who just moved to town?"

"What doctor?"

"She's a gynecologist."

"Just what you need."

"Oh, so now you're a comedian."

Richard grunted.

"She brought a nurse with her. She's a looker too, but I've got dibs on the gyno."

"I've got a wife, remember?"

"For how long?"

Richard regarded him a moment. "Until death do us part," he said and headed to the shower wondering if he really could make it last that long. He'd been sure by now she'd come around. In the past his attention to her had always worked. But nothing seemed to be working now. *Nothing*.

Richard pulled his shirt over his head and stepped out of his shorts. Had she really fallen out of love with him? Was what they'd shared and meant to each other so insignificant?

Deep fears began to seep in. He didn't want to go through the dating scene again, not when he was married to the woman of his dreams.

If Crystal didn't love him, could anyone else? She was making him remember the questions he'd asked as a child, like why hadn't his father loved him enough to spend time with him the way other fathers did with their kids? Then he asked himself if he was doing the same to Crystal. He hated this feeling of insecurity, resented Crystal for bringing it to the surface, because he was only trying to do what he felt was best for their family.

He turned on the shower. Every time they saw each other, they parted either with anger or indifference. What was he to do to change the tide? God, he wished he could take some time off and just deal with it. But would even that do the trick?

Hot water pounded him. One question he feared most lingered on the edge of his consciousness. He'd refused even to acknowledge it in the past. Had Crystal fallen out of love with him? Was love that easy to lose? What could he do to bring his dear wife back to him, especially when she didn't even want his presence?

That bedraggled relationship book still sat on his desk. He'd read it tonight and see if he could bridge the gap. No, not *if*. He refused to give up. He'd seek out *what* he could do to bridge the gap—not *if*, but *what*.

He lived in the here and now. Why couldn't Crystal do that? The past was gone. Why belabor it?

The more time Crystal spent with her literacy group, the more they trusted her. Today she planned to read food-can labels. That at least was something they all could use. They'd progressed at an extraordinary rate. They knew the major pronunciations. They knew how to break down syllables. Aunt Annie had taught them well.

"Your doctors have probably put some of you on restricted diets, which means you need to read food labels to plan your daily meals."

"I don't be worrying about that," Able said.

Able sat at the table behind Sadie. Sadie turned around in her chair and said, "That doesn't mean your doctor doesn't want you to eat right."

"I let Ruth take care of that."

"Well, now you can read it for yourself."

"Hmmph. Maybe a mechanical booklet would do me more good," Able grumbled.

"We'll get to the mechanical booklets later. For now, let's look at what you'll see on a can."

Crystal had printed off copies of food labels from the Internet and handed them out.

Sadie proudly angled her glasses on her nose and squinted. "Hard to see that itty-bitty print."

"Your glasses should help," Crystal said. She should have gone to the library to get the print enlarged on the copier. Oh, well, they'd have to make do.

"Can anyone read the top line for me?"

"I can read 'facts,' " Gertrude said.

"Can you sound out the word before it? Let's start with 'nu.' The *u* has a long sound."

Gertrude pronounced it syllable by syllable.

They were able to work with most words. Polyunsaturated and monounsaturated gave them problems. It would probably be a while before they were up to words that complicated, but they could read fat and sodium, which would help them tremendously.

The first part of the lesson ran longer than usual. Ricardo finally raised his hand. "Do we get a snack break today?"

Crystal glanced at her watch. Time had gotten away. "We certainly do."

Betty stuffed her papers in her book. "What did you fix?"

"I fixed an African dish. Ground nut stew. It contains peanut butter. I hope no one is allergic."

"Not me," Able said, frowning. "I don't eat strange food though."

"At least try it," Crystal said.

"I'll try anything once." Sadie placed her precious glasses in the case. "Sounds good to me."

"Me too," Betty agreed.

Crystal went inside and dished the food into serving bowls. Gertrude helped her.

Able may have voiced the only complaint, but he didn't

waste time filling his plate once she'd set the serving bowl on the table.

"This is good," Ricardo said, biting into a homemade roll. "You're a good cook."

"Thank you." Crystal guessed the young man had come straight from work. He probably didn't get an opportunity to eat before class.

"A little spicy, though," Able said before he dished a heaping forkful into his mouth.

"It's not stopping you from eating," Sadie said.

"There you go again. Always butting in."

"At least I don't complain," Sadie said before she gathered another mouthful.

"Say, Gertrude, I saw your brother with Annie the other day. Is he courting her now?" Betty asked.

"There's gonna be some mighty sad women with him off the market," Sadie said. "Louise has been going after him for more than a year. Bet she's marked a path up to his house, Gertrude."

"She's not the only one," Able said, shaking his head. "Just about every single woman around here has lost their minds over him."

Betty laughed. "I don't know. He's got a way about him. The country gentleman."

Able snorted. "Bunch of crazy old biddies."

"You wouldn't be knowing about gentlemen, Able," Sadie teased. "Women like them quiet, muscular, and handsome."

"You know what they say about farmers," Betty said.

Amusement glittered in Sadie's eyes. "And they're right."

"How would you be knowing?" Able said. "Your husband wasn't a farmer."

Sadie patted her hat covered in toile, and narrowed her eyes at Able.

Unable to win any argument with Sadie, Able shook his head and bent back over his plate.

* * *

Richard was shocked when Crystal asked him to accept the invitation for dinner with his parents on Saturday. His father, John Dupree, met them at the door. He was casually dressed in a short-sleeved knit shirt and slacks.

"Crystal, it's good to see you." Richard's father kissed her on the cheek.

"And you. It's good to be back."

They had only run into each other once since her return. Crystal felt somewhat awkward after the long absence. They were certainly aware of the state of her marriage, but she couldn't avoid them.

"I'm barbecuing ribs out back. Come and join me. Everyone's there," he said, walking beside her. "Barbecue ribs are the judge's favorite. Claire has prepared all his favorites this evening," he said in a conspiratorial voice.

Crystal smiled as she placed her purse in the closet and walked through the stately family room to the deck.

Judge Reynolds was nearing seventy. He had been a stern judge. But fair. He'd started a very successful program for troubled teens. Richard often worked with the program. He also handled their cases pro bono.

Windy Hills had the lowest crime rate in the state—probably one of the lowest in the country. Still, crime was here just like anywhere else. Annie's case had been one of the worst. The most troublesome area here was domestic disputes.

"Well, Richard. You're trying to follow in my footsteps, I see."

Richard glanced at his wife. He hadn't told her about the application. "We'll see," he said.

"He's eminently qualified," his mother said, offering a platter of hors d'oeuvres.

Richard raised an eyebrow at her. She ignored him. "He's the most qualified applicant for the position. As you well know, he's been a smashing success as a lawyer."

Judge Reynolds patted her hand. "I'm well aware of his skills. But it's not my decision."

"Too bad," Claire said.

"Anyone ready for ribs?" John asked.

"Yes, indeed." The judge rubbed his hands together and selected a plate from the glass patio table.

The other three adults hovered around the grill. Crystal lingered back with Richard. "What's this about an application?" she asked.

"I applied for Judge Reynolds's position. He's retiring in a few months."

"I guess it wasn't my business."

Richard sighed. "Of course it's your business. I wanted to wait to see if I get the appointment. Then I wanted to surprise you."

"Some surprise."

"I'll have evenings off."

"I see," she said, selecting a plate and joining the others. Richard wondered exactly what she saw.

Ten

Travis approached the porch where Annie was catching the late morning breeze. "It's a mighty fine day out today, Ms. Annie. How about letting me take you on a picnic at my place? Gertrude packed a nice basket for us. Said she'd love to see you."

Annie used her cane to ease herself from her chair. "I'm not going out with the scoundrel who's trying to sweet-talk me out of my theater."

Travis chuckled. "Now, Annie, I'm not trying to take anything from you. I want to *buy* it."

"You're not going to romance it from me, either," she said, placing a hand on her good hip.

"I know that. This picnic has nothing to do with the theater. I want to take a pretty lady out." To emphasize his desire, he swept a glance from her head to her toes.

Leaning forward on her cane, Annie narrowed her eyes at him. But Travis caught the slight quiver in her voice. "I'm immune to your silver tongue."

There were a lot of things he'd like to do with his tongue right now other than argue with Annie. Instead, he thought it was safer to discuss this. Riled, Annie was a mighty tempting figure. Her color had heightened. Her body was stiff with indignation. If he approached her now, she'd likely dump one of those hanging baskets on his head.

Travis held up both hands. "I'm offering food. Not sweet talk." He approached the steps cautiously, easing his way to make sure Annie didn't whack him with her cane. She was all feisty this morning. Her lovely eyes were lively and spirited. He wanted to kiss her.

"The picnic's already packed. I've got a nice bottle of Chablis chilling."

"It's the middle of the day. I don't drink in the middle of the day."

"It's the weekend. We can afford to indulge as long as we don't make it a habit."

"I don't know about that."

He detected interest, nevertheless. "I've got nice cold lemonade, too. It's all in the truck—waiting for you. I drove the truck so it'll be easier on your hip." He glanced back toward the Rambler he'd shined up for the occasion. "The seat's at the perfect height."

Annie looked interested but hesitated. "I'm still not selling you my theater."

Travis grinned. "You already told me that. I heard you loud and clear."

Annie looked indecisively toward the truck, thinking of the lemonade and Travis's broad shoulders and how striking he looked standing on her steps. To her annoyance, she found herself starting to blush. The scoundrel had inched up to the porch. He was a slick devil. She always liked slick devils.

"Mighty fine day for a picnic," he said with a devilish teasing grin.

"Only if you keep to your word."

His voice lowered. "You can count on it." The theater was the furthest thing from his mind today.

"It's going to take me a few minutes to get ready."

"I've got all the time in the world." His voice was now a husky rumble.

He watched Annie disappear into the house. He sat in the warm seat she'd just vacated. He smiled. An entire day with Annie. He'd been working his way up to this for a while. He'd sent Gertrude to her home. There would be no one around to interfere.

Annie was some kind of woman.

Richard had meant to be here earlier, but because of the case he hadn't made his way up the mountain until almost noon. Today he vowed not to talk about issues. They needed peaceful time together. Maybe he'd tackle another issue next week. He only hoped Crystal was still at home and had not taken off for the day. Richard exhaled a sigh of pleasure when he spotted her car in the yard. Even as he parked his SUV beside her car, she exited the house with Princess. She looked disappointed when she saw him. *That's just great,* he thought.

"Going somewhere?" Richard asked as he exited the SUV and approached her.

"I thought you weren't coming."

"It's our day together," he reminded her with an edge to his voice.

"As if I could forget it."

Richard tried not to let the day continue on a sour note. "Where were you going?"

"It can wait."

"Maybe we could go together."

"I was taking Princess to see Raymond. I told his daughter I'd try to get out there soon."

"I'll go with you."

She glanced questioningly at him. "Are you sure?"

He opened the door to his SUV, dreading the fur he'd have to clean up after the dog—not to mention dirt.

He made uneasy small talk along the way. "How are your students working out?" he asked Crystal.

"Just fine." She smiled for the first time. Putting up with the dog was worth one of Crystal's precious smiles.

"They really enjoy and appreciate the classes," she continued.

"I think you've tapped into a need we should have addressed long ago." In his work, it wasn't unusual for him to run into clients lacking reading skills.

"It's not just in our area. Illiteracy is a problem throughout the country."

Richard was silent for several minutes as he slowly drove down the winding road. "You really like what you do, don't you? I can see the sparkle in you that I haven't seen in a long time."

"Yes," she said quietly. "I really like teaching them. How could I not? They're so enthusiastic."

Richard reached over and caught Crystal's hand with his own. "I'm glad, Crystal. I'm happy for you."

It seemed for the first time since he'd arrived that Crystal relaxed. On a straight stretch of road, he hazarded a glance at her. Princess's head was between them as she looked out the window, breathing hard with her tongue lolling.

For a moment Richard thought of them as a regular American family. But they weren't quite a family any longer.

In another twenty minutes, they arrived at the retirement home where Raymond lived. Richard parked and sat in the car with Princess while Crystal went inside and gained permission to let Raymond spend time with the dog. In ten minutes, Crystal came running out.

Something was wrong. Richard was out the door before she reached the SUV.

"What's wrong?" he asked.

"Raymond is going to be arrested. They've called the police. You've got to help him."

Richard threw the keys at Crystal. "Park the car," he said and ran inside.

There was a commotion at the desk and Richard hurriedly asked to be directed to Raymond. "I'm a lawyer."

"This way, sir. Security has finally contained him."

The woman led the way down a long corridor papered

with lavender and cream, giving the area a warm homey feel.

There were three security guards. One restrained Raymond and another held a geezer Richard didn't know. The other was standing between the two. The geezer's eye was red. Richard was sure he'd sport a black eye by tomorrow. A nurse handed him an ice pack. A bruise was beginning on Raymond's cheek. The doorway was cluttered with people. A couple of women were yakking in the corner. Richard introduced himself and asked to speak to his client alone.

They escorted him to a small room but said that the police were on the way. They also informed him that Raymond would be arrested for attacking the other man.

Richard led Raymond to a chair. He was still throwing daggers with his eyes at the other man. Before they could begin to talk, a knock pounded on the door. He opened it to Crystal.

She rushed over to Raymond. "Are you all right?" she asked, regarding him closely.

"No."

"Where are you hurt?" she asked.

"My pudding's gone."

"Your what?" Richard asked.

"My pudding. It got splattered on the floor when he dropped it." He pointed an imperious finger at the door.

Richard cleared his throat. "This fight was about pudding?" he asked.

"It was banana pudding. We don't get it much. It was my turn. The ladies said so."

Crystal patted his hand. "I'll make a whole pudding for you and bring it to you soon."

"Really?" His eyes lit up. "It's my favorite. I'll be waiting for it."

"Tell me what happened," Richard started again.

"The ladies at the table said that since Warren got the banana pudding the last time, I could get it this time." He shook a finger at Richard. "But that old coot Warren snatched it before I could get to it."

The room was silent. The quiet, gentlemanly man had turned spastic over a bowl of banana pudding, and Richard didn't quite know what to say.

"Who threw the first punch?"

"I did."

"Oh, boy."

"I had good reason to." Raymond balled his hands into fists as if he wanted to pummel Warren again. "I should have hit him again. He wouldn't give up my pudding."

Richard glanced at Crystal, who looked beseechingly at him—as if he could or *should* save the world for her.

"He had just cause," Crystal said. "It is his favorite. Warren had no business taking something that belonged to Raymond."

Richard glanced at her incredulously. He couldn't believe she was agreeing with Raymond.

Another knock sounded. Crystal stood and opened it. An older woman ambled into the room.

"Are you all right, Raymond, dear?"

Raymond pinched his lips together and nodded once.

"It wasn't his fault," she said. "We all told that nasty Warren that he couldn't be greedy this time. We know banana pudding is Raymond's favorite. We all agreed to do without so that he could get it this time. But that Warren is a scoundrel." Her jowls shook as she pronounced the word. "He just wouldn't share. He always gets the best." She gazed toward the door. "I hope they put him out of here.

"It was my turn anyway but I told Raymond here that he could have it."

Didn't they feed these people? Didn't they have enough activity to keep them entertained? Richard wondered.

With Annie beside him, Travis drove up a dirt path and turned left at the fork. He looked at the fresh tire tracks leading to the old cabin his parents had built, and wondered why anyone would drive over there. He hadn't been to the cabin in months. No one else had reason to go there, either.

Just the other day Craig Johnson's workers had been caught growing marijuana in a patch in the forest. They weren't there for farming as they were hired to do. They were there to grow their illegal crop.

A farmer had to keep an eye on things nowadays. He could lose his land and everything fooling around with illegal substances. The government would be happy to get its hands on his land. He couldn't afford to get lax. He'd been putting too much work on his nephew, though. Perhaps he should take a look around to see what was going on.

He drove to the enclosed gazebo that overlooked the Smith River below. It held comfortable benches and a table. He'd had it enclosed with screening this week just for his picnic so the mosquitoes and bugs wouldn't pester Annie.

The water flowed gently past them. The trees grew up to just a few feet off the water and kept the area cool and comfortable.

"You've done a lot of work here," Annie said. "My goodness, how many years has it been?"

"Seems like a long time, doesn't it?" he said.

"It certainly does."

Travis hopped around the truck and assisted Annie to get out. She was getting on very well right now. Her limp was less noticeable. He liked touching her anyway. He'd think of any excuse to do so, he thought as he helped her to the gazebo, then returned to the truck for the picnic basket and cooler.

He glanced in the direction of the path again as he gathered an old quilt for Annie.

She'd started to unpack the picnic onto the table. A pretty red tablecloth covered the wooden surface. Gertrude had picked everything out to look romantic. Just the setting Travis wanted. Too bad they couldn't use candles. But the lush wilderness setting was enough scenery in itself.

And Annie was there. What more did he need?

"I'm famished."

"Me too." But food wasn't what he was starved for. It was the woman sharing the afternoon with him.

Annie watched the rascal observe her. Her fingers fumbled with the plastic bowl of strawberries. She shouldn't really be out with Travis. She wasn't selling him her theater. There was something about him that drew her like honey to a bear. Not only her, but many women.

Louise wouldn't speak to her at the drugstore the other day when she went to get her medicine refilled. Everyone knew that Louise had been running after Travis since the day his wife passed away. He hadn't responded to her attempts. He'd been very cagey about keeping his distance. Annie knew a randy man like him had to be parking his truck someplace. She just didn't know where. And now she knew why he'd parked it in her yard. She'd had such high hopes.

She really shouldn't have let him talk her into this picnic, but she was tired of her own company. And he was good company. He knew how to entertain a lady.

She dug two china plates out of the bag, and real silverware. Crystal wineglasses were meticulously packed. He'd put a lot of thought into this picnic. The least she should do was enjoy, she thought as she selected the potato salad and fried chicken. She closed her eyes. Fried chicken. She hadn't had fried chicken in . . . she didn't know how long. There was ham and Brie with crackers. Fresh whipped cream for the strawberries. A bottle of Chablis. She opened another container. Was that caviar? It was. She'd never developed a taste for the delicacy. She'd keep that a secret. She pulled out a vinaigrette salad with tomatoes, onions, cucumber, and more. They'd both have to eat the onions.

She'd try not to eat like a pig. Hopefully they'd be here long enough for her to do justice to the picnic.

"I heard about the old boyfriend, Annie. The one that might be troubling you. If you want to stay with me you can. I'll protect you."

Annie glanced away from her bag to him. "I don't think that'd be a good idea."

"Why not? I can protect you."

"Hmm. Who's going to protect me from you?"

His mouth stretched into a sly grin. "Do you want protection against me?"

Annie declined to answer as she dug into the cooler for the drinks.

"I didn't hear an answer, Annie."

Annie scoffed, placing the last container on the table. "All the protection I need is from you."

Travis narrowed his eyes in a sexy kind of way. He did everything with style. "Hmm. But let's get back to this guy and why you think he's a threat."

Annie really didn't want to talk about Rufus. It had been so long ago. "It was right after I graduated from college. I'd obtained my first teaching job in New Jersey. Rufus's parents owned the apartment I rented. It was an old house that had been turned into four apartments. He was the fix-it person. He collected the rent sometimes too. Anyway, we dated a couple of times, but it wasn't working out for me."

"You tried to cut it off?"

Annie nodded. "But Rufus wouldn't take no for an answer. He was always around. I had a year's lease on the apartment. I had to get to the end of the school year. I had my locks changed. And you know back then there wasn't any protection from stalkers." Annie shuddered at the thought.

"Go on," Travis said gently.

"Anyway, at the end of the school year, I packed my bags in the middle of the night. I didn't attend the last day of classes. It's a throwaway day anyway. I'd recorded all the children's grades. I got recommendations from my principal. I had talked to her about what was happening. I left town in the middle of the night. But Rufus knew I was from D.C. On the apartment application I'd given my parents' names and address as an emergency contact. A friend said she knew of teaching positions available here. And this is where I ended up. Information wasn't as readily available then as it is now. I even had my last name changed. When I married I felt more comfortable."

"Stalking doesn't get any better. What makes you think he's after you after all this time?"

"A friend who still lives in New Jersey down the street from Rufus's sister told me he just got out of prison. He'd stalked someone else a few years ago and killed her. He may have made it here."

Travis thought for a moment. "Annie, if he was the one, he would have killed you by now."

"I don't know what else it could be. I had money in my pocket that night. The man didn't take it. I don't have any enemies here."

"That you know of anyway."

"I haven't done anything to anyone."

"Who knows what goes on in twisted minds?"

"Certainly not I."

"Have the police looked into this Rufus?"

She nodded. "Right after I told Richard about him. They said he hasn't been out of New Jersey."

"My offer still stands. It might be a good idea for you to stay at the farm until after this is settled."

"There's no telling when it will *be* settled. It's been two months. They don't know any more now than they did from the very beginning."

Travis wondered what insecurity twisted the mind to the extent that a man couldn't treat women decently, or leave them alone if that's what they wanted. He may not have been educated, but he had common sense.

Annie, he thought, right out of college, budding with hope and enthusiasm for the future. Her parents probably told her to come home and teach, but knowing her, she wanted to spread her wings, only to have them clipped by someone with a twisted sense of reality. He wondered if her parents told her that most dreaded line, "I told you so."

At least the experience didn't break her spirit. Travis was thankful for that. Annie still stretched her wings. She still worked harder than most men. She wasn't afraid to live. That's what he liked most about her. She was her own woman. He wanted to share his life with her. He couldn't until he got his diploma. Every night, Travis spent hours on his studies. He didn't get much sleep these days. He could sleep after he'd accomplished his goals.

It wasn't just Annie that made him work so hard. He wanted that sense of freedom. He didn't want anyone to read to him. He wanted to read his own contracts. He wanted to know what a sign read, not by the color and shape, but because he could read the words. He could read signs now. He'd progressed that far in the last few months.

He remembered the first time he read SLIPPERY ROAD AHEAD. Something had squeezed his heart at that moment as tight as a fist. At that moment, he knew that soon he'd be able to travel and read the signs. No one would have to read them for him. He wouldn't have to remember landmarks to get to a place. A gas station here, or a blue house there. He'd be able to read the words on the sign.

Most of all, he wouldn't have to hide his fear any longer. Fear that Annie would think less of him. That she wouldn't love him if she knew.

Richard read the information the officer had gotten him on Annie's old boyfriend. It seemed that Rufus had been in New Jersey for the last year. He dated a woman he'd grown up with. She'd visited him in jail all those years and now they were preparing for a huge wedding. He doubted the woman knew what awaited her.

Richard doubted that Rufus was settling old scores but one never knew. He had Theresa make plane reservations. He was having a talk with Rufus. He snapped his suitcase closed as Crystal came into the room. The last time she stood there, she'd announced she wanted a divorce. What did she want this time?

"Theresa said you're going to New Jersey."

"I am."

"I want to go with you."

"Forget it."

"Why not?"

"I don't want you near that man."

"Oh, is this a guy thing?"

"It's potentially dangerous. I'm going strictly as a lawyer."

"I'll pretend I'm your secretary."

"It'll never work. Rufus has learned a few tricks since he's been in prison."

"She's my aunt."

"Mine too, by marriage. I want you safe, Crystal. I don't want him to follow us here if he doesn't already know about Annie's whereabouts."

"Don't worry about me."

Richard sighed, rounded the desk to sit on the edge. "I spend more time than you know worrying about you."

Crystal glanced away from him.

He chuckled. "Bet you don't want to hear about that."

"We were talking about Aunt Annie."

"I was talking about you." He touched her face. She didn't pull away. He loved this woman. Above distraction. He tugged her close and kissed her. She hadn't let him close to her since that night. The night they made love. His body fitted tightly against hers as he rubbed his hand along her back, along her cheek. Her skin was soft to his touch. His body tightened at the sensual desire that flowed through him.

He kissed her neck.

"Richard," Theresa said, coming to the door.

Richard groaned. He and Crystal pulled apart. He should fire Theresa, he thought.

She had a smile on her face.

"Well?" Richard snapped.

"Your flight's all set."

"Make reservations for Crystal."

Theresa narrowed her eyes. "I'm not going to have to cancel it, am I?"

Crystal smiled. "Not this time."

Theresa returned her smile. "Good," she said and returned to the reception area.

"I'll pack a carryon."

Richard was afraid to hope. Hope that something wonderful would happen while they were away. But with Crystal, seesawing from emotion to emotion, he didn't know what to expect. He could only hope.

Eleven

Rufus lived in a house that had been divided into four apartments, which he had reconverted into a single-family house, Richard noted as he exited the cab with Crystal. He wasn't comfortable about taking her with him. This Rufus could still be crazy and Richard could be leading her into trouble. He had taken karate in college and sometimes practiced with Leon, but that made him no match for a hardened criminal with a weapon. His fights these days were with words.

He paid the cab driver and promised a sizable bonus if he'd wait.

"I wish you'd stay in the cab," he said to Crystal.

"I want to see this man."

Richard sighed and knocked on the door. When did she listen to him?

A man who fit the snapshot he had of Rufus answered the door. His salt-and-pepper hair was cut short and he had long sideburns and a tattoo on his upper arm. The sideburns were out of style for today, but then Rufus hadn't needed to worry about style for years.

"May I help you?" he said.

"Yes," Richard said, giving Annie's maiden name. "I'm an attorney representing Annie Butler."

He frowned. "Annie?"

Richard knew the moment recognition hit.

He smiled. "Annie?" I haven't seen her in years."

"I'm aware of that."

He came out onto the porch. "What can I do for you? How is she?"

"Annie was shot two months ago."

"Shot?" There was anguish on his face until he got the point. And then his expression cleared. "I see. You think I shot her?"

"I'm asking questions."

"I know that I lost it when I was dating Annie. But that was over thirty years ago. I was young then. I haven't seen her since she left here in the middle of the night."

"The police can't explain why anyone would shoot her."

"So because the woman I dated was killed and I was charged, it must have been me who shot Annie."

"I'm just gathering information," Richard assured him.

He studied Crystal. "You sort of look like Annie did back then. You must be related."

"Yes . . ."

"We were talking about Annie," Richard said.

He sighed, focusing on his shoes. When he lifted his eyes, pain flickered there.

"I didn't try to kill Sissy. I know she was running from me, and she fell to her death, but I didn't push her and I didn't kill her. It was dark that night. We'd had an argument. Just like with Annie. I know I scared Annie. I came on too strong. But I wouldn't have hurt her. I'd had some therapy by the time I dated Sissy. I still had a long way to go, but I didn't kill her. I just couldn't prove it. And my past was the kiss of death. My parents insisted I get therapy for my aggressive behavior. But no one would listen to me when I said I didn't murder that woman." He sighed again, dropped into the chair on the porch.

"Where were you on May seventeenth?" Richard asked.

"Right here," he said, pointing to the house. "Fixing this building. I'm engaged. My fiancée and I are going to live right here."

Just then a woman in her mid-fifties walked into the tiny yard. Rufus's expression softened. "That's Dana, my fiancée. I spent May seventeenth with her. We went out to dinner. It was the night we got engaged."

Richard watched the woman come up the sidewalk. He didn't have much hope in Rufus's therapy. But Dana confirmed his statement. They'd spent the night celebrating. If that was so, then Rufus couldn't be in Windy Hills hurting Annie. That didn't mean, however, that he couldn't hire someone to do it. He could have run into all kinds of guys willing to do his dirty work for him.

For now, Richard let it go. He and Crystal left, and although originally he'd planned to take the next flight back home, he decided to spend the night in Manhattan. He bought tickets for a Broadway play and after, they ate at a restaurant that remained open for the after-theater crowd. As they ate the famous New York cheesecake, his body responded to the upcoming night in the one hotel room they were able to get.

Richard tossed and turned in bed. The room had *two* beds. Crystal slept peacefully in the *other* bed.

New York was a noisy city. He stared at the ceiling, listened to the sirens outside. The most he heard from his bedroom at home were a few crickets.

The play had been thrilling. The food delicious—as New York cuisine was known to be. But that had been the end of his good fortune.

Richard pushed back the covers. Damn. It looked like this hell wasn't going to let up any time soon. He was getting tired of this nonsense. Crystal needed to get over it and come back to him where she belonged. But he wasn't going to force her.

He went into the bath and took a cold shower. His behind was going to get frostbite from all those cold showers.

Travis met with his nephew in the office in back of the house. He wore jeans and hung his straw hat on the peg by the door.

"I was near the fork to the cabin yesterday—up there by Cedar Creek—and I saw fresh tracks on the road leading to the cabin. I'm heading out to check on things. You know what happened at the Johnsons' place. I don't want any wrongdoings out here. At the first sniff, the government is ready to take your land, home, automobiles, everything. I've worked too hard to lose everything."

Sam glanced up from his accounting. "The band and I go there sometimes to hang out and practice. It's quiet. We don't disturb anyone like we do in my apartment. Don't have folks hollering about turning the noise down. I go there sometimes when I need to get away, too. You don't mind, do you, Uncle Travis? I mentioned it a few months back."

Travis shook his head. "Must have slipped my mind. Of course I don't mind. Just wondering, is all." He frowned at his nephew. "How do you play without electricity?"

Sam placed his pencil on the pad. "I had it hooked up. I pay for it. I don't expect you to."

Travis nodded, satisfied. He shuffled papers on the desk. "Just don't leave anything of value in it without insuring it. I don't have any insurance on that shack. A good strong wind will blow it clean away."

"Don't worry. The only thing of value is a CD player, tape player, and TV. We like to watch movies to wind down where nobody will bother us. Nothing else of value is in there. Just some old broken-down computers and band equipment we thought we'd fix one day when we get the chance—junk we don't use anymore. Doesn't look like we'll have the time for it though between the job and practice and gigs." He leaned back in his seat, linked his hands behind his head. "I'll probably take all of it to the dump before long,'' he said. "What were you doing out that way? Anything I need to know?''

Travis picked up a piece of paper. His reading skills were improving greatly. He could pick out a few words. At least he was advancing. He glanced up from the paper. Two months ago he couldn't read that much. "Took Annie to the pavilion,'' he said with a smile, placing the paper back on the desk. "Thought it would be nice for her to get out of the house for a spell. It was a nice day for being outdoors.''

"How is she doing?'' Worry furrowed Sam's brows.

"Mending well. I'm still worried about her, though. Richard doesn't think the Blake brothers shot her. He's checking out an old boyfriend. I'd feel a whole lot better if we knew for sure.''

"An old boyfriend? I haven't heard anything about Mrs. Annie dating.''

"Happened a long time ago, right when she got out of college. Dated some crazy guy up New Jersey way. Richard's up there now. I think I'll go on out to see Annie. Keep an eye on her. You got things going okay here?'' He collected his hat from the peg.

"Yeah. We're spraying the peanuts today. I got plenty of paperwork after that.''

"I don't know how you do it all with that band taking up so much time and not paying worth spit.''

A soft expression crossed the boy's face. "I love the band, Uncle Travis. It's my dream.''

Travis shook his head. "I know you do, boy.'' *He's just setting himself up for disappointment—again,* Travis thought. He just had to convince Annie to sell him that theater. Then his nephew would have *something* to hold on to.

The outer door banged open so hard it hit the wall. In came "the Shadow.''

"Morning, Mr. Walker,'' Troy said, grinning and plunking himself into a chair in front of the desk. He stretched out his long legs, resting his dirty tennis shoes on Travis's prized mahogany desk.

Travis grunted. "Keep your feet off the desk," he said.

That boy irritated him more and more every time he saw him. He had no fault with him, just that he was always underfoot as if he had no direction without Sam. As if the boy would be lost without him. Travis thought for a full minute. Perhaps he *would* be lost without his nephew. It was a waste for a man not to be his own person—to follow instead of traveling his own road. There was nothing wrong with working in their band together, but there should be some individuality, some self-expression. No. A man shouldn't always follow.

Travis glanced at his watch. "Well, I'll be getting on to town. Got a meeting later on." Actually, he'd started to meet with Gertrude and her group. They met at a back room before the place got full. He hoped his news didn't get back to Annie. He liked to keep his business to himself. Since he was further along than they, most times he helped them out on things they'd forgotten.

"See you later."

Travis got into his truck and drove the ten miles to town thinking about his date with Annie. Annie was a sweet woman. Feisty, but sweet. Lord Almighty. He liked them feisty, a little frisky. Kept excitement in the air. Travis smiled. She might offer him a glass of lemonade.

He might sneak a kiss.

Richard stopped by the restaurant for breakfast around ten Monday morning. He wanted a moment to clear his head before he went to court. His seat faced the banquet room. Travis and a bunch of senior citizens were hanging out in there with books. Crystal's students. The bustle of the restaurant prohibited him from hearing what they were saying, but he observed the thin primers they held up in front of them and the way Sadie bent over the book to read. He admired them for taking this step at this age. Most people would have given up in their sixties or seventies. Not these geezers. They were plowing on. Their strength was lined with steel.

He couldn't give up on Crystal. Saturday had been good. For once she wasn't second-guessing him. For once she acted naturally. Raymond only got to spend a little time with Princess. Richard had delivered a lecture on fighting to the older man. Raymond ignored it, continuing to grumble about his pudding, until Crystal led him to Princess. He seemed to enjoy the dog and didn't want her to leave. The officers arrived and took statements from the staff. Then they spoke to witnesses.

Richard had called the sheriff's office to set up an interview with Raymond. Two hours had passed before he and Crystal left. He'd expected to deal with teens and fighting, not senior citizens.

He scanned the restaurant. The Parkers were sitting at the table while their new son slept peacefully in a stroller. Janice had taught with Crystal at Windy Hills Elementary. Only last October Crystal and she had compared their pregnancies. Was it only last October when his world was riding high on a cloud? It seemed so much longer.

As the couple conversed and giggled over the menu, Richard wondered when the last time was that he'd taken Crystal out just to be together—before she left for Japan. He was ashamed that he couldn't even remember.

Although Crystal had been ecstatic about the baby, Richard admitted to himself that something still wasn't quite right. He had begun to work long hours again. He and his mother had worked tirelessly on one of her pet projects. Crystal had simply given up complaining about his absence. And since she had, he'd breathed a sigh of relief and gone on as things were.

He didn't deserve her. Still, he couldn't let her go without a fight. He realized that to keep her he'd have to make more changes than hiring someone to lighten the workload. He thought back to the relationship book he'd scanned a couple nights ago. It mentioned that he should write out his personal goals. He thought about Crystal and about the children he wanted.

He remembered swearing as a teenager that he wouldn't raise his children as he'd been raised. He wanted time with his children—wanted them to be raised by both parents. Not by one, with the other too busy with his career to take an active role. Although his father was the mayor, politics was as much his mother's life as his father's. He hadn't set up his life that way. And he'd thought that if he became a judge, things would change.

Richard rubbed his temples. He was fooling himself there, too, because as soon as he became judge, he'd fill his free time with other projects and obligations that would still take time from the family. He realized that he couldn't give up all of his volunteer work. He'd been blessed and he needed to carve the way for others less fortunate. But his first priority was to his family—Crystal and any children they might be blessed with—if it wasn't too late.

Change was required and his quest was to discover a way to get Crystal to trust him again. Lord knows he hadn't given her reason to.

He glanced at the Parkers. They were sharing an appetizer now, chatting and smiling, making love faces, showing tender intimacy that only those in love shared. The baby still slept peacefully in the stroller.

Richard pulled out his cell phone. He called Theresa to make sure his schedule was still clear for the afternoon. He was taking time off to spend with Crystal—even though it wasn't his day to do so. What could she do? Toss him out? The question was, what *would* she do?

He hadn't made love to Crystal last night. He hadn't slept well. He twisted in his seat. This separation was getting old really fast.

Crystal had prepared her students' classes for tomorrow, but she was getting bored with so much time on her hands. She'd planted flowers all around the house. Delicate mountain flowers that wouldn't bloom for too long but that would be appreciated nonetheless for their brevity.

Resisting Richard was getting harder and harder as time went by. She wanted to give in to his desires, but she'd be right back where she was months ago if she did. She heard a car approaching. She got up out of the dirt, pulled off her gloves, and straightened her straw hat. She rounded the side of the house just as she heard a car door slam. It was Richard's mother.

"Oh, there you are. Could you give me a hand here?" Claire asked. "I brought you a few things." She was dressed casually—at least casually for her—in cream slacks and a navy short-sleeved silk blouse. A fine straw hat—unlike Crystal's wide-brimmed one—covered her short hair. Women of her generation abhorred getting too much sunlight.

"Hi, Claire. What do you have?" Crystal asked, dusting her hands.

"A few books. I went to a book fair in Roanoke. They were well discounted. Didn't cost much at all. I thought you might be able to use them. I also have a couple of computer programs you might be able to use."

"That was kind of you. Thank you," Crystal said, surprised that Claire would think of her students. Then again, Claire was always chairing some committee, so Crystal shouldn't be surprised.

Claire opened the trunk. Two boxes of books were inside. The women carried each heavy box together and made two trips to the house. They deposited them near the small table by the window in the great room.

"I made a pot of tea this morning. Would you like a cup?" Crystal asked.

"A glass of iced tea would hit the spot." Claire dabbed at the perspiration gathered around her forehead. She was graced with flawless skin and didn't require makeup. She only wore it for special occasions and she stayed away from it in the heat of the day.

"Make yourself comfortable," Crystal said and went to

the fridge for the pitcher. She retrieved two glasses from the cabinet, set everything on a tray with napkins, and brought it to the great room, setting it on the cocktail table in front of the couch.

"Thank you for the books and computer programs, Claire. The readers will love them."

Claire waved a hand. "It was nothing."

Crystal poured two tall glasses of tea. "It's already sweetened, I'm afraid."

"That's fine. I like your tea." She accepted the glass from Crystal. "This is a lovely cabin. I see why you like it so much in the summers. So peaceful."

Crystal smiled, still wondering why the woman really came. "You're welcome to spend the night sometime."

"John and I might do that. We don't get away often enough."

Claire sipped and set the glass on the coaster. She regarded Crystal.

"I never knew what Richard saw in you. But he loves you and I guess that's all that counts."

"Claire . . ."

The older woman held up a hand. Her fingernails had been painted a delicate off-white. "Just give me a moment, please. This isn't easy for me. I know that our relationship has been strained. I've always been focused on my husband's career, and of course my position at the college."

Crystal nodded.

"I do now understand why he needed you so much. He needed someone to focus on just him."

Crystal set her glass on the table. "Richard isn't the only one in the relationship."

"I know that." She gave Crystal a shrewd look. "You're good for him, I think. You can give him the things he's missed. I just hope you two can work it out."

Crystal merely stared, tongue-tied. She thought that Claire would think Richard was better off without her. That he needed a wife more like . . . well, more like Claire.

Claire took one more sip of her tea. The air conditioner

had cooled the room. Claire looked much more comfortable. "I have to go. I have a lunch engagement." She grabbed up her cream purse and keys and headed to the door. Once there she turned to regard Crystal one last time.

"Take the time you need to heal. I lost a child so I know what you're going through."

Crystal was shocked—again. She hadn't known that either. "Richard never mentioned that."

Claire gave an ironic smile. "He doesn't know. It's not something I like to talk about. It happened years before he was born."

She wouldn't talk about it, Crystal realized. Claire was the type of woman to wipe failure from her mind and get on with her next project.

"I'm sorry."

Claire tilted her chin as if to muster up courage. "It was a very long time ago. People tell you that you'll have another child and you'll get over it. You do have other children. And you do get on. But you never forget. The good thing is, with time, the pain does ease."

Crystal hadn't gotten to the place where she could be philosophical about the situation, but one day, she guessed, she would be.

"Well, what can you do but go on and try to put it behind you? I'm sorry that Richard wasn't there that night—that none of us were there. He would never have left you if he knew you were ill. Deep in your heart you must know that." Claire pursed her lips.

Easier said than done, Crystal thought. She knew that Richard would be there in the future if he could. But she also knew that she might not be able to give him another child. "Thanks again for stopping by."

Crystal walked Claire to the car and waved when the woman pulled out of the drive. Who would have thought? The pain of the miscarriage was lessening every day. It wasn't as sharp as it had been in the beginning, but the sense of loss hadn't completely abated. As time went on, Crystal began to feel that things would be better, the ache would cease, eventually. She didn't blame Richard for the miscarriage. There was nothing he could have done. It was that on top of everything else his constant absence had been the final straw.

Crystal was still turning Claire's short visit over in her mind when another car drove up. This time it was Richard.

"Did you get your days mixed up?" she asked him after he'd parked his car.

"Why was my mother here?"

"She bought books for my students."

He shrugged and planted his hands in his pockets. He'd loosened his tie and left the jacket slung over his seat. His chest was broad in the print shirt. Crystal looked away. He might need her. For the first time she was willing to admit she might need him. It had been good to talk to him last week. Talking to him was like purging something awful. But most times he certainly wasn't good for her, was he?

Crystal was tired of fighting him. Not tired enough to go back, but she'd like a pleasant evening without the arguments and recriminations. He looked a little tired himself. Crystal closed her eyes briefly. What would the future bring for them? What did she really want? Long ago she'd realized that it wasn't just what she wanted—she knew she couldn't change Richard. He was his own man. You couldn't make someone want what you wanted—believe in what you believed—just because you willed it, just because you needed it.

And she'd finally realized that she'd love Richard forever, but she couldn't live *with* him. That love could just as easily turn to something else. This separation was best for the both of them—to hold on to what had once been precious and dear.

But she was tired of fighting him and Richard seemed to realize it.

The warm pressure from his lips and the sweetness of his breath sent the pit of her stomach into a wild whirl. Raising his mouth from her skin, he gazed into her eyes. It was as if he'd found the window to her soul, and she had found his in turn.

Crystal hadn't realized her hands had snaked beneath his shirt to caress the strong contours of his back where strength met softness.

Burying her face in his neck she breathed a kiss. He closed his eyes on a moan and teasingly kissed the edge of her mouth, the tip of her nose, her cheek. And then he brushed his tongue across her mouth. Then their tongues moved together to a sexual rhythm, his heartbeat pounding against her chest, his breath quickening. His gentle, passionate assault, sent shock waves through her body and Crystal felt as if she were dissolving in his embrace.

She missed him so much, she thought as their foreheads rested against each other.

"Did you like that?" he asked in a husky voice.

She was incapable of speech so she nodded, and in moments she found herself in their bedroom in the center of the bed.

He combed his fingers through her hair, taking his time as if he needed to get to know her all over again. And although she knew him like the back of her hand, she reached up and touched his face, gently tracing her fingers along his ear, stroked his neck, his back, his sides. She grasped his shirt and pulled it off and tossed it aside. He slid her shorts down her hips, planting darting kisses on her skin, sending waves of heat through her body.

Tenderly he kissed her hands and the inside of her wrists and then sucked gently on each fingertip. She closed her eyes with the burning desire, the aching need to have him in her, but he took his time.

"Open your eyes," he said through a fog of emotion.

"What?" she asked, opening them of her own volition because she hadn't really heard a clear word he'd said.

"I said . . ." He ran his tongue down her arm, stole her breath away. "Open your eyes. Look at me." And she did. She saw the need that was searing her burning in his eyes. She took her other hand and caressed the inside of his thigh.

Then he pulled her top over her head. Slowly, deliciously, he stimulated every erotic nerve ending on her breasts, her nipples. Rubbed his face softly against her stomach. Covered it softly, teasingly with kisses, slid a hot tongue around her navel, then he stroked her legs, brushed his lips against the backs of her knees, and kissed her inner thighs. He squeezed and kneeded her feet and brought them alive. Gently sucked a toe.

All this amid her cries of pleasure.

By the time Crystal had touched every inch of Richard's body, by the time she'd kissed him, stroked him, ran her fingers over every inch of his lean muscular form, her body felt liquid. And she felt as if she were going out of her mind from his thorough foreplay. He stroked her inner moisture. She begged him to enter her. Only then did he cover her and guide his penis into her. She closed her eyes. Enjoying the exquisite sensations spiraling through her, she was lifted to a different dimension.

Once in the middle of the night, Crystal wakened, felt Richard's warm body surrounding her, his heavy arm around her waist, pinning her to him, and it was the most pleasant feeling.

Twelve

Richard left early the next morning. That night, sleep hadn't been their priority. Crystal knew Richard didn't mind and truth be told, neither did she. He'd looked fresh when he kissed her good-bye. She was exhausted, however, and went back to bed for another two hours.

Now she looked at the prophylactic that had fallen into the trash can. Alarm skittered up her spine. They had started out using prophylactics. By the last time they made love they hadn't bothered. She was due in . . .

She'd missed a period. She remembered they hadn't been careful about using one that night weeks ago either. She'd missed a period before. So this wasn't unusual. Since it took several months for her to conceive the first time, they had become accustomed to not using protection. And since she'd been married, protection hadn't been an issue.

My God, could I be pregnant? She rubbed a hand across her abdomen. She was still naked. If she had bothered last night, she wouldn't have kept her nightgown on very long anyway. Nevertheless, she felt the same. She gazed at herself in the mirror. She didn't look any different.

The first time around she'd had huge bouts of morning sickness. It was too soon to think about that.

A child. She'd welcome a baby. Richard would see her pregnancy as the answer to their dilemma, but even if she were pregnant, she couldn't return to him right now. He'd think that things would go on just as before. No, if she were pregnant, it was more important than ever that they settle their differences.

A year ago, she wouldn't have wished Richard as a father for any child. Now, she wasn't so sure. He was making an effort. The question was, would he continue to do so? Would he be willing to be the father their child needed—the husband he'd been the last few weeks?

A trip to town. That's what she'd do today, and she'd buy a pregnancy kit. No, make that Roanoke. Everyone knew everybody here. The news would spread all over town before she made it back up the mountain—before she'd even know the results of the test. And she couldn't go to the doctor's office immediately. Dr. Marsha Davis's schedule was always filled. The nurses in Marsha's office were more discreet than the employees in the pharmacy, Crystal thought as she headed to the shower.

She sniffed the air. Was that smoke she smelled?

Summer fires were a wilderness nightmare, especially when the weather was hot, the season was dry, and the heat seemed to extend to forever. She grabbed a long yellow T-shirt and tugged it over her head. She quickly went to the front porch. The smoke billowing in the air in the distance through a tuft of trees constricted her breath. If that fire spread it could destroy hundreds of thousands of acres and burn countless homes before it could be contained. Summer fires had been the nightmares in California, Arizona, Colorado, Florida, and the list went on. God, they didn't need one here too. It was so close to many homes, and the beauty of the area would be destroyed.

Crystal hurried to the phone and dialed 911. All emergency calls went directly to the sheriff's office. This neck of the woods supported a volunteer fire department, but the forest service became involved in larger fires. Whenever one started, as many volunteers as they could rustle up ran to the department to get trucks and headed to the fire. More likely than not, the house would be half burnt by the time they even arrived.

Tulip, Janice's cousin, was manning the phone at the sheriff's office.

"It's Travis's old cabin there near the lake. That thing was a firetrap waiting to happen," she said.

"I hope they can contain it." Crystal looked warily at the smoke billowing and not seeming to be abating even a little. She got moving.

It had been years since Crystal had been near that cabin, but she remembered it being right in the middle of the forest, not that far from her. The rain from last night might hamper the fire a little—at least Crystal hoped it would. Last night's rain had been the first they'd seen in more than a week. In spots, the grass was brown, flowers wilted from lack of water.

Crystal told her she'd keep in touch and disconnected. She took a very quick shower and dressed. Taking only enough time to grab a red apple from the bowl, she snatched her keys and purse and ran out the door to her car and headed to the fire. Travis's old cabin was only a little over ten miles from her place. But ten miles in the mountains along twisting roads seemed three times that distance on the highway. Ten miles along the highway decreased to three as the crows fly.

When she reached the scene, the building was still blazing. The firemen had wet the surrounding area to contain the fire. Still, the blaze had gone up the branches of a maple tree, but the firemen had fought tenaciously to keep it from spreading.

Several cars were in the vicinity, keeping a safe distance from the danger. Crystal joined a group standing around observing. The heat from the fire was intense. Even from their distance Crystal could feel the wave of heat in the air.

She saw Able talking with a group of men. He'd probably followed the fire trucks to the scene.

"It's a good thing those boys got out in time," someone said.

"Somebody was staying in the cabin?"

"Yeah. The band got finished practicing late last night. Took out their sleeping bags and slept over."

"Shoulda knocked the building down years ago," Able said, positioning his hat.

"Nothing but a firetrap," a geezer said.

"I could hear the noise from the playing over to my place late into the night," Able said. "A darn disruption, I tell you." It wasn't like Able not to find something to complain about.

"They do play well," Crystal interjected. "Richard and I went to see them a few weeks ago at Jimmy's place. Jimmy has done a good job with that restaurant and nightclub, don't you think."

"Don't go there," Able muttered. "I go to bed early at night. Don't believe in partying and carrying on. Get enough singing at church on Sunday. That's where these boys need to be instead of highfalutin it off to New York. Nothing but trouble in New York," he warned.

"You and Richard back together at last? Glad to hear it, glad to hear it," someone else said.

"No—"

"About time," Able agreed. "A wife needs to be with a man. Her place is to support him. Richard is a hardworking man. Not enough of them left. I can tell you that."

"I . . ."

Since they hadn't officially announced a parting, and since she might be pregnant, Crystal decided to keep quiet about it. Everyone would find out soon enough.

Crystal glanced to the side where Sam stood with the other members of his band. They stood apart from the other gatherers. With soot-covered faces they stared forlornly at the burning remains of the building. She walked toward them. What could one say at a time like this? Was there anything to be said to lessen their burden? There wasn't. But sometimes just being there, just offering a kind word was enough.

"Hi," she said to the boys.

They all grunted replies and looked at the fire as if they'd lost their best friend.

"There's nothing in that fire that can't be replaced. You can't be. I'm glad you all got out in time."

"We couldn't save our equipment, though," Sam said.

"None of it?"

"Happened too fast."

"You have insurance, don't you?" she asked.

He shook his head.

"Oh, my goodness."

"We've lost everything," another band member said, swiping a hand across his face. "Everything."

Crystal touched his shoulder and stared at the building with him.

"How did it happen?"

"Don't know. We conked out after practicing."

"Like we always do."

"When we woke up the fire had started."

Just then the fire marshal from Windy Hills arrived. As soon as things cooled down, he would try to assess what caused the fire—what destroyed the dreams of these boys. More likely than not it was from dry lightning. That happened so much in the dry season.

Another dream destroyed. Like it was a freak of nature that had destroyed her dreams last November. It had taken her months to begin to recover. She was still recovering. Again she looked at the somber group.

She'd see what she could do to help these young men recover sooner. She hated to consider that this would end their dreams. They were so good at what they did. More. They were dedicated. They worked hard to succeed.

The band's agent, Gary, approached them. He seemed a nice enough guy in a clean-cut sort of way. She often wondered why he hadn't gotten them better or bigger gigs by now. They were certainly talented enough. But she realized that bands all over the country were just as talented and they were trying to make it in the expensive business just as this group was.

Gary seemed to be in the area quite frequently. She'd think most of his work would be in New York or California. Why would he stick around Windy Hills?

"How are you, Mrs. Dupree?" Gary said a half hour later.

"Not a good day, is it?"

He looked on at the dwindling, smoldering flames, the crestfallen look on his face a palpable thing. "I agree with that."

"Were you here when it started?" As much as Travis didn't trust him, at least he cared about the boys and their dreams. At least he was helping them.

He shook his head. "I'm renting a house in town. Came for the weekend to hear them play. We were supposed to start recording the CD in a couple of weeks."

"I'd heard."

He nodded and they both watched the firemen work with the dwindling blaze. "I don't mean to get personal, but I understand that your relationship is over with your husband?"

Crystal opened her mouth to reply.

He indicated her bare ring finger. Crystal constantly rubbed the space where the ring used to be.

"I'm not trying to be forward or rude. It's just if you *are* free once again, I'd like to take you out."

She thought about that. She'd never considered dating another man since college when she first met Richard. She wondered how it would feel to date again and she couldn't picture herself with this man—with any other man.

"I'm not free," she simply answered.

He nodded and dug his hands in the pockets of his expensive khaki slacks. "If you ever are free, would you let me know?"

"She's married. Out here married women don't date other men," Richard said, to Crystal's surprise. When had he come up?

"Excuse us." It wasn't a question. Richard grasped her hand and led her across the brown grass.

"Putting the cart before the horse, aren't you?" he hissed at her.

"Says who?"

"You're still a married woman."

"Don't lecture me."

"I won't put up with other men dating my wife," he said. His angry steps propelled her across the yard.

Her temper flared. "I'm not dating other men. If you gave me my divorce, you wouldn't have to worry about it, would you?"

"Don't start that again."

"I didn't. You did." They sounded like juveniles. She regarded the stern set of his jaw. Something that shouldn't have, swirled within. She should have been thrilled at the knowledge that she was still attractive enough to warrant a look. Yet she thought nothing of the agent. She was still attracted to her husband. Deep down, hadn't she always known that? She took her arm out of Richard's. She wasn't going to let him manhandle her across the yard.

She felt Richard's anger as they walked together across the lawn. Love couldn't give her what she desperately wanted. With love must come trust. Richard was feeling territorial. This went far beyond him marking that territory. Their issues went to the very heart of their survival together.

She regarded the band and the agent as they huddled together. Sam shook his head at something the man had said. He seemed very agitated. He had good reason to be, she thought.

Richard stopped near Travis, who had smudges of smut

covering his clothing from helping to put out the fire. His arm had been burned, but the damage seemed to be minor. A medical technician had bandaged it.

"With all that equipment gone, maybe he'll stop throwing good money after bad," Travis said.

Crystal looked at the dejected young men and again wished there was something she could do to help them. She knew what it was to have dreams and for them all to come crashing at your feet.

"Dreams aren't a bad thing," she finally said.

"No. But there has to be a cut-off point. This is the second time they've been at this. Both times, he's lost everything. If he'd just put that money in the bank, he'd be much better off financially."

"There are worse things he could be doing," she said. "Much worse."

Travis regarded her and glanced at the boys. "I guess you're right about that."

"I'll tell you what they need to do," Richard said as he threw a sour look at the agent. "They need to get a decent agent. The one they have isn't worth two cents. If I handled my cases the way he handles his agency, I wouldn't be able to get a client." This from the heat of jealousy.

"Richard, I'm sure he's doing a good job."

Richard threw a scathing glance in their direction. "Not from what I can see. They don't need him to get gigs here in Windy Hills. They could do that on their own."

Crystal had thought the same thing, but what did she know about the music business? "He gets them shows in New York and other places. They're always going there. And now they're making a video. That has to advance their career."

"Always thought there was something shady about him," Travis said.

Crystal threw up her hands. "For goodness' sake, will the two of you stop it! Don't encourage Richard, please."

Richard drew his brows together. "Think I'll check into that guy."

"Mind your business, Richard. I wasn't going to date him," she hissed.

Nodding, Travis said, "Still needs looking into. I'm with you on that. I'll even pay you." Travis looked at his nephew. "It's time Sam started looking out for his future. He's still young. Got a good head. Just needs to be steered in the right direction. I've been trying to do that, but you know how addictive playing in a band can be. It's an attractive, glorifying job. What boy's head wouldn't be turned at the thought of all the women worshiping him? Look at the stuff the big band players go through. Looks good to a young man from a small town."

Crystal rubbed her forehead. The fire was out now. She didn't need to pack and leave the cabin. "I'm going home. If there's anything I can do, Travis, please let me know."

"I appreciate that, Crystal."

Instead of driving home, Crystal drove to the winery and ordered sandwiches for the group at the fire. Although she didn't think the boys would be able to eat after the devastation, she'd take the food anyway. After the manager of the winery discovered what she planned to do, he refused to accept her money. He offered to deliver it along with a cooler of punch for everyone to drink.

Crystal went back to help serve. It was afternoon before she made it to Roanoke. She couldn't wait for the almost two-hour drive to her house to find out the results of her test, so she spent the night with her parents, who lived in Roanoke.

She disappeared into the bathroom and took the test, held her breath, then stared at the results. She'd been so worried that she wouldn't be able to get pregnant again. The doctor said she had a fifty-fifty chance for success.

She was pregnant.

Tears streamed down her face. She was pregnant. How would she ever tell Richard? He deserved to share the joy with her. But she wasn't ready to share just yet. She wasn't telling anyone.

She called her gynecologist and made an appointment.

She'd feel a lot better once the pregnancy was confirmed. This time Crystal would stick closer to the rules to give her baby the best chance she could. She rubbed a hand across her abdomen, loving her child already. She walked outside to the porch and looked up into the clear blue sky and the mountains and said, "Thank you, God."

Richard paced in his office. He still smarted over the incident at the fire. He had a good mind to check up on the agent who tried to put the make on his wife.

Who did the guy think he was? This was Windy Hills, not a big city. Men didn't try to snatch another man's wife around here. There was the family respect and a code of honor to consider. But the agent was an outsider. He wouldn't understand.

And Richard wasn't going to forgive the insult.

He needed to get to Annie's place. He was changing into sneakers when he heard Crystal's voice in the outer office. He went to the door.

"Do you have anything scheduled for the next couple of hours?" he asked.

"No, why?"

"I want to take a look at the property around Annie's house. Want to go with me?"

"Sure, but why are you checking out Annie's property?"

"Just to see if we missed anything," he said, sliding out of his dress shoes into sneakers. Then they started for the door. Crystal looked comfortable in beige shorts and an orange sleeveless top. He'd seen her dressed like this a thousand times, and each time she looked just as sexy as the last.

"What exactly are you looking for?" she asked as they walked out into the hot sunshine. She pulled her sunshades over her eyes.

Richard shrugged and walked the few paces to the SUV. "I don't know. I'll know once I see it," he said, opening the door for her.

Traffic was sparse. It took only a few minutes to drive to Annie's place. Crystal went inside and borrowed long pants and sneakers.

After Crystal changed, Richard drove about a mile from Annie's place and they started walking toward the wilderness away from the house.

They walked the first few minutes in silence.

"Are you really attracted to Gary?" Richard finally asked.

"Don't be silly."

"Would you date him if I wasn't in the picture? If you divorced me?"

She glanced at him. She seemed surprised by the question. "I haven't thought that far in the future but no, I wouldn't date him."

"You thought far enough ahead to seek a divorce," he muttered.

"You couldn't have been getting any more out of the marriage than I was."

"We're different. That's not a bad thing."

"Only if each of our needs are met."

"You're saying I'm not meeting your needs?"

"Lately you have been."

"It won't always be like this. We don't live in a perfect world."

"I don't expect it to. I don't expect you to wait on me or entertain me twenty-four-seven. I just want to feel like a married woman."

Richard pressed his lips firmly together to keep his anger in check. By now they were more than a mile from Annie's house. He almost stepped in a hole. He scrutinized the area closely. A huge burn spot was evident. He walked the area around the camp. Over in the bushes he spotted a canning jar. He picked it up and opened the top. The smell was strong. High-proof moonshine.

He'd bet that Tiber had been making moonshine right here. Did the old man suspect Annie had seen something out here?

Thirteen

When Crystal finally returned home that afternoon, euphoria engulfed her. She hugged the knowledge of her pregnancy as snugly as an infant wrapped in a warm blanket. She didn't know how she'd last four whole days until her appointment with Marsha to confirm it. Perhaps work would keep her too busy to explode.

One project required her attention immediately, however. Sam and his band needed help with getting their new equipment. Crystal closed her eyes and looked toward the heavens. Thank God those boys got out in time. Travis might not believe in them, but she believed in dreams.

Everyone had dreams. All the students in her reading group had their own dreams. Dreams made living worthwhile. Dreams kept the band practicing in the wee hours of the morning. Dreams kept a person striving long past what a normal person would view as reasonable. Dreams forced one to push further than one's capacity.

Crystal sighed. She and Richard had had dreams. Long ago dreams of love and happiness ever after. Not in the fairy tale sense, but in the sense of love and respect.

Until death do us part, Crystal thought. *In good times*

and bad. When she pondered the many women who were beaten by their husbands and still stood by their sides, her reasoning seemed awfully frivolous. But she didn't marry to live a totally separate life. She married to live interdependently with Richard. Was she asking for too much? Was she being unreasonable?

Now that she and Richard once again had a child on the way, she needed to reassess the entire situation.

Crystal stood leaning against the railing, looking out on her mountains. She had the best view in the world. The Blue Ridge with the bright sunshine beaming down. She didn't feel alone. She felt . . . wonderful didn't describe the peace that surrounded her. She was at peace with herself. Hopeful was a better term. Hope for the future. There was the fear. Fear that she could miscarry again. Crystal touched her abdomen. But she believed. Dreams kept her going, too. Dreams had her believing that this time—this time things would work out. She was going to follow her doctor's directions to the letter. Because for the first time since November, Crystal had dreams, too.

Perhaps not the first, she thought. Being with Richard these last few weeks had given her a new burst of life before she discovered the news about their child.

She left the railing, went inside, and pulled out the phone book. She started to call some friends to set up a meeting for that evening in town. But before she dialed the first number, she remembered that she had a class to teach and materials to prepare. She took out a pen and paper and for thirty minutes she jotted down ideas for a fund-raiser. Sam had an opportunity to make it big, she thought, whether he accomplished his goals or not. Sometimes the will was enough.

As Richard drove to Roanoke, he was still smarting over the incident with Crystal and that idiot agent. The only positive note was that Crystal had told him she was married. What got his goat was that she hesitated in answering as if she really wanted to date that philanderer. Richard frowned, tightening his grip around the wheel. If he absolutely didn't have to go to Roanoke today, he'd be at Crystal's right now.

A lump formed in his stomach. She was actually considering dating another man. The thought of his wife with another man dripped at his insides like acid. Here he was doing his best to make the relationship work and some other man was moving in on her. She was his wife. And by God, she wasn't fooling around with another man while they were married. If the agent spent more time on managing the band, maybe the boys would be much better off. He spent entirely too much time in Windy Hills to make them successful.

Richard couldn't wait to get back to the office to start the wheels rolling for the information he needed. He pulled into the courthouse parking lot and with the motor still running dug the Palm Pilot out of his briefcase. The air conditioner blasted comforting cold air into the car. He retrieved the number for a former law school buddy in New York and dialed the number. He wasn't in so Richard left a message. When he exited the car, the blast of ninety-nine-degree air hit him like a sauna as he made his way to the courthouse.

Months had passed since her hip replacement and Annie had yet to venture out on her own. Having people near had been an extra measure of comfort that if she slipped, there was someone there to pick her up. Although she hadn't told anyone, a smidgeon of fear of being shot again was always close to the surface. The reason for being shot had never been established.

Annie couldn't forget that the man hadn't immediately snatched her purse. She thought about that often. He was looking for something specific—but what? She'd turned the situation over in her mind for what seemed thousands of times. She carried nothing valuable—she carried even less now. She owned a few nice pieces of jewelry, including her anniversary ring, but they hadn't given her ring a second thought. She wore expensive pearls that her father-in-law had purchased for his wife in Korea during the war. Before her death, her mother-in-law had handed the pearls to Annie as a gift—for loving her son. The thief hadn't given the pearls a second look, which still left the question of what he was really after.

And there was Rufus. She didn't know where the man stood. She didn't know if Rufus was still carrying a grudge against her. Richard said he hadn't detected anything about him that indicated he did. But that didn't mean much. Was he going to come right out and say, "Hey, I'm settling old scores before I tie the knot"? But somehow, Richard didn't believe it was Rufus. Although he didn't discount him either—yet.

Annie knew that she couldn't hide away forever. It was time she let her fear go. She needed to get on with life. Yesterday, she told Crystal not to come in, that she had things to do.

Annie used her cane and made her way to her car, which Stacey had backed out of the garage that morning. That old house had meant a lot to Travis. It had been his parents'. It had been the first house he and his wife had lived in until they could afford to build a more suitable one for themselves. She'd called him earlier to offer regrets and he'd assured her that he was fine. She wasn't so sure though. Old memories were hard to set aside. It wasn't that long ago that his wife had died. She should know. Her husband's memory still touched her at times. She may have moved on. But she never forgot. She wouldn't leave Travis alone on a day like today.

Yes, indeed. Even though he now had a lovely home and he was one of the successful farmers, there were still the memories of when things were simpler and of the people they had loved.

That afternoon, the reading group arrived early. By now everyone knew about the little group, and Sadie brought her grandson to the lessons. He usually sat with Princess and read.

"Goodness," Gertrude said as she folded her spare body into the seat on the deck. "Every year this time I swear I'm going to get air-conditioning put in my car and never do."

Crystal poured a tall glass of lemonade and handed it to Gertrude.

"You're a dear," the older woman said as she took a sip from the frosted glass. She closed her eyes briefly and sighed. "It's so hot this summer I just might break down and do it." She took the napkin and wiped the sweat from her face.

"I can get my nephew at the garage to do it," Able mumbled. "He's good."

"I appreciate it, but it makes my arthritis act up. I'm going to try to do without for as long as I can."

"Did you hear about Travis's house?" Betty asked, shaking her head. "How is he doing, Gertrude? It's a real loss for you, too. I'm surprised you're even here."

"Life goes on. The house was more memories than anything else."

"Wish there was something we could do to help," Sadie said, shaking her head.

"I was thinking the same thing," Crystal said, grateful for the opening. "Maybe we could plan an event to raise money to help Sam's band replace their equipment. They had been practicing that night. They lost all their equipment and they didn't have insurance."

"Now why would they do a thing like that? Insurance is the first thing you get when you dish out a lot of money," Ricardo said.

"They're young and foolish," said Jimmy.

"Insurance wouldn't cover all of it anyway," Able said. "Never does."

Sadie scrunched up her face. "Lots of things we could do, but it'll all take time."

"They don't have time. Got that demo to make in a couple weeks," said Able.

"That doesn't give us much time to raise money," Betty muttered.

"It's early in the week. What about a rock-climbing contest, kayak-racing contest?"

"Down by the river? Throw in a fishing competition and you've got a winner." A rare smile creased Able's face. "Haven't gone up against the guys in a while. Got some pretty good fishing spots already picked out."

"You tell me how we're going to get the word around in one little week," Gertrude said.

"Tell the local radio stations and TV news stations. Bring in folks from Roanoke and all over, betcha," Able said, all knowing.

"You can make the signs on the computer to put into the local stores," Crystal said.

"You want us to make signs?" Sadie asked.

"On the computer?" Betty murmured with interest.

Ricardo went to the ground and poured some lemonade for Princess. In the dog's eyes, Ricardo was a friend for life.

Able frowned, rubbing his stubbled chin. "Never used a computer before."

"Oh, Mama," Ricardo said as he rounded the corner for the deck. "What'sa this with the computer?" His accent was more pronounced when he became excited or angry.

"We're making signs to raise money for my nephew, on the computer," Gertrude said. "It sure is nice for you all to do this. Travis doesn't believe it's going to come to anything. He thinks the boys are wasting time."

Ricardo shook his head. "Heard about the fire at the college. Sad thing. What we gonna do to raise money? I want to help."

"Can I help too?" Sadie's grandson asked. "We use computers at school."

"Sure you can," Crystal said.

Everyone had finally arrived. It was still a class day and Crystal thought they could use the session as a learning experience. After they went over last week's lessons, she handed out sheets of paper and suggested they first write out what they wanted on the signs.

Annie took a deep breath and opened the car door. She'd parked beside Travis's truck, leaving enough room for her to maneuver. Using the cane for balance, she cautiously exited her car. Three of Travis's dogs rounded the corner in a race to greet her. "Nice doggie," she said gingerly, patting the hundred-pound mutts, who could knock her to the ground. Obviously, they remembered her from earlier visits.

"Annie!" Travis smiled at her. "Get away, boys." The dogs obediently left her side, but doing so left her feeling vulnerable, as if she were stepping out into unfamiliar territory. She glanced at the dogs and watched them take off after a squirrel that skittered up a tall oak.

Travis took her elbow in his hand and looked lovingly down at her. "It's good to see you."

Annie glanced at him. "I'm sorry about your house. I know what it meant to you."

"At least no one was hurt."

It was then that she noticed the bandage on his arm. "What happened?"

He patted the bandage. "Just a little burn. Not worth mentioning." The gaze he sent her was as piercing as a laser. "I'm glad you came," he whispered.

A zigzag of lightning streaked up Annie's spine as they walked the flower-strewn walk to his front door. Black tires filled with dirt and pansies surrounded the huge porch.

Annie shrieked and dropped her cane when she felt Travis lift her into his arms. "What do you think you're doing? Put me down this instant."

"Carrying you up the stairs is what I'm doing. You're a nice armful."

"Put me down," she repeated, but not too strenuously. Being in his arms felt darn good. "The doctor wants me to walk more," she said weakly.

He looked her over closely. She saw the heartrending tenderness of his gaze. "You'll have plenty of time when I'm not around." The deepened timbre of his voice affected her so much that she hardly noticed as he took the six steps up to the porch, carrying her as if she were as light as feathers. But he didn't stop there.

"Grab the door, will you?" His eyes held her as if entranced. Annie couldn't have looked away if her life depended on it.

"It'll be nice to sit out here. There's a nice breeze flowing through," Annie said.

He shook his head, the look on his face indicating that he had more on his mind than sitting in the breeze. Was that why she really came to his home? Was she ready for what the look on his face suggested?

Annie caught the screen door and opened it. He moved effortlessly through the opening. The door banged shut behind them.

Travis slowly lowered her to the floor. Her legs almost gave out from beneath her. Her good hip.

He took one calloused finger and tilted her chin.

"My cane," she whispered.

"You don't need it. I'll support you," he whispered back, as if they were sneaking in, making sure no one heard them, even though they were the only ones there.

Annie knew that the wide, thick breadth of his shoulders, the strong lines of his body were more than capable of doing so—and more.

He eased the other arm around her lower back, and lowered his head to hers and kissed her urgently. She needed support, but not because of her hip. It was the drugging sense of warmth that filled her like liquid fire that brought on weakness.

"Sweet Jeez," he whispered against her lips. His gaze roved and lazily appraised her. "Do you know how long I've wanted you?"

Such an attraction should be perilous, she thought. "About as long as I've wanted you?"

Pulling her closer, he rumbled deep in his throat. "Don't play with me, woman."

"Who's playing?"

Travis moaned and kissed her again, swiping his tongue around her mouth with a gentleness, an authority, a skill that weakened her knees. She worked her hands beneath his shirt to feel the strength of his back, his masterful shoulders. The texture of his skin was a paradox. Smooth skin and sinewy muscles met beneath her fingertips and palms. Annie closed her eyes and savored the pleasure, remembering how wonderful it felt to be in a man's arms once again. How especially nice Travis's touch was.

"How's your hip?"

"What hip?"

Laughter rumbled against her cheeks. He kissed her there and then her neck, the prickly mustache and soft lips creating pleasurable sensations as his fingers danced along her spine. He stoked a glowing fire.

Annie's breath quickened to match his. Before she knew it he lifted her into his arms again and was strolling down a corridor, barely giving her time to take in the view along the way. The only view she really wanted right now was of him. His regard sent her spirits soaring.

He kicked a door open and Annie found herself placed gently on a spread. She was barely aware of the king-size bed. "If you don't want this, tell me now," he said, leaning over her, his eyes serious as a heart attack.

"I want it."

He opened a bedside drawer and pulled out a box that was still covered in plastic and dropped it on the bed. "I made a trip to Roanoke weeks ago."

She leaned back, took his measure. "You think mighty highly of yourself, don't you?"

He gave her that twisted smile, the one that raised goose bumps all over her. Something intense flared through his entrancement. "I could only hope."

Annie wrapped her arms around his neck, dragging his

lips to hers. "I've been hoping, too," she said before his lips brushed hers.

He kissed her body from the tip of her forehead to the tip of her toes, removing each stitch of clothing. Then she became self-conscious of her scars. When she stilled his hands, he looked askance at her.

"You're a beautiful woman, everywhere. I've got plenty of scars of my own. I care about you—all of you."

Um. Um. Um. Her body was squirming in need by the time he stood over her and stripped every inch from his big, beautiful body. With shaking fingers she opened the prophylactic and slid one on the long, throbbing penis.

Then he was on her. Her body ached for his touch. "I'll take it easy with your hip," he whispered against her ear. His voice sent her right over the horizon.

"I can't wait another minute."

"Bet you can."

"I need you and now."

The smile left his lips, the teasing left his eyes. "Annie, you couldn't know how much I crave you."

And then he eased his way into her. Annie closed her eyes, feeling the strong length of him to her core. It felt so damn good she wanted to cry out—she did cry out. She wished her hip would let her tighten her legs around him. She wished she could push up as she did in her younger days. He felt so wonderful that she tried anyway. Her need for him outweighed the slight pain in her hip. She knew she'd suffer later, but right now she ached for the fulfillment of his lovemaking.

He sank even deeper into her, filling Annie with need as their motions quickened.

"Take it easy now," he said gently.

"The heck with easy."

His deep voice rumbled as he laughed and kissed her forehead. His hands grasped her hips and they moved until every drop of sensation spiraled within.

Time in a loving woman's arms relaxed a man like nothing else on earth. The last thing Travis said as he eased himself to her side and tenderly gathered Annie in his arms was, "You're some kind of woman, Annie."

Hours passed before Travis walked Annie to her car. She sat on a lawn chair near the garden while he picked her some vegetables out of his garden.

"You still plant a lovely garden," she said.

"Gertrude does more with the garden than I do. I just make sure it's planted and plowed. She usually gathers the food, cans and freezes it. I told her it would be better at her place—closer to her. She swears it doesn't grow as well there. She and Rosalee used to always have it here so there's no talking her out of it."

"I'll help you with that, Uncle Travis," Sam said. "How are you, Ms. Annie?"

"I'm fine."

Sam and Troy each grabbed a bag and carried the food to the car. Annie opened the door. Just as they put the bag of peaches behind the backseat, the bag burst.

"Hold on," Travis said. "Run up to the house and get another one. You know where it is. Double it up this time," he hollered to Sam's back.

"All right, all right."

As soon as Sam returned, Troy held the bag while Travis gathered up the peaches.

He paused, tugged at something. "Looks like you've got something stuck under your seat."

"What is it?" Annie asked, craning her neck to get a better view.

Travis leaned down, the strong shoulder muscles capturing her attention as he fumbled under the seat a few seconds and dug out a tape.

"I've been wondering where that got to. It's something I taped for my nieces." She'd brought it home the night of the accident. Since then she'd completely forgotten about it. "I don't know when I'll see them. I'm glad it's not damaged or melted in the hot sun. I'm going to take it into the house as soon as I get home.'' She put the tape on the passenger seat along with her purse and gingerly slid into the car. She put the cane beside her purse.

She smiled up at Travis. He leaned into the door as if he wasn't quite ready for her to leave. ''Thanks for the fruit and veggies.''

''Any time,'' he said in that husky bass and closed the door securely.

She started the motor, waved to the three men watching her, and drove off.

Annie felt wonderful. Her hip was a little tender, more so than usual, she thought as she shook her head and headed down the long dirt drive. But Travis's lovemaking had definitely been worth it.

The sex life of older women could be almost nonexistent. It had been a long, long time since she'd had a tumble in the hay. She didn't even want to think about how long it had been. *My goodness,* she thought. She felt like a new woman. She was glad that her abstinence was broken with Travis. He was some kind of lover. She'd reached the tar road. She looked both ways and pondered in which direction she should go. Travis's home was halfway between hers and Crystal's. It would be nice to spend a night in the mountains. Of course she lived in the mountains, but not as high up as Crystal.

Crystal had a lovely view. She also had enough room. Annie hoped she wouldn't be intruding by dropping in on her niece without calling.

Richard made his way up the back roads to Tiber's place. Everyone knew where Tiber lived, but few—other than those interested in purchasing his moonshine—ventured here. The road was one of the worst kept in the county. Not only that, there was almost four miles of dirt road to travel after leaving the blacktop.

Dust swirled, thick and heavy in the air. Richard slowed his pace. After this he'd need a trip to the car wash. Up ahead he saw another dust cloud. Someone was approaching him. Damn. Now he'd have to drive through the dirt—putting another layer of dust on his car.

The road was narrow. He drove through a wall of trees. He and the approaching driver each had to hug the shoulder to pass. Richard glanced at the driver in the other car. It was the blue Lincoln he saw at the fire. It was Gary.

Richard frowned. What was he doing out here? Richard made the last leg of his journey.

Tiber stood beneath the listing porch with a toothpick in his mouth. He was a tall man—around six-four—with a long beard, trimmed neatly, and a mustache that nearly covered his lips. He wore overalls without a shirt beneath and run-over sneakers. A ragged straw hat covered his head.

"Well, as I live and breathe, what brings you to my neck of the woods?"

"Afternoon, Tiber." Richard eyed the shotgun leaning against the wall.

"Depends on what brings you here," Tiber said.

"Annie."

"Annie? How is Annie?" The older man shook his head. "Heard about her troubles. Couldn't have happened to a nicer woman."

Richard took a few steps closer to the porch. "I've noticed you've been out her way."

He regarded Richard for a few seconds. "Naw. You couldn't have. I don't have call to go to Annie's place. Haven't seen her in ages."

"I didn't say you were at her house, but close by. From the looks of things, right around the time she was shot."

Tiber stopped working his toothpick. "You accusing me of shooting her?"

Richard shook his head. "I don't think you're that dumb. I just want to know what you saw."

Tiber relaxed, started working his toothpick again. "If I'd a seen anything, I'd be the first to tell. Annie's a nice lady."

"Tell me about Gary."

"That New York feller?"

Richard nodded.

"Likes my moonshine. That's all."

"Who came by your place the evening Annie was shot?" Richard asked.

"Lots of people."

"We're talking about Annie here. I need to know who's after her and why."

"Wouldn't make sense for them to come here if they planned to shoot her."

"Let me decide that."

"The New York feller and the band, to name a few."

"They all came together?"

Tiber shook his head. "All at different times."

"Business was light that night."

Tiber shrugged.

Richard nodded, turned toward his car. "If you remember anything, give me a call."

"Don't have no phone," Tiber said. "Don't like being worried with them."

"You know how to reach me," Richard said and climbed into the SUV for the long drive to town. Tiber tried to make himself as unnoticeable as possible, Richard thought. He sold his moonshine to anyone who could climb this godforsaken path. Everyone knew about his business. Even the local bar carried his stuff—under the counter, of course. But in all the years he'd been around, Richard had never known of Tiber taking after someone unless they fooled with his stash. Annie wouldn't come near Tiber's moonshine.

Fourteen

Crystal was pleasantly surprised to see her aunt at her door.

"Aunt Annie," she said, pleased to see her. "I would have driven into town to get you."

"I can drive myself. As a matter of fact, I'm feeling good about driving myself. I'm beginning to feel more and more like the old Annie."

"You're looking like her too."

"I hope you have a nightgown and don't mind me spending the night. I hadn't planned on it."

"Clothing isn't a problem. I'll enjoy your company," Crystal assured her.

Annie glanced around, took in the peacefulness. "I see why you love it so."

"Oh, yes," Crystal said, hooking her arm with her aunt's and walking her inside. "I just put dinner on. I have enough for two. It should be ready soon."

"Take your time," Annie said, walking to the French glass door that led to the deck. "What a view."

Crystal smiled, and stirred the pot simmering on the stove. Princess sidled over to Annie for a pat and Annie reached down and obliged. "Why don't I fix you a mimosa? Go on out. I'll be right there."

Crystal mixed the mimosa for Annie and orange juice for herself. No more drinks until after the baby. She felt different already, like a protective mother.

She took the drinks to the deck and handed Annie hers and sat across from her.

"Was it just my company and my mountain view that brought you here?"

"Isn't that enough?"

"To me it is."

"I had dropped by to pay my respects to Travis."

"What a shame."

"That old house held lots of secrets. Lots of sadness." Annie sipped from her drink.

"What kind of secrets? And what sadness?"

Annie shrugged and sipped her drink. "Travis's youngest sister. Always getting the wrong man. You know she never married Sam's father. I remember Travis being upset about that."

"Being an unwed mother was a big thing back then."

"It was. They shipped her off to Roanoke with a wedding band on her finger. Told everybody she was married. She never married, though."

"What happened to Sam's father?"

"The family tried to keep it quiet, but he and Troy have the same father. He didn't marry either woman."

"That accounts for why the boys are so close."

"Don't know if they even know."

"They have to know."

"Who was going to tell? I know Travis didn't. Neither did Gertrude. They were always hush-hush about family secrets. A year after the baby was born, she married some guy from Roanoke. Sam took on his name. He thinks of him as his father. I don't think anybody ever told him different."

"He knows. That he was illegitimate anyway. When they get to be teenagers, and learn about the birds and the bees, they start counting years."

"Maybe so. Kids learn so much now, too young, if you ask me."

"They do grow up fast."

"Umm." They were silent for moments, each deep in her own thoughts, then Annie said, "What's with you and Richard?"

Crystal thought about the baby. "We're working on it."

"That's a nice change from a month ago. You wouldn't even consider him then."

"The country air has mellowed me—and Richard, he's trying."

"I always liked him."

"I know."

"You know, Crystal, I know you're serious and you don't like to play games. But sometimes with men, you've got to keep things hot to keep them interested."

"Aunt Annie . . ." Crystal started, speechless.

"Don't Aunt Annie me. I wasn't born under the turnip patch. Men like frisky women. If not in public, they love them in their homes and in bed."

Crystal could fry an egg with the heat searing her face. This was something she never discussed with her dear older aunt. And then she thought about the last time she and Richard had made love.

"The bedroom was never a problem," she finally said.

"He's a healthy male. He's probably got a lot of stamina. Tell me if I'm wrong."

"There's more to marriage than sex and stamina."

"Said like someone who's satisfied on a regular basis. If you had to do without for a while like some of us, you wouldn't be so blasé about it."

Crystal needed to change the subject. "I hope Travis has stamina."

"He's a farmer, isn't he?"

Crystal laughed. "Is that all it takes?"

Annie sipped her drink, a sly look on her face, making her look years younger. "All I'm saying is that he lives up to the reputation."

"Things are getting serious then."

"I'm not saying it is or it isn't. Just that he has possibilities."

"Don't you end up pregnant out of wedlock," Crystal teased.

"Oh, please. That's the nice thing about my age. I don't have that to worry about anymore."

"I hear the women are running after him. You've got a lot of competition."

"He's not looking."

"You're sure of yourself, aren't you?"

"That's what I'm telling you. Keep Richard guessing. Give him a reason to leave those papers in the office and come running home to you. It's something wrong when he'll let you stay up here while he's down there week after week. Make him climb that mountain after you."

Crystal sighed. "I can't *make* him do anything."

"Hasn't that sister of mine taught you the basics? Of course you can make him do anything you want." Annie leaned forward in her seat. "Take Lisa. You know Lisa Brown, don't you?"

"I know her. Everybody knows her."

"Well, her husband started looking at Shanny many years ago."

"Who's Shanny?"

"She used to live around here. With a little help, she decided to leave town a few years back."

Alarm chilled Crystal's spine. "Run out of town? They don't do that kind of thing here, do they?"

"Nobody ran her out of town. She was estranged for chasing so many husbands." Annie crossed her legs, then thought better of it. "Hmmph. You deserve what you get when you start messing with another woman's man."

"I'm not going to ask how you all ran that poor woman out of town."

"Poor woman, my foot. She tried to steal Lisa's husband away from her."

Crystal thought of the man who resembled a bulldog. He

didn't exactly fit the type who would have women clawing each other over him.

"She'd tried for my William too. I hauled him up right and tight. I don't put up with foolishness. And there were a couple more husbands she was trying to snatch too. She was better off setting up business some other place."

"Uncle William was stepping out?"

"I would have taken a skillet upside his head."

Crystal howled at her aunt's expression. "And I always thought you were sweet."

"When I want to be. I caught on to her frisky ways before he did. It was during the time we were going through some problems. All marriages go though them one time or another. Just like you and Richard. When you weather this, you'll be stronger for it."

"There's no excuse for him to go tipping out." Crystal thought about Richard and frowned. She couldn't picture him stepping out on her. Look at the way he reacted when Gary tried to weasel a date with her. She trusted Richard. Then, too, she was the one who asked for a divorce. He gave no indication that he was ready to get satisfaction from some other woman simply because they were going through a crisis.

No, she trusted Richard. They were still married—or so he kept reminding her. He wouldn't step out. She rubbed her stomach.

"Got the tummy ache?" Annie asked.

Crystal shook her head. "No," she said and watched the satisfied look on Annie's face.

"You're trying to start trouble, aren't you?" Crystal said to her aunt.

"I'm trying to give you something to think about. Stop taking Richard for granted and get your marriage back where it should be. Move back home where *you* belong." Annie sat back in her seat, her words hitting Crystal like a hammer blow. "Before it's too late."

"Aunt Annie, I'm not going back to Richard out of fear. If or when I return to him, it will be because I believe he can be the husband I need—I can be the wife he needs. Not because I'm afraid of him stepping out when things are tenuous between us. If he's that shallow, I don't want him—don't need him.'' Crystal hoped her baby would forgive her.

"Always got to take the high road, don't you? The high road can't keep you warm at night. You remember that!''

The night Annie stayed with Crystal, Annie's house was broken into. Nothing was destroyed, but things had been tumbled out of place as if someone was looking for something. The police left after taking fingerprints. She didn't hold much hope in their finding who did it. Again, nothing was stolen.

"Richard, do you think it was the same person who shot me earlier?''

"I don't know, Annie. Did anyone know you were going to spend the night with Crystal?''

She shook her head. "No one. It was a last-minute decision. I had to borrow a gown from Crystal. I didn't even take a suitcase with me.''

"I'm grateful you were away.''

"What do we do now?''

"I'm going to check on some things. You sit tight. In the meantime, I don't think you should stay alone.''

"I'm not letting anyone force me from my home.''

"Don't be stubborn, now. I'll talk to the police and make sure they keep extra officers posted here.''

"Thanks, dear.''

Richard kissed Annie and left.

As soon as he reached his office, he called his investigator in New York to have someone check out Rufus's whereabouts last night. The investigator wouldn't be able to do it, but he worked with an agency in New Jersey who would be able to.

He also checked on the Blake boys. They'd had dates until late. Then they said they went home. Their parents attested to the fact that they arrived home on time for the eleven-o'clock curfew they'd imposed on them.

Richard worked over that night. But when he left at eight, he stopped by Annie's. A light was still on in the kitchen. When he went to her door, he was surprised to see Travis sitting at her kitchen table. Annie was dressed in a nightgown and robe. Travis had on slippers.

Richard stayed no longer than five minutes. He had the feeling Travis's truck was parked in the garage. It was obvious the older man planned to stay the night—for Annie's protection, of course.

Richard glanced at Crystal's convertible in her parents' yard and got angry just thinking about her allotting him days to visit like some high-school flunky. Friday wasn't his day with her but the hell with it. He'd been invited to the cookout at her parents' home—not by her parents or Crystal, but by Annie, bless her heart. He wasn't sure of his reception by the rest of the family, but he'd called Crystal's parents occasionally and tried to keep a decent relationship flowing. Actually his relationship with her parents was much better at this point than the one with their daughter—after they'd made it known that they held him responsible for holding the marriage together. At least they hadn't yet banished him from their home, he thought.

As he pulled into the yard, Travis's truck drove up behind him. Annie was sitting in the passenger seat. The sexual awareness between the couple was glaringly obvious.

Travis must be doing something right, Richard thought. He tried to pull himself together while exiting the SUV.

Travis was hopping around that truck like an eighteen-year-old. In contrast, Richard felt as if he were going on seventy, when actually the opposite should have been true. Not that Travis was seventy. He looked to be between fifty-five and sixty.

"Mighty fine day for a cookout," Travis said with a pleasant grin.

Speak for yourself, Richard felt like replying, but merely nodded in agreement. "How are you, Annie? Thanks for the invite."

"Couldn't be better." Travis opened her door and eased her out of the truck. He handed her the cane, and gathered her left arm into the tuck of his elbow.

She was walking much better, Richard noticed as he fell into step behind them. He could hear the children playing in the backyard, and smelled a tantalizing aroma from the grill. They bypassed the house and followed the smells and sounds.

The first person he saw was Crystal standing beside her dad grilling burgers. The whole blasted family was in attendance. They weren't dressed in chic casual either as at his family dinner days ago. No, the kids wore shorts. The adults wore the same, or jeans, and others wore sundresses.

But Crystal. His wife wore shorts. Her long legs springing from beneath looked good. She wore a cool tank top with spaghetti straps. She looked too sexy by far. Their eyes met. Joy bubbled in her laugh and shone in her eyes. There was something different about her. A radiance that he hadn't observed in months. A radiance that had been lost since her pregnancy.

Richard had ambivalent thoughts on that. Ever since Gary had asked her for a date the image of his wife with another man had disturbed him. Separating hadn't seemed real before.

He thought their situation was improving. Crystal seemed to respond well to their time together. But she still refused to move in with him.

He hoped the healing process was finally working. Was she coming to terms with the baby? Had she finally accepted that they belonged together? So many questions. So few answers.

Right now, Richard wished the crowd would disappear. He wanted his lovely wife to himself.

Something was tugging at his arms. It took a moment for him to realize Crystal's mom stood at his elbow.

"Hello, Mom."

"How are you, son?" She gave him a warm hug. He enclosed her in his arms.

"I'm fine," he said.

"I'm glad you came. Why don't you join your wife at the grill?" she said when a grandchild bided for her attention.

"I think I will," he said, but before he could, someone charged toward him and Annie.

Crystal's heart almost stopped. She hadn't expected Richard here. This was a reprieve. A time to think about other things—not her failed marriage. Not about her husband. Not about telling him about the baby. She couldn't tell him until she saw Marsha and received a definite confirmation.

"Aunt Annie, you're here." Her niece raced to Annie and hugged her around the hips. She smiled up at Richard, showing two missing front teeth.

"Did you bring me something?" she asked Annie.

Annie took her hand out of Travis's elbow and stroked her niece's hair. "Yes, I did. I have a tape you can watch later when it's dark and the mosquitoes try to eat you for dinner." She tickled the child in her ribs.

"What tape? What tape?" the little girl asked, hopping from foot to foot.

"It's a surprise. But you'll love it," Annie said, tweaking her pigtails.

She gave Annie one last hug and ran to join her cousins on the swing.

Crystal watched as Richard shook her father's hand. Her parents had always loved Richard. Thought she had married well. She was thankful they weren't interfering. Her mother just nodded and said everything would work out for the best. They were there if she needed them. Her father merely grunted, almost bit his tongue to keep from lecturing her. Crystal had a feeling her mom had lots to do with his silence. Her father believed a woman's place was beside her husband—through thick and thin.

And then Richard was in front of her. He seemed to be peering at her intently. Suddenly he hauled her into his arms and kissed her. It was so easy to get lost in the way she felt in his arms. The rest of the world seemed to disappear. Her feelings had nothing to do with reason, but the excitement that wrapped around her like a warm blanket.

The kids giggled and clapped in the background. The kiss had occurred so quickly Crystal barely had time to think. Then he was looking over her shoulder and stepped around her to flip a burger.

"Hello," he whispered against her lips.

Her mother nudged his hand away. "My goodness. The two of you. We'll never eat tonight." The burger had almost charred. For a moment there, Crystal had forgotten about the food—her thoughts had centered on Richard alone.

A couple of hours later, the children had played hard and eaten well. Her niece asked about the tape again and Travis retrieved Annie's tape from the truck. The kids then sprawled in front of the TV in the family room.

"Don't sit too close to the TV," Annie said. "You'll ruin your eyes." She inserted the tape into the player. A whizzing sound inside indicated the tape was ready. Then the movie started to roll.

The movie she'd expected was *not* the one that had left her theater only two months ago and was *not* yet on tape.

"Thanks, Aunt Annie. This is great!" A loud cheer went up from the kids.

"I thought you said we couldn't see this, Aunt Annie," one of the nieces said.

"Will you shut up," a nephew hissed.

The child punched him on the shoulder. "You can't tell me to shut up."

"Be quiet now." Annie pushed the stop-and-eject button. She looked at the tape that she'd left in her car after the shooting. She had never gotten around to sticking a label on it. But it was the tape from her car. She'd carried it around in her big purse for days after Travis had retrieved it from beneath her car seat.

"See what you've done? You're such a blabbermouth," Annie heard through a thick fog.

"Enough of that," she said to the kids.

Richard came into the kitchen. It was so quiet that he glanced toward the tube. Annie stood with a puzzled look on her face.

"Is something wrong, Annie?"

"Find another tape, Eric. Please." Using her cane for support, she slowly made her way toward Richard.

He grew alarmed by her cryptic behavior and leaned toward her. "What is it?"

"This tape," she said, holding it up. "I had it in my car the night of the shooting. I must have picked up the wrong tape in the office. I remember there were two on my desk, but I was certain I got the children's movie. Instead I got the movie that was showing in my theater. It hasn't been released on tape yet. How could this be?"

Richard took the tape from Annie and pulled out a chair for her at the kitchen table. He heard the video begin to play in the background as he sat beside Annie.

"Just the other day, I kept wondering what was really going on that night. They never tried to steal my purse or valuables. They must have been after this tape."

"Which means there's an underground bootleg ring in this area. Chances are, they're actually doing the taping in your theater."

"My movies are cheap. I get the movies weeks after the release date. They're half the price of regular movies. Why would anyone do that to me?"

"It's not a matter of your costs. They charge more for these tapes than you do for your movies. There has to be a distribution outlet around here."

Annie shook her head. "Confound it. A ring of thieves operating right in my theater." She hit the table with her hand. "I won't have it, Richard! I'm going to grill every last employee until I get to the bottom of this."

Richard patted her hand. "You can't do that. That'll tip them off. They'll close down shop and you'll never find out who's taping—or who shot you. It's out of your hands. If it was just the taping, you could fire the person and let him go. But he shot you. That's another matter.''

''I'm not going to let it continue.''

''Of course not. Let me talk to the sheriff. It's his job to deal with this.''

''It's my business we're talking about. William and I started that theater.''

''Let's go about it the right way, okay, Annie?''

Annie pinched her lips tight. ''Damn it, my hip still hurts from that shooting. All because they want to steal a stupid movie. It's not worth it, Richard. What makes people take stupid risks like that—endanger other people's lives? I'm barely making a living for my daughter and me out of that theater.''

Richard could tell her that courtrooms were lined with kids taking stupid risks. Lined with kids throwing their lives away at young ages. Could it be as simple as their knowing no other way? He knew that wasn't the answer either because many of them did. Blame it on drugs—blame it on bad influences. Blame didn't change reality.

''I don't know, Annie,'' he said simply. If it were up to him, he'd yell at them all to *think* before they did something insane—something they couldn't reverse. He knew that his work with the boys club was more important than ever. If he could reach them early enough, maybe they would think before they took a step like bootlegging tapes, holding up a liquor store, or any of the hundreds of illegal activities boys could get themselves into.

''When does the next movie arrive?'' Richard asked.

''Not for a week and a half.''

''We'll set something up for then. In the meantime, we'll get this copied and returned to your car. Whoever shot you is still trying to get it back.''

Soon after his findings, Richard left for home—alone. Crystal was spending the night with her sister. As he traveled the lonely road home, he dialed the cell phone number for the Blake boys.

Rodney answered.

Richard heard loud music and a deep drumroll in the background; then the volume lowered.

"Sorry about that," the boy said. "Yo."

"Dupree here. Meet me at my office . . ." He checked out the time. "In forty-five minutes."

Silence followed his directive. "We've got dates. It's Friday night."

"Take them home."

"Are you kidding?"

"Forty-five minutes." Richard disconnected to some swearing in the background.

Forty minutes later he drove down the bricked street in downtown Windy Hills. The Blake boys' car was parked in front of his office.

"Good choice," he told the boys as he passed the car for his office. They dragged their feet behind them. They were dressed in identical jean shorts and T-shirts.

Richard could have asked them the questions out in the parking lot near the muted glow of the halogen light, but he wanted a clear view of their faces when he interrogated them. Once he settled behind his desk, he started the interview.

"Tell me what you know about bootlegged tapes around here," he said.

The boys shrugged. "Don't know about any here. We get them from Roanoke." The boys looked innocent enough.

"From whom?"

"Some guy we know gets them from his cousin," Alonzo answered.

"Why do you want to know?" Rodney asked.

"It may involve your case."

"Wait a minute now. We aren't into bootlegging."

"Find out what you can about those tapes. Don't endanger yourselves. Just get me the info and let me deal with it. Otherwise keep this under your hat."

"You coulda asked this over the phone. You didn't have to mess up our whole evening."

"You'll get over it."

"Man, you need a life."

Richard sighed. "Don't I know it?"

When Richard made it home, the red light was blinking on his answering machine. He depressed the message button.

"Richard, dear," came his mother's voice, "I'm calling to remind you of the benefit dinner in two weeks. Your father will be speaking. A show of family support is called for. Please convince your wife of her duty."

He could just imagine Crystal's reaction to a message like that.

Richard sighed. He'd asked his mother weeks ago if she'd look into a literacy program in Windy Hills. He wondered if she'd made any progress.

Fifteen

Saturday at ten was overcast, humid, and hot. Crystal glanced at the horizon and hoped that the impending rain would hold off until after the festivities. The weather forecasters never knew for sure. They only knew that when it arrived, it would be a heavy thunderstorm.

They were gathered at the park at Crater Landing where the ropes had already been tethered on the rocks for the climb. SUVs, trucks, and cars bearing families with kayaks filed into the park one by one.

Dozens of families arrived to prepare secret recipes of ribs and burgers to sell at the tailgate party. Some brought their own grills while others used the few that the park provided. All in all it was a festive atmosphere.

Crystal glanced at the signs. All of them had been made by the members in her literacy group. Funny how she'd been reluctant even to start the group and now she claimed ownership. They were her group now.

Her students were even more proud of their progress on the computer. Crystal made a mental note to have them use it more. The Internet made them feel more up on the twenty-first century. They were very proud of the publicity they'd provided. Ricardo, Betty, and Sadie had even been interviewed on the radio station. They were local celebrities now.

Sadie had had a lot of say in how the huge banner was made. They'd chosen felt. Two huge smiley faces were placed on either end.

Right now, Able stood on a ladder with hammer and nails, and under Sadie's strict direction hung the banner between two trees.

"Lift it up a little higher," Sadie demanded, squinting to make sure the sign was even. She was bossing things as usual.

"Hurry up and make up your mind. I wish you were up here on this ladder. *Then* you'd see how it is," Able grumbled, complaining as usual. He stood at one tree, Ricardo at the other. Ricardo took it all in stride. Crystal smiled. She'd also learned to take their arguments in stride.

Aunt Annie arrived with Travis. The number of people in attendance had more to do with their respect for Travis than for the band. He'd long ago given up hope that anything would ever come of the band. Still, he participated in the festivities.

Gary drove up and soon after, the actual band members. Sam stood for a moment, taking in the setting. A wide smile spread across his face. He seemed pleased and surprised that so many people attended. He also seemed somewhat embarrassed.

They deserved the generosity of the community, Crystal thought as her father drove up in his pickup truck. He unloaded the huge grill. Richard came over to help him with it and the four coolers packed with food. She spread out a cloth on the nearby picnic table and piled hamburger and hotdog rolls on top of it.

Sam approached her and hugged her.

"Thank you," he whispered, a catch in his voice. He cleared his throat twice.

"You're more than welcome. You deserve this."

He looked at her in surprise. "I don't know about that."

One of the band members called him. He looked toward where they stood with Gary.

"Come on. We've got to get started."

"Catch you later," he said to Crystal and took off with the others.

Then suddenly the Blake boys arrived. They had the nerve to approach her aunt, who smiled at them as if they were as welcome as rain.

The air suddenly grew heavier. It seemed as though everyone standing around stopped and observed the scene in as much shock as Crystal did. They took the folding chairs and cushions out of the back of Travis's truck and carried them to a shady spot under a tree near Crystal's family and opened them.

They spoke politely to everyone. Then they asked Annie if they could do anything else for her. Annie thanked them and told them no. The boys went about their business. Their frail mother two tables down looked as if she were about to have a heart attack.

Crystal glanced at Richard, who called after them. The boys loped over to him. What in the world was going on? As Richard talked to them, slowly people began to resume whatever tasks they were doing. The rumble of conversations started up again.

Richard was well aware that the scene had captured everyone's attention. A few continued to stare as the boys approached him.

"What have you discovered so far?" Richard asked them.

"Not much," Alonzo said.

"Anything that will help anyway," Rodney agreed.

"We talked to a cousin. He got the tape from a buddy who gets them from some dude in D.C."

They stood a better chance of staking out Annie's theater when a new hot movie arrived. This was much more than bootlegging tapes. The bootlegger had been so frightened of Annie getting ahold of that tape that he'd been willing to take her life. And that was the crux of his mounting frustration. Annie wasn't safe in her own home or anywhere until these people were caught.

Richard and his father participated in the kayak race. His father hadn't been in the running, but he'd been close behind the Blake boys, who came in almost nose-to-nose. Now the others had gone on ahead of them. He and his father were paddling slowly back to camp.

"I hope you can work things out with Crystal. Election time will start in a few months and we need a show of family support, Richard."

"We're working on it." Richard didn't want to talk about his relationship with Crystal right now. They paddled rhythmically side by side.

"I never had to worry about your mother. She was always satisfied with supporting me. Now men almost need a college course in dealing with women."

"I don't know. They're just more vocal about their needs. That's not a bad thing."

His father narrowed his eyes at him and paddled the kayak. "It is when it destroys marriages."

"How are things with you and Mom?"

"Couldn't be better. She's gearing up for the election. Right in her element."

Richard broached the subject that had been bothering him lately. "Have you ever thought about taking more personal time with her?"

His father chuckled in that self-assured manner. "No need to worry about us. We don't have a problem, son. We spend plenty of time together."

"On politics, on charitable events. But what about just the two of you? When is the last time you've gotten away— just to spend time with each other? Like a vacation?" Richard asked. And then it struck him. He was sounding like Crystal.

His father frowned. "We can't take a vacation when the

election is around the corner. There will be time for that later.''

''Hmm,'' Richard said. They paddled a few more strokes. ''It's not like you have a competitor. Sometimes I wonder if she takes on so much because she doesn't have enough time with you. She looks to me as her significant person. I can't be that for her. I have a wife I'm trying to keep. She needs you, Dad. And I need to be with Crystal more.''

''Look, son. Just because you're having problems with your wife, don't try to put them off on me as if your mother and I are the reasons for your problems.''

''I'm not saying you have anything to do with my problems. But, Dad, you're never there—you haven't been for her or for me. I don't need you for me, now. But I need to be able to concentrate on my marriage without worrying about Mom. You need to be there for Mom.''

His father's eyes turned as stormy as the clouds overhead. ''Look, I brought you into this world. I'm not taking any criticism from you.''

''I'm not criticizing. I just want Mom happy. She loves you.''

His dad gave a vicious stroke that almost toppled him. He turned so red, Richard wondered if his father was going to keel over with a heart attack. ''Of course she loves me. And I love her. We're just fine. We don't need your meddling!''

''She's been wanting to see a play in New York for months. I bought tickets for the two of you, and plane tickets. My treat. Take her to see it.''

''Are you crazy? Have you listened to anything I've said? This is the middle of an election year. I don't have the time to go gallivanting about the country. If I leave the door open for a second, I could have a contender. Your mother understands that even if you don't. It's obvious that you don't know what's important any longer.''

''I know what's important. If you don't think I'm right, tell Mom you bought her tickets for the show and the plane.

Ask her if she can get away for a couple of days. Let her decide.'' Richard had issued it like a challenge.

''Hell, no.''

Richard smirked. ''Because you're afraid. You know I'm right.''

''Give me the damn tickets. I'll prove to you the stuff your mom is made of once and for all. This business with Crystal has damaged your brain. Got you thinking of nonsense. Suddenly you can't take care of your woman, and the whole damn country can't take care of theirs, either. You'll see what I'm talking about once I show those tickets to your mom. When she turns them down, you'll see what she's made of. But it's your money to waste.''

''It's not about that. It's about a woman who wants her husband to think she's important enough to take time out of his busy schedule for her. She wants to know that you love her more than you do your election.'' Richard stopped paddling and toppled into the water. He came up sputtering.

''What's with you? You've been paddling since you were knee high to a grasshopper,'' his dad said as Richard righted the kayak and swiped the water from his dripping face.

''Nothing,'' he said. But he'd just had his V-8 moment. This was what the breakup with Crystal had been about. How on earth was he going to get her to trust him now?

The benefit had been going on for hours now when Elzey appeared.

''I'm glad you could make it,'' Crystal told him.

Wearing dress slacks and a pressed shirt with the shirtsleeves rolled up and the top buttons opened, he looked as if he'd come straight from the office. She'd seen very little of him this summer and imagined Richard had kept him glued to the office chair even on the weekends. She was surprised that Richard got away. But lately, she'd seen more of him.

Elzey stopped in front of her. ''Would have been here earlier. Had to meet with a client.''

She nodded. How often had she heard that from Richard? She started piling a plate high with her daddy's ribs, her mama's spiced beans, greens and potato salad and handed it to him.

He thanked her and dropped some bills in the cash box. They made their way to a picnic table where he started eating like a man who hadn't had a decent meal in weeks.

"Do you like working here?" Crystal asked, half listening to the activities going on around her.

He bit into a tender rib. "Love it," he said, wiping barbecue sauce from his fingers. "Richard handed me this major case. He's consulting with me, but it's mostly mine. I didn't expect that so soon. Thought he'd need more time before he trusted me that much."

Crystal was shocked at Richard handing over a major case. Richard never would have done that a year ago.

Crystal's mother called her over to man the cash box and deep in her thoughts, Crystal left Elzey to his plate.

Crystal watched, mystified as a dripping Richard pulled his kayak out of the river to the teasing of the teens.

Richard was an experienced paddler, she thought as he approached her. Once he reached her, she handed him a towel, but he dodged the towel and lifted her in his arms, soaking her shorts and T-shirt.

"Ohhhh, you're all wet," Crystal squealed, leaning back from him, but not too far. Even through the dampness, she felt the heat from his body.

"Misery loves company," he said just before he lowered his head and kissed her.

A warm liquid feeling flowed through her. "You lost the race. You don't deserve a kiss," she teased, when he let her up for air. She ran her hand across his head.

"But I've got the girl."

There was something in his eyes that melted Crystal's heart. Something that drew her like a magnet, and she found herself kissing him. She had forgotten that a crowd was about. Forgotten that she was splitting from him. She knew she loved this man. . . .

"Oh, for goodness' sake," Mrs. Dupree said. "There's a crowd about, Richard. Please confine your baser instincts to privacy."

But it was a full thirty seconds before he let Crystal ease herself out of his arms.

"One little kiss isn't going to cost John the election, Claire," Annie said. "Chill."

Claire ignored Annie as she gave her son and Crystal a stern glance. "Please be on your best behavior. There are lots of voters here today."

Richard let Crystal go and grabbed his mother in a hug, lifting her feet off the ground to the delight of the gathering crowd.

"Put me down this instant, Richard." As soon as her feet touched the grown, Claire Dupree straightened her navy sailor shirt, dabbed at the wet spots on her pristine white slacks, and sent a speaking glance at her son, who looked as innocent as a ten-year-old who'd just hit a ball through a neighbor's window. Guilty as charged. Only in this case, he didn't care. Claire needed a little excitement in her life.

When she noticed the crowd, she whispered furiously at her son, then smiled the politician's-wife smile and went off to politick.

"I enjoyed myself today," Annie said as Travis walked her to the door.

"Day's not over yet. How's your hip holding up?"

Annie didn't know she could blush. "My hip's just fine, thank you very much."

Travis smiled that devilish smile that turned her insides to jelly. "I'm glad to hear that, Annie."

"I made a pitcher of my good lemonade this morning."

"I love your lemonade."

They went into the cottage and after filling two glasses they sat on the back porch to take in the evening breeze.

"Annie, I don't want you mad at me, but we need to talk about the theater."

"Travis, I'm not selling you my theater. My daughter runs it. My husband opened that place and he wanted to leave something for the children."

"It needs fixing up. I can do that."

"I know what it needs. We'll get around to that when we can." She kept it cheerful by having it painted regularly. But she knew the place needed new seats, new carpeting that wasn't a patchwork quilt, the concession stand updated. Annie felt old. Lord, so much to be done and not enough money to do it all.

"Why is my theater so important to you?"

"Sam isn't going to make a go of that band. I don't have any faith in that manager of theirs. He's just taking their money. But Sam has good ideas. He could make a real go of that theater."

"It's just a theater. We show movies, sell food. It doesn't need a genius."

"If you take me on as a partner, you can buy the things you want for it."

"And you'll take over—or try to."

"We'll discuss things. I wouldn't take over."

"Hmm."

"Think about it, Annie. You and I can work together on this."

Annie wasn't so trusting.

"Woman, don't be giving me the eye." And then the laughter left his eyes. "I need to talk to you about something. I want to tell you before you find out from anyone else."

Annie grew immediately concerned. "What is it?"

"I can't read—at least I can't read well. Crystal has been giving me lessons." He got up and walked to the end of the porch.

"I started learning when you started teaching the reading group. Gertrude would teach me what you'd taught them." He told her about the phonics set he'd purchased, and how his reading had progressed. "Gertrude and I didn't have it easy. Neither did my younger sisters and brothers. We missed so much of the school year we couldn't keep up. Eventually we just stopped going. Our family was poor, Annie. We had to work to eat. But that meant we never got an education.''

Annie let out an inward sigh, but admiration was in her voice. "You had me worried there a moment.''

"You aren't ashamed of me?''

"What do you take me for, Travis? I don't know how you can ask me a question like that. Why would I be ashamed? I'm angry that you thought I would be.''

"I'm not proud of the fact that I'm not educated. I want to be. I'm going to get my GED. Then I'm going to take some college courses. Farming is changing. You have to keep up with the times—with new technology.''

Tears gathered in Annie's eyes. "You can be proud of your accomplishments. You've taken that farm and developed it into a growing, profitable business when many were going under.''

Annie thought of how many students today found it a chore to get out of bed and catch the bus to school. She'd had to walk several blocks to school every day. And she knew how farm workers worked when Travis was young. They'd usually be in the field with the crops soon after daybreak to spend the entire day there, only breaking for lunch and water. And he did this at the age of six. Many thirty-year-old men didn't work as hard today as he had at six.

"I'm going to get my GED, Annie,'' he reassured her.

"I know you are, Travis.''

Annie knew that with many men their word meant nothing. Travis's word meant everything. If he said he would get his GED, then he would. If he said he'd take college courses, he would. He was a man of his word. But a college course would never make the man. It was the core of Travis Walker that made him the special man that he was.

"Thanks, Annie.'' Travis approached her and sat beside her on the rocker. He leaned closer and tried to kiss Annie.

"You may be an enticing man, but sex isn't going to get you my theater, Travis. Anyway, I'm still mad at you for not trusting me."

His lips brushed against hers, sending a spiral of sensations to the pit of her stomach. "Your theater has nothing to do with the way I feel about you, woman."

He gathered her into his arms and lifted her onto his lap and kissed her deeply. "You find me enticing, hmm?"

Annie ran a finger along his shirt collar, triggering a masculine groan.

"I'm too old to be making out on the back porch," he whispered against her lips.

"Let's take this show inside—in private."

As they entered the house, Travis stroked Annie. "I've been wanting you all day," he said in a heady voice.

"You've got me now."

"Yes," he said with pure masculine pride. "You're all mine."

Annie tried to think about how she felt about his possessiveness, but his hands were doing such delicious things to her body that other thoughts evaporated like puffs of smoke. Slow hands caressed her body, sending her into a blazing bliss.

She closed her eyes and luxuriated in the sensations of his hands stroking her breasts just before the heat of his breath seared them with nipping kisses and contrasting with tiny prickles from his freshly trimmed mustache.

By the time he finished he turned her to her stomach and, goodness gracious, by the time he'd moved to another spot she was a mess of emotions and sensations. But Annie wanted to reciprocate. She wanted him to feel the pleasure she felt.

She urged him to stretch out on her big king-size bed. It looked smaller with him in it. And she went to work on him. He didn't last as long, though, because before she knew it, she found herself flat on her back. But this time she slowly stroked him as she rolled on the prophylactic. Tight thigh muscles strained with need. A tense expression on his face along with a healthy erection let her know more than anything he was ready beyond need.

"Damn, woman." He groaned one of those deep masculine moans that turned her knees to butter. And then he was entering her and the teasing left her only for her to be engulfed with the pure pleasure of his body filling hers.

Sixteen

At the next meeting, Crystal decided the class was ready for chapter books. Claire had purchased seven copies of each book and Crystal handed a book to each student at the end of class.

"All of us are getting the same book?" Sadie asked, craning her neck to see what everyone else was getting.

"This week you're getting the same reading assignment." The book ran fifty pages. She hoped they could complete it by the next class.

"This is going to be like one of those book clubs. We can discuss the story when we meet at the restaurant," Sadie said, flipping through pages.

"Book club?" Able said, frowning at Crystal. "That's women's stuff."

"Some book clubs have both sexes," Betty said. By the smile on her face, it was apparent that she liked the idea of a club as much as Sadie did.

Able shook his head and punched Ricardo on the arm in a man-to-man gesture. "They going to have us reading Oprah books before you know it."

"I don't think we're ready for that yet," Ricardo said, frowning.

"We'll get there," Gertrude said. "One step at a time is all it takes. A year ago we couldn't read at all. Look how far we've come."

"That's right, we're on our way," Sadie said. "And we have our own book club." She narrowed her eyes at Able. "What are we going to name our club?"

Able was still studying the book. "Do we get to keep these?"

Crystal hadn't thought about that. What if other students were illiterate and came to her for instruction? She wouldn't have books for them. But everyone looked expectantly at her. "Why don't we use the books like a library. Whenever you want them, you can check them out."

"Who's going to be responsible for keeping records?" Sadie asked.

"We'll use the honor system," Crystal said. This was getting complicated.

"I don't trust Able," Sadie said, her fancy hat bobbing in the wind.

"I don't trust you either," Able rebutted.

All this over a few books? "You don't have to fight," Crystal said.

"I'll keep the records," Gertrude put in. "The two of you are old enough to know better."

"She started it," Able said.

"Do you think you can read the entire book by the next class?" Crystal asked.

Her question put an end to this argument. Crystal could count on an argument between Able and Sadie each class.

"You'll be getting a test on the reading assignment next class."

"A test?" Betty said. Pensively, she shook her head. "I don't know about that."

"Think you're going to flunk?" Able asked.

Crystal wanted to roll her eyes. "No one will fail. I

want to test your reading skills. How else can I assess your progress?''

"You can't cheat, Able," Sadie said.

Able nearly sprang out of the chair. "You don't have to worry about me cheating. I'm going to keep an eye on you, though."

"Lord have mercy. Do we have to go through another argument with you two?" Gertrude said.

Able pointed a finger at Sadie. "She started it."

"I want the two of you to stop talking to each other during class," Crystal said gently. How on earth did their study groups go, she wondered, if they couldn't get along for two minutes in class? "Class dismissed," Crystal finally announced. This was one day she was glad to see the end of—just as it was when she taught her fifth grade class. There were good days and bad days. She knew to expect this.

I'm good at giving advice, but not so good at taking it, Richard thought. He'd talked his father into at least offering to take his mom to New York, yet he hadn't done a thing with Crystal.

Everyone in town knew that the literacy group met in an empty banquet room to practice their reading. If they'd tried to keep it a secret, the secret was out. By the time he knocked on the door, they were well into an argument.

"Good to see you, Richard," Sadie said, glancing up from her book.

"You too."

"What can we do for you?" Able said, cutting to the chase as he was known to do. Richard discounted the fact that he was a tad nosy.

"I need a small favor," he said, taking a seat at the head of the table.

"What is it?" Sadie asked.

"I want to take Crystal out of town tomorrow. Would you mind rescheduling your class?"

Sadie narrowed her eyes. "What are you going out of town for?"

"None of your business," said Able.

Sadie straightened her shoulders. "If I've got to change my class date, I need to know."

"It's not like we're paying Crystal to teach us," Betty reminded her.

"I take her some of my eggs—better than the store-bought ones."

"She can't pay the bills with those eggs," Gertrude said. "I take her eggs, too."

"The day don't make no difference to me. One day's like the next," said Able. "Give us more time to prepare for my test." He puffed up when he mentioned test.

"Any day is fine for me, too," Ricardo said.

The others nodded.

Sadie still screwed up her face, squinted through her glasses. "I guess it'll be okay. I don't see why you have to be so secretive about it."

"I really appreciate it," Richard said and left the group to their reading.

Crystal hung up the phone after the last person in her reading group called to cancel tomorrow's class. Actually, every person in Crystal's reading group canceled. Odd, she thought. Usually one person didn't make it and made up for it with their private meeting. *But every last one of them?* Something was definitely afoot. She knew sooner or later she'd find out. In the meantime, she had a free evening to spend with her aunt, or whatever.

She was about to pick up the phone when a car drove into her yard. She glanced through the French windows. Princess barked, wanting to go out.

Richard climbed out of his car.

Last night she was sure he'd planned to initiate lovemaking. By the time the evening was over, she probably wouldn't have turned him down. After a night of tiny touches, sneaky kisses—she'd die before she told a soul she'd loved every minute of it. But he'd headed for home.

She opened the door before he knocked.

He hauled her into his arms and kissed her solidly. "Pack your bags. We're taking a mini vacation."

"To where?"

"It's a surprise."

Crystal could have fought him, but she didn't want to. "For how long?"

"Just overnight. I have a case on Wednesday." He let her go so she could pack.

Twenty minutes later, Crystal was in the passenger seat, headed out of town. Princess was in the backseat. "You could give me a hint." He'd been closemouthed since they entered the car.

He winked at her. "Just wait and see."

They dropped Princess off at Annie's. This was only the second time Crystal had spent a night away from her pet. She'd grown accustomed to the golden retriever and missed her immediately.

She watched Richard in profile as they drove along 81. She could no more contain the excitement building within her than she could the love that grew stronger by the day. Even he seemed less serious—more lighthearted as they drove farther away from Windy Hills.

Two hours later they pulled into a winery—one of many sprinkled throughout Virginia the last few years. They had lunch and then drove another half hour, ending at the Natural Bridge.

It had been years since they'd been there.

They rode the bus to the entrance. From there they walked, passing the cave where saltpeter was mined centuries ago. A tired man carrying his son approached them from the opposite direction. Another couple asked how long to the waterfall.

"Too long," the father answered, hefting his son to a more comfortable position.

"How are the sights?"

"It's not worth the walk," he said and trudged on, shifting his son.

His wife had a different opinion, however, but she wasn't carrying a four-year-old on her back. "It's nice," the wife said. "There's an Indian village, a hidden river, and the waterfall is very pleasant."

"Thanks," the couple said and decided to continue on.

The mock Indian village was from a tribe that had roamed this land centuries before. Deer and squirrel skins were drying on portions of the fort as they would have been two hundred years ago. A small vegetable garden was just outside the fort.

"It's amazing that even today, scientists can't tell where the hidden river originated."

They neared the opening and could hear the water rushing inside a rock cropping. Years back, engineers had dug to find the source, but were unable to.

"Even with scientific advances, there are some things that science still can't do," Richard said.

Even without their knowing, it was beautiful and peaceful. The trees provided so much shade that one couldn't tell that the temperature had climbed to ninety degrees.

Crystal was tired once they reached the waterfall. They sat on the benches there for a few minutes watching the miniature falls.

"Thanks for bringing me here," Crystal said to Richard.

"You're welcome." He kissed the top of her head.

She felt the heartrending tenderness in his gaze and relaxed, sinking into his cushioning embrace.

They sat there for what seemed a half hour before they started their trek back. By the time they reached the bridge, the sun was starting to set and the music had begun to play.

Crystal loved the romantic music played at sunset—the colorful lights flashing on the waterfall. There was a certain peace that enveloped her as she sat beside Richard. His arm was thrown around the back of her chair. They sat close and intimately together.

And still . . .

They sat there for an hour before they left for dinner and the hotel. She got in the shower first but while she was there, Richard walked into the bath naked as the day he was born. And he looked gorgeous. His eyes met hers, analyzing her reaction.

At that instant, she realized she was waiting for him.

His eyes had a sheen of purpose. His large hand took her face and held it gently. He kissed her lips, a tender gesture at first, then deeper. Tonight there were no shadows across her heart. Two people who loved each other—who belonged together—sought ecstasy in each other's arms. As the water fell on them, her hands caressed his sleek slick skin. He lifted his head and looked her over seductively and she stared at him with longing.

He took the soap from her hands and rubbed it into his palms with his fingers. Then he smoothed the soap over her body in slow, electrifying motion. It was more a caress than a bath. The mere touch of his hand sent a warming shiver though her. She moaned.

"You like that?" he asked.

"Oh, yes. Yes," she said, drawing her fingers down his slick chest.

He drew his fingers along her breasts. The water falling there washed the soap away. He bent, flickered a tongue over her breasts, sucked on her brown nipples.

His touch sent lightning strikes of pleasure through her. For someone trying to get away from her husband, they were much too intimate. That thought didn't stop her from enjoying what he was offering—enjoying the pleasure of his magical touch. The pleasure was pure and explosive. In a moment, she wasn't thinking at all. She was only reveling in his touch. Warm water cascaded over her body like a miniature waterfall, continuing to rinse off the soap as it fell. Richard's mouth and touch seemed to follow its path.

And then he lifted her and slid inside her. She clutched his back, the hard muscles straining against her palms. Her senses were intensified by the touch of his body. He lifted her against the wall. And then they were moving—moving to a familiar drumbeat. Her legs wrapped around his body. Pleasure intensified. Passion escalated, and it overwhelmed her as waves of ecstasy throbbed through her. And then she heard his deep masculine response, her heart bursting with love and anguish.

Crystal didn't know why she let Richard talk her into the benefit dinner for his parents. She was sending out the wrong message—or was she?

She sighed, but kept the pleasant look on her face. She loved this man. There was no question of that. She knew she wouldn't be happy with anyone else. He'd been supportive and had spent the time with her that she'd longed for for years. But could she trust this to continue?

Ultimately she guessed it came down to whether she trusted him enough.

She glanced down on the audience. She and Richard sat on stage in a place of honor with her in-laws. Although it would never be her favorite thing, attending a few political dinners wasn't the end of the world. Richard's father had done a lot for this town. And although his mother was hard to take sometimes, she too had done much for Windy Hills.

Two hours later, they met at the Duprees'. Crystal had spent much of her marriage debating political strategies. She expected the same tonight, but was surprised when her mother-in-law announced that she and her husband were taking a short vacation to New York next week.

"We have tickets to see a Broadway play. I've been dying to see it." She took her husband's hand in hers and brushed her lips across his cheek—a rare public show of affection even though only family was about.

"Thank you, darling," she said and her husband—the politician who could outtalk his most strident opponent, who could placate the most irate constituent, who could stonewall it with the best of them—actually blushed at his wife's show of affection.

Liquid warmth flowed through Crystal. Not everyone

wore their hearts on their sleeves as her family did. Even this queenly woman needed to know she was special. Needed to know that she was loved, that she wasn't just a pawn to further her husband's political career.

Crystal knew that her mind was almost made up. She may have a fight on her hands for the rest of her life to see her as someone deserving of Richard's time when he forgot. But she wouldn't be happy elsewhere. Why should she? Everything she wanted was with him. She knew she'd never fall out of love with Richard.

She remembered the song that sent her into laughing fits when she was a child—the song to which her uncle would catch her aunt in his arms and execute an exaggerated dance—went something like "I will never ever love another, after loving you." Who sang that song? Crystal wondered. The words expressed exactly what she felt right now.

The next day life returned to reality, and though their trip had been short, it had been invigorating and hopeful. Suddenly Crystal realized that Richard was really doing the things she'd asked of him for years.

She knew well that he couldn't give her his undivided attention twenty-four-seven, and she wouldn't want that. But just a little time together to make them a couple was all she sought. And it was the little things that gave meaning to life. Like the gift of flowers now and then, to let someone know they were special. There was no reason why she couldn't send Richard flowers, was there? Maybe, she'd just show up with them.

Crystal shook her head. "No," she said aloud. *I'll send them,* she thought, digging out her phone book. As she flipped through the pages, she heard a car drive into her yard. She left the phone book on the table and went to the window. Her father exited his truck wearing his prized fishing hat. He reached into the back of his pickup truck and dug out a cooler and fishing pole.

By the time he started for her door, she was standing in

the middle of the porch. Princess stood beside her, eyeing the cooler.

"What brings you here so early?" Crystal asked. Usually he called her to let her know he was arriving.

"I was sent to talk some sense into you."

Crystal crossed her arms beneath her breasts. "I don't need a lecture."

"Good, then we can get in some fishing," he said, heading along the back. "Grab your pole."

Crystal hadn't been fishing with her father since his last visit. It would be good to fish again. "Wait up," she said and went inside to don her gear.

Twenty minutes later, Crystal made her way down the embankment. She'd dressed in fifteen minutes, but she'd taken five minutes to call the florist. She smiled. She'd love to be a fly on the wall when Richard received the flowers. She was also a little nervous about his reaction. It was almost like starting over again.

Crystal gingerly picked her way down the rocky slope to the Smith River. Her father stood hip deep, several yards out, casting his fly into the water. He loved to fish. She counted on spending much of the day here. Crystal pulled on her own hip boots and stepped into the water.

"The one who catches the biggest fish gets to watch the other one clean them."

Crystal would stand here all day if she had to to make certain she caught the largest. She loved a challenge.

"You're on," she told her dad and cast her rod.

Half an hour later, her father said, "You know, there's a thing called forgiveness."

"Hmmm," Crystal said. So far her father had caught the largest fish. She hated cleaning fish. "Do you need forgiveness for something?" Crystal asked.

"I'm talking about you and Richard." He was never good at father-daughter talks.

"And?" she prompted.

"Why don't you just forgive the man and let it be done? He's learned his lesson."

"I wasn't teaching him a lesson."

"Women always teach men lessons. Or at least try to," he said.

"You can rest. I've decided to give our marriage another try."

Her father sighed a heartfelt sigh. "Good. Now let's enjoy the fishing. Looks to me like you're going to have your work cut out for you."

Just then Crystal felt a tug on her line. She pulled it up. A huge catfish wiggled on the hook.

"Who's going to be cleaning?" Crystal asked with a sly smile.

Seventeen

Richard should have been working furiously on his Stonehouse notes. Instead he stared at the two dozen roses that had just arrived on his desk. He glanced at the note again. Dared he hope that his wife was finally coming around? *It's about time,* he thought as he lifted a blossom from the vase and brought it to his nose. He inhaled the subtle scent.

"You going to stare at those roses all day like some lovesick fool or get some work done?" Theresa said in her usual brisk manner.

Richard ignored her—refused to let anything detract from his joy.

She tsked, sighed, and returned to her desk—where she belonged, as far as he was concerned. A man should be able to enjoy a pleasure or two without censure from women.

In the background he heard Elzey enter and ask about the brief.

"He's back there meditating over flowers," she informed him.

"What?" the younger man asked.

"Go figure."

Richard sighed, stuck the rose back into the vase, and got

back to work. Didn't have the time to enjoy his flowers in peace. It wasn't the flowers themselves that had him in a trance. To him the flowers represented much more than a feel-good gift. He was hopeful of the motive that had prompted his wife to send them.

The Stonehouse case was progressing as expected. Elzey was doing a fine job but Richard forced himself to return to his notes.

Richard sent his brief to Theresa through the office network and grabbed his briefcase. He was on his way to Crystal. His body was already revved for the night ahead of them.

"I'll be late coming in tomorrow," he said, backing against the door.

The phone rang.

Richard turned to leave.

"Richard . . . hold on," Theresa called before the door shut behind him.

Impatience furrowed his brow. "What is it?"

"Telephone."

"Take a message," he said.

"It's Annie."

Richard expelled a breath and took the phone in his office and shut the door.

The new movie had arrived and the projectionist was splicing it for viewing. Annie was at the theater with her daughter. The two women were keeping a close eye on things.

"Annie, I want you and your daughter out of there right now. You aren't usually there when the splicing is done."

"We have to act normal," she said. "Besides, I'm not running away. This is my business."

"Don't be stubborn. We're talking about your life. It's more important than any business."

"I'm making up some excuse for Stacey to leave, but I'm staying. I'm feeling up to spending a few hours here."

"Stubborn women! Let me get someone over there."

Annie had gone into the theater today and Travis felt safe with leaving her with a group of people.

He glanced at the street sign, MAIN STREET. He turned right on Meadow Drive and drove a few miles. Then he turned on High Mountain Road. He read the signs to streets he'd known most of his life, not because he could read them, but because it was something one picked up along the way. But now he could actually read them. He felt different somehow. More in sync with the community.

He trusted Annie. He loved Annie, but he was still uncomfortable with his reading and writing skills. He practiced writing an hour each day. He practiced reading every spare minute. He didn't realize how difficult simply writing would be until he began forming unfamiliar letters. Before the class, the only thing he could write—and not comfortably—was his name.

He called Crystal and asked her if she could spare a few minutes. She could. He patted his brand-new checkbook in his left shirt pocket and turned into Crystal's driveway. He grabbed the bills he'd stacked in a folder and took them with him to her house.

She opened the door just as he reached it.

Travis didn't grin often, but the pure pleasure on his face clutched at Crystal's heart as they made their way to the deck. He placed the folder he carried on the table. Beside it, he placed his new checkbook. The warning page was still attached on top.

"I want to try paying my bills by check this month instead of driving to the bank and different offices."

"All right," Crystal said.

She watched as he selected the electric bill and glanced up at her. "My wife used to write out all the checks," he said. "I can read what's on here. I owe $148.36 for the electric on the house." He frowned, pondering that for a moment. "I must be using a lot of electricity."

"Air-conditioning can be expensive."

He nodded. "It's about the same as last month."

"It is," Crystal said.

She demonstrated how to actually write out the check and he followed her instructions. Then she had him record it in the check registry so that he would keep track of his balance. He had a very nice handwriting for a man. He stuck the check and stub into the envelope and sealed it. Then he marked the envelope with his return address.

"I'm going to have to send away for labels," he said.

"Or make them on the computer. You have one in your office, don't you?"

"Yeah, I can do that, can't I?"

Crystal nodded. "Only temporarily. Ordering them is cheaper."

"I guess we'll do the phone bill next."

"Okay."

He completed the check himself this time. He may have been illiterate, but he was an intelligent man, she noticed not for the first time as he completed the stack.

Crystal was going to miss teaching this group once she started back to school. Summer would be over soon. Aunt Annie was much better. She'd be able to take over her class once again.

It was then that Crystal realized that she really enjoyed this. If given the opportunity, she'd continue to teach adults. They enjoyed every step of the learning process. She realized that her class was a bit unorthodox. Most students wouldn't fight as much as Sadie and Able. They, too, reveled in every scrap of information imparted to them. You were never too old to learn. If nothing else, Crystal had learned that in the last two months.

She smiled as she watched Travis separate his envelopes into the folder pockets. In June, she'd returned with no direction for the future—not about her marriage or her career. Now she knew that she could either teach children or adults. With all the effort Richard put into keeping their relationship together, she felt that they could make their marriage work.

She really would like to explore an adult education program in Windy Hills. Perhaps she'd look into it tomorrow. Joy bubbled in her. In the meantime, she had an appointment with her doctor this afternoon.

Richard had tried to reach Crystal all evening, but hadn't been able to. She must have been with her parents or at her sister's place. Why tonight of all nights did she plan to stay away? After he finished at Annie's it was too late to go to the mountain cabin, so he made his way home.

Once there, he saw a light in the house. He must have forgotten to turn it off. But when he entered the garage, he saw Crystal's red Jaguar parked in its rightful place.

Crystal was home.

He rushed into the house looking for her. The aroma from something delicious hit him immediately.

"Ah," he said. Memories from the past.

Crystal had fallen asleep on the couch. He felt like a heel. How many times had this happened in the past? God, she'd never come back to him if he kept these hours. He looked at her dressed in a pretty sundress. He wanted to kiss her, but she looked so peaceful there.

He headed to the kitchen. Food was on the stove waiting for him. But he really didn't want food. All he wanted was his wife.

Richard set his bag on the entryway floor and discarded his jacket. He forced himself to eat the pork chops smothered in a rich sauce, the rice and salad. Not realizing how starved he was, he ate the entire dinner. Then he went upstairs and took a shower.

When he came downstairs, he kissed Crystal lightly on the lips. He couldn't wait another second. "Wake up, sleeping beauty," he whispered against her lips.

"Ummm, that must be me."

"You better believe it," he murmured. "Dinner was delicious."

"I couldn't wait for you."

"I'm sorry about that."

"It's okay."

That was certainly a change of tone, but he wasn't going to look a gift horse in the mouth. "Let's go upstairs," he said, lifting her from the couch. He kissed her one last time as he carried her up the stairs.

"Ummm," Crystal said as he released her on the bed and did wonderful things to her body. She was completely awake now. He had on tight briefs that showed his physique to a definite advantage. Just looking at him raised her blood pressure to dangerous levels. But as he kissed and touched her body, she wasn't thinking about briefs. She was thinking about what was in them.

She lifted her hand, rubbed it back and forth over his crotch.

A deep moan was followed by a whispery, "You keep that up and this slow pace I'm setting is history."

"I don't want it slow," she whispered back and brought his mouth down urgently on hers, sucked on his tongue, nearly blew the top off his head. Worked her hands beneath his briefs, down his thighs.

"Hold on, baby. I've got to be sure you're with me." Richard was teetering on the edge himself, but he wanted this to be special for her.

"I'm with you, I'm with you."

He slid his hands in her panties, felt the wetness, and stroked her with her hips grinding against his hand as he felt her pulse quickening, her moans, her pleas music in his ear. And when she came he watched the miracle. Watched her breath come in staccato beats, her eyes closed tightly, her muscles slowly unclench. He stroked her softly, held her gently until her heartbeat slowed.

Then gradually, together they stroked the lingering spark to a glowing fire. Her mouth did wondrous things to his body. He dissolved in the splendor of the feelings. Gentle nails slid back and forth along his back and buttocks; then she stroked him with the palm of her hand. The contrasting sensations drove him crazy with need. This time he covered her body with his, entered her with desperate force.

And as they embraced in the dance that was as old as time, her body catapulted him directly to the stars.

The next morning, Richard wanted to stay in bed with Crystal an hour longer, but knew he had to get to work. Plenty was happening at Annie's. The film had been spliced and put together. Any time now, someone would be taping the new movie to sell as videos. He was very nervous about Annie and her daughter. But he saw no other option. At least Travis was spending time there. He'd talked to Travis last night just before he left Annie.

Richard quietly dressed as Crystal slept in their bed.

Their bed, Richard thought. It had been a long time getting to this. They'd made love so many times last night, they didn't have much of an opportunity to talk. He didn't tell her about Annie, he thought as he knotted his tie. He'd leave a message to call him when she awakened.

Richard descended the stairs. He passed Crystal's purse and a slip of paper on the kitchen bar. It was a bill from her gynecologist. He frowned toward the stairs. Was anything wrong with Crystal? Hadn't she healed well? Richard knew the number. She was friends with the doctor. He couldn't wait. He picked up the phone and dialed her home number. He wakened her from a sound sleep.

"Marsha, I'm calling about Crystal."

"She's fine, Richard. The baby, too. I don't foresee any problems with this pregnancy. She has a list of instructions I gave her yesterday."

Crystal was pregnant? Richard found a chair and stumbled into it.

"Richard, are you there?"

Richard cleared his throat. "Ye . . . Yes, Marsha, I'm here. Is there anything I need to do?"

"Just be a supportive husband. And unless it's an emergency please call me at a decent hour. I had a delivery at three this morning."

"Sorry."

"No problem. Congratulations," she said and disconnected.

Richard punched the off button and set the portable phone on the table.

Crystal was pregnant again.

He glanced toward the stairs. Last night had been her first night spent at home since January. Had she come home to him? Or was it for the baby? Crystal believed with every fiber of her being that children should be considered first beyond all else. So what if one married for the sake of the child? It was only right, she'd said so many times. At least the child would have a head start in life. Sometimes it wasn't about the husband and wife. It was more about the child. Make the best of things for the child's sake, she would say.

A sick feeling drifted to the pit of Richard's stomach. Was she making the best of things now? Crystal had been so hurt by the loss of their child. She'd promised emphatically that she didn't want their marriage any longer. Did she use him as a baby-making machine? Come to think of it, she hadn't worried about protection. Since it had taken so long for them to conceive the first time, he didn't think much of it. When they were in college, he couldn't touch her without a prophylactic. She carried those things around with her—was always prepared. Yet, although she swore she wanted a divorce, she didn't mention protection once— not once.

Richard felt sick. He grabbed his jacket and briefcase and left the house. He needed time to think.

When had she planned to tell him? he wondered as he opened the garage door. She had plenty of time last night, he thought as he slung the briefcase into the seat.

Then he saw the wilted rose he'd put on the dash with

intents to bring it home and put it in a vase by his bed. When he saw her car, he'd forgotten about the rose on the dash.

Were the roses a thank-you for the baby? Roses weren't something Crystal ever sent him. Yes, she'd made other loving gestures. But roses?

Come on, Richard. Has Crystal ever used trickery before? His only answer was no. She was always up front about her needs and wants. She didn't believe in deceit.

Crystal had changed since the miscarriage, though. The question was, how much had she changed? Had she strayed that far from the woman he knew and loved?

You're so selfish, he thought to himself. He was happy about the baby. He loved his wife. He just wasn't happy about how it all came about. He felt tricked. Used. He didn't like either emotion.

He didn't have a problem with taking care of his responsibilities. He married Crystal for love. He expected truth from her, not this deception.

Crystal stretched and felt the empty pillow next to her. A note was on Richard's pillow. It said *I love you. Call me when you get up.*

She reached for the phone. Theresa answered the call.

"May I speak to Richard, please?"

"He's not here, Crystal. He asked me to set up a lunch date for the two of you if you're available."

"I'm available."

Theresa chuckled. "Sounds romantic. I hope it puts him in a better mood. He's been a real tiger today."

Crystal smiled. She felt like a college student again. She couldn't wait to see him again. She would have much preferred hearing his voice, but at least she'd see him soon. She got up and showered. She enjoyed the oversize shower once again. They had built a smaller one in the cabin. She was back among her personal things. From the looks of it, Richard used the same bowl he'd always used in the double-bowl bathroom. She used her bowl, easily breaking into the routine.

She'd left her winter clothing in the closet. Many of her other clothes were still there also. Finding something to wear wasn't a problem although she'd packed a suitcase with makeup and items she just couldn't do without.

She ate a quick breakfast of oatmeal, drank a glass each of juice and milk. Then she took the vitamins Marsha had prescribed for her. Wearing Richard's bathrobe, folding up the sleeves, she retrieved her suitcase from the car and completed her dressing ritual for the day.

Crystal saw Richard at a table in a secluded corner in the restaurant. When she approached him, he wasn't the man she'd shared the night with. His composure was completely inflexible. He must have been working on a difficult case, she thought. After all, when she'd called Theresa, he was unavailable.

He stood as she approached him, and kissed her on the cheek. It wasn't a warm, welcoming gesture, but cold and stiff—as if she were a stranger, not his loving wife, the wife he tried so hard to hold on to.

"I hope you're hungry," he said.

"Famished," Crystal replied, opening her menu. She glanced over the top to regard him. He glared intently at the menu as if he were unaware of every item on it. There weren't that many restaurants in Windy Hills. They ate out often. He more so than she on business lunches.

Crystal returned her attention to the menu.

"Have you decided yet?" he finally asked.

"I'll have clam chowder and a chef's salad." Plenty of calcium, she thought.

He ordered a steak and baked potato and closed the menu.

"Tough case this morning?" she asked.

He shrugged. "No worse than usual."

"I see."

He regarded her as if he was waiting for something.

Crystal wanted to share the good news about their baby with him. They also needed to discuss their relationship. She should have done so last night, but once he'd touched her, all other thoughts flew from her mind. Then, too, she wanted to share it with him at a special time. Now should be perfect. He would be as ecstatic as she.

There was a coldness and stiffness about Richard, however, that stymied her actions. She wanted to tell him in a warm and comforting way. She wanted them both to share the joy of their child. They made small talk until their lunch arrived. The food was delicious but Crystal couldn't tell anything by the tension at their table. What on earth was bothering Richard?

"Is anything wrong, Richard?"

"You tell me."

Crystal put her fork on her plate. "What are you talking about?"

He wiped his mouth, threw the napkin on the table, and glared at her. "Are you keeping secrets?"

So, he found out about the baby. "No, I'm not keeping secrets, but if you want to know if I have some news to share with you, it's obvious that you already know."

"Did you do it purposely?"

"Did I do it— Are you out of your mind?" Crystal straightened in her seat and pointed an imperious finger at him. "I have never needed to sneak to do anything. I don't work that way and if something bothered you, all you had to do was come right out and tell me. I don't operate on deceit and lies." She took her napkin off of her lap and dropped it on her plate. "It's obvious our relationship has more problems than I thought if you react to me this way. Nobody treats me like this, Richard. You've taken something precious and special and made it into something sordid and cheap. I'm not a child. So you just sit on your high-handedness and sulk."

"Everything has been your way for the last few months," Richard said. "I've been dancing to your tune like a puppet. I'm supposed to do all the trusting, yet you don't trust me.

Trust is a two-way street. You trust me, you get trust in return."

"I heard you loud and clear." Crystal turned on her heel and left the restaurant. She didn't see the patrons watching her as she left.

Richard, you've just acted like the biggest fool in the county. He motioned to the waiter to bring the check. He couldn't let Crystal get away. He grabbed his wallet out of his pocket and snatched out some bills, throwing them on his table. He took long strides out of the restaurant.

His cell phone rang. Crystal was pulling out of her parking space. His first reaction was to ignore the phone. Then he thought of Annie. "Damn it." He took it out of his pocket and answered.

"Richard? It's Theresa. You need to get on over to the theater. There's trouble over there." As he walked toward his car, he watched Crystal's car disappear from sight.

"All right. I'm on my way." He disconnected, climbed into his car, and made his way the few blocks to the theater.

Eighteen

Crystal was hopping mad by the time she collected her bag from the house and drove up the mountain to the cabin. She'd had such high hopes for lunch—for telling Richard about the baby. How could he think her so small-minded? She was never going to speak to that idiot again.

Accusing her of tricking him? If she ever! She was so agitated that she was startled at the ringing doorbell. She didn't care if he did drive up the mountain after her. She wasn't going to speak to him. The doorbell rang again. She ignored it.

"Crystal! You in there?"

That wasn't Richard's voice. Now she felt even worse. He didn't think enough of her or the baby to come after her. She marched to the door and let in Travis. He was carrying a folder again. And he seemed very agitated.

"I need to talk to you."

"Come on in." They settled at the kitchen table.

"I want you to take a look at these."

Crystal wasn't in the frame of mind to deal with anybody's papers, but she read the receipts anyway.

"I was looking through the checkbook while Sam was

away. I came across this check and wanted to know what it was for. You see it's got the receipt number on the bottom. This is a music place. I don't buy music stuff for the farm so I had him fax the receipt to me."

A list of recording equipment was listed on the receipt.

"I don't understand. This is high-quality video recording equipment. Not the everyday brand we buy for home use." The equipment came to nearly twenty thousand dollars.

"Now look at this deposit. It's the exact amount. I keep tabs on all the checks that come in. I don't remember that one."

It was the exact figure. "It looks like the money was replaced," Crystal said.

"I don't know what that manager got them into. The boy's headed for trouble. I can feel it. It's like a storm's coming and there's nothing I can do to stop it." Travis hit his hand on the table. "I knew that manager was no good right from the start."

"Let's not be hasty," Crystal cautioned. What had that manager gotten the boys into? She hated even to consider calling Richard, but he was better at this than either she or Travis. Perhaps he could stop them from making a drastic mistake. From ruining their lives. "Let's call Richard."

"If you think it'll do any good. They're fixing to catch the person who's making tapes off of Annie's movies right now?"

"What?"

"Richard didn't tell you? The tape at your parents' house the other week hasn't been released yet. Annie picked it up by mistake at the theater. Richard's looking into it. They're trying to catch who's recording it out of her theater. I guess we know."

"Let's call him right now."

Crystal dialed his cell number. He answered on the second ring.

"Yes?" was his curt response.

"Richard. It's Crystal."

"I know your voice. I'm busy right now. I'll call you back."

"Wait. Travis is here. Sam purchased some high-tech video equipment a few months ago."

"I'm not surprised, Crystal, but I have to get back with you. I'm with Annie right now."

"Is she all right? Is she hurt?"

"She's okay, but some arrests are going to be made." He disconnected.

"He's at the theater. It seems they just caught who's been taping Annie's movies."

"I'd better get on over there."

"I'm going too," Crystal said, grabbing her purse and keys and following Travis out the door.

On the porch Travis suddenly stopped. "You know, the boys dragged some stuff out back to an old van that doesn't work anymore before we got to the fire. I think I need to take a look to see what's there."

"I'll follow you," Crystal said.

Crystal took the time to put the top down to her car and plunk a straw hat on her head as she followed Travis the ten miles down the mountain to the old house that had burned down. The day wasn't too hot. Just a little overcast. That kept the sun from pouring down on her.

In a few minutes, they arrived at the house and, passing acres of peanuts, maneuvered the dirt path, which led more than a mile from the highway. She parked next to Travis's truck and exited the car.

Most of the debris from the fire had already been cleaned away. "You worked pretty fast in getting rid of things," Crystal said, looking at the empty space that once held the old house.

"Sam took care of that. Said he wanted to do it."

They didn't take the time to appreciate the sound of birds, bees, and the rushing water. They looked in the windows of the old blue van. The windows were covered with raggedy curtains. The curtains held together well enough to keep them from seeing what was inside.

Travis tried the doors. They were all locked.

"I guess that's that," Crystal said, disappointed.

Travis went to his truck and took a coat hanger out. "These work just fine on the old models," he said and went to work. It only took seconds to unlock the van. She could see the dread on his face as he geared up to go inside. Travis climbed in and looked. Then he climbed out looking ten years older.

Crystal gently tugged him aside and clambered inside. The scent of smoke was strong in the air. The interior was dim and cramped. Stored in the back from floor to ceiling was row upon row of recording equipment. There were three stacks of tapes leaning against one side.

What a mess, Richard thought as he walked the two blocks to the theater to meet Annie. The employees were not yet there. In a half hour three of them were due to arrive. A couple of officers were hidden inside. He didn't think anyone would be foolish enough to try to tape today.

In the meantime, the tape was back in Annie's car, on the floor of the passenger side, as if she'd never taken it out. Richard entered her office. The projectionist would look at the film for the first time when he arrived to verify that nothing was wrong. Annie was leaving then. Today the theater wasn't open for business.

The projectionist arrived half an hour later with Troy. Troy carried a gym bag. They worked with the film for a couple of hours before they began to show it. As the film played, Troy videoed the screen. This was a long one. It was nearly two and a half hours before the screening finished.

They locked the door. The authorities wanted not only to discover who was filming but also to locate the place where they made productions.

Before Troy could leave, Crystal and Travis ran into the theater. Travis jacked him up. "What have you gotten Sam into?"

"Travis, we don't know that he's involved," Crystal said, trying to hold him back.

"Let me go, man." Troy was shocked for a moment or two before he grabbed Crystal.

Richard came flying out of the theater. "Let her go," he said.

"Back off. Tell everybody to back off." He held a knife to her throat.

Richard looked into Crystal's eyes. They were wide with fear. The same fear shook his body. Troy held the fate of his wife and baby in his arms.

"Let her go," Richard said, quietly. "You're in enough trouble. If you hurt someone else, things will be a lot worse. I'm a lawyer. I know."

"I'm already in trouble."

"Not nearly as much as it can get," he said.

Tires squealed behind them. Richard didn't pay any attention. He concentrated on Troy and the knife at Crystal's throat.

"Let her go, Troy."

A door slammed. "What the hell are you doing, Troy? Why do you have that knife at Crystal's throat?"

Troy's own face was full of fear. "Man, I've got to get out of here."

"Hey, buddy. A few tapes isn't worth a life." Sam walked closer to Troy.

"It's more than the tapes." He pointed the knife at Richard and the officers. "They know it."

"What are you talking about?"

"Annie."

"Annie?"

"Man, she got the last tape. I thought everything would be over. I didn't mean to shoot her."

"Oh, man." Sam looked sick. He walked toward Troy, put his hand against the blade at Crystal's throat. "Let her go. You can't hurt her. It's gone far enough."

"I can't," Troy said.

"I'll help you."

"How? You're in trouble, too."

"We'll make it. We've always stuck together. We'll make it somehow."

Troy loosened the blade. Sam took it away, and then Troy released Crystal.

Richard sprang forward and grabbed his wife in his arms, impervious to his surroundings. With Crystal in danger, he saw his life flashing before him. He couldn't have lived without her.

"Are you out of your mind?" he roared. "What are you doing here? Didn't I tell you we were working on this thing?"

"Just stop it, Richard. Don't talk to me like I'm a two-year-old. I had to tell you something."

The fear still lingering in her eyes rocked him to the core. He tried for a calm voice even though his insides were charged up.

"Whatever it was could have waited. It wasn't worth your life." He was still queasy. She and his baby had been in danger.

"It was important."

Richard groaned. There was no reasoning with her. "You haven't thought rationally for months," he said, tugging her to him. But she resisted.

"If you're going to act crazy, I'm leaving."

"You're not going anyplace." Richard was so frustrated he could barely stand it. It was either shake her or kiss her. He opted to kiss her, nearly squeezed the breath out of her. It was a long time before they came up for air.

"I love you, Crystal," he said.

Annie knocked on Travis's door. Gertrude answered it.

"Annie, I can't tell you how—"

"Stop right there. You didn't do it." She stroked the woman's arm. "Don't give it another thought. I'm looking for Travis."

"I'm here."

He looked as if the weight of the world rested on his shoulders. Gertrude left the two of them alone.

Travis opened the screen door and they walked outside to the porch. Annie sat on the swing, but Travis held on to the porch column.

"Annie, I've never been so ashamed in my life. What can I say to you? What can I do to make up for what Sam did?"

"You've got nothing to be ashamed for. I don't want to hear any more of that nonsense, do you hear me, Travis Walker?"

He sighed. "The boy has ruined his life. He was like a son to me. I—I feel like my life is over, too."

"He didn't shoot me, Travis. It's not going to be as bad for him."

"But he stole from you. He was part of the whole thing."

"That's not your fault. You can't carry that on your conscience," she said. "Richard will help him."

"He doesn't deserve it. I don't deserve you."

Annie got up and approached him, lifted a hand, and touched his shoulder. He flinched as if she'd struck him. How did they get back to the place they were? she wondered. She knew Travis was a proud man. How did you reach through that pride?

"I love you, Travis."

He shook his head. "You can't, Annie. It just won't work. There's too much standing in the way."

"Oh, no, there isn't. The only thing standing in the way is you and your pride. Please don't let your pride rob us of our happiness. I'd give up that theater any day before I let that happen. Tell me I mean more to you."

He was silent for a long time—too long. Fear gnawed at Annie's insides.

"You mean everything to me, Annie."

Tears ran from Annie's eyes and she sent a look heavenward. "Thank you," she whispered so that only she and the Man Above knew she'd uttered the words.

* * *

Crystal and Richard were in the swing on their deck cuddled together. He stroked her arm.

"I didn't purposely try to get pregnant, Richard."

"I know."

"I didn't return to you just because of the baby. It was us. We've been through so much. I love you."

"I know that too." He tilted her chin to look directly in her eyes. "I shouldn't have said those things. I knew they weren't true when I said them."

"We've been through so much this last year, haven't we?"

Richard sipped his mimosa. "You can say that again."

"What's going to happen to those boys?"

"Do we have to talk about them right now? I get nightmares every time I think of the danger you were in."

"I want you to handle their case."

"Forget it."

"I mean it. I blame Gary for getting them into this."

"He is responsible—for part of it. He talked them into reproducing the films temporarily so they could make fast money for the music videos, but he's been lying to them. He's made a ton of money. He never planned to make those CDs."

Anger simmered in Crystal. "I hope they lock him up and throw away the key."

"Yes, well, you just may get your wish."

She snuggled against Richard, caressed his chest.

"I have more good news," he said.

"What's that?" she asked.

"The literacy program. They're starting one here. The school board will be talking to you soon."

"Really? How on earth did you pull that off?"

"Claire Dupree."

"Did I hear my name?" Richard's mother asked as she rounded the corner of the house with Richard's father.

Crystal started to sit up.